Discover the
Award-Winning and . . . *or*

JODI THOMAS

"Jodi Thomas's writing is exquisite and often lyrical . . . a very talented writer."
—*Inside Romance*

THE TEXAN AND THE LADY
The unexpected romance of a lovely young Harvey Girl and the danger-loving lawman who stole her heart . . .

"Another wonderful western romance from the author who made Texans tender . . . Jodi Thomas shows us hard-living men with grit and guts and the determined young women who soften their hearts."
—PAMELA MORSI, bestselling author of *Runabout* and *Marrying Stone*

"Five stars. One of the most moving and tender love stories I've read this year. A fascinating tale, beautifully told . . . Don't miss it!"
—*Affaire de Coeur*

"Remarkably touching . . . Another winner from Jodi Thomas. Five star reading!!"
—*Heartland Critiques*

CHERISH THE DREAM
The best of friends, Katherine and Sarah were swept up in the thrilling lives of two young pilots—men who dared them to love . . .

"A story of friends who love enough to give their all . . . This is a story for all times, a story for all readers!"
—*Heartland Critiques*

Continued on the next page . . .

PRAIRIE SONG
Her most sweeping novel of love and glory in the heart of Texas . . . and of Maggie and Grayson—whose passion held a power and fury all its own . . .

"A thoroughly entertaining romance."
—*Gothic Journal*

THE TENDER TEXAN
Winner of the Romance Writers of America Best Historical Series Romance Award in 1991

"Holds all the warmth of LaVyrle Spencer's
The Endearment."
—*Heartland Critiques*

"Excellent . . . Have the tissues ready; this tender story will tug at your heart. Memorable reading."
—*Rendezvous*

"This marvelous, sensitive, emotional romance is destined to be cherished by readers . . .
a spellbinding love story, guaranteed to move you to tears and fill your heart with joy.
The Tender Texan is filled with the special magic that makes a book a treasure."
—*Romantic Times*

And now her newest novel . . .

TO TAME A TEXAN'S HEART
The delightfully romantic adventures of a woman writer who meets the hero of her dreams—from the master of Wild West love stories, the one and only Jodi Thomas . . .

To Tame A Texan's Heart

Jodi Thomas

DIAMOND BOOKS, NEW YORK

This book is a Diamond original edition,
and has never been previously published.

TO TAME A TEXAN'S HEART

A Diamond Book / published by arrangement with
the author

PRINTING HISTORY
Diamond edition / December 1994

All rights reserved.
Copyright © 1994 by Jodi Koumalats.
This book may not be reproduced in whole or in part,
by mimeograph or any other means, without permission.
For information address: The Berkley Publishing Group,
200 Madison Avenue, New York, NY 10016.

ISBN: 0-7865-0059-X

Diamond Books are published by The Berkley Publishing Group,
200 Madison Avenue, New York, NY 10016.
DIAMOND and the "D" design
are trademarks belonging to Charter Communications, Inc.

PRINTED IN THE UNITED STATES OF AMERICA

10 9 8 7 6 5 4 3 2 1

I would like to dedicate this book
with much love to
Jim and Julia Koumalats

PROLOGUE

TIMBER CREEK, TEXAS
JULY 1898

Seth Atherton closed the ledger book to his hardware store and shoved it into an ancient safe behind his desk. He stretched his long legs as he stood and lifted his dress coat from the back of the chair.

"Want the last of the coffee?" Nell Owens asked, already twisting her shawl around her thin frame.

If women could be compared to trees, Seth thought, Nell would have been a willow in both grace and plainness. Though, like him, she'd hardly touched thirty, he could never remember regarding her as young.

"No, thanks." He smiled, thinking for the hundredth time that Nell's coffee was thick enough to sell as paint after a day in the pot. "Without Dad and Johnny at home, I thought I'd go over to the hotel cafe for a bite before I turn in."

Nell nodded in that sad way she had of silently saying she felt sorry for him. "I'd invite you home for supper, but I'm catching the train to my sister's in less than an hour."

She'd been inviting him to supper almost every month since his wife died five years ago. And Seth had been turning her down every time with a gentle no. He looked at her now almost wishing there could be something between them. Nell was a kind woman, devoted to him and the business as though she were far more than a secretary. If the truth were known, she could probably run better than he could the hardware store that had been in his family for almost fifty years.

"I appreciate the concern, but you'd best be going." He forced his voice to lighten. "Enjoy your two weeks off before I change my mind and decide not to close."

Nell opened the door. "And you enjoy your time away from both the store and family. Do something for yourself, Mr. Atherton. Do something different." She smiled, lighting her face with a touch of youth. "Maybe even get a haircut."

"I plan to." He waved as she disappeared. He'd made a habit of never stopping by the barbershop until Nell reminded him at least three times.

For a moment after she'd gone, he stared at the door wondering if he had the nerve to take her advice and do something different. Since he'd been eighteen, he could only remember the store being closed on Sundays and for family funerals. His mother died that year, and he'd started helping his father full-time. Before he turned twenty, his father lost interest in running the place. Seth had lifted the load onto his own shoulders. He'd even worked until noon on the day of his own wedding, but he'd closed the whole Monday two years later when his wife, Marcy, died. With a store to run and a year-old boy to raise, there had been little time for grief.

Then, he'd needed the work to fill his life. Now, at thirty, Seth found himself alone for the first time. His father and son were back East visiting relatives, and Seth had decided to close the store during the last few weeks of July.

He pulled the blind closed over his office window and reached for a dusty box on a top bookshelf. Slowly, as if opening a great treasure, he pulled a worn gun belt and holster from the box. With the skill of a practiced gunman, he strapped on the belt. The holster seemed mismatched to the man in tailored trousers, white shirt, and leather suspenders.

Seth reached in the box and gripped the handle of a polished Colt. Smooth and easy, he lifted the gun and slid it into place at his side.

All his life he'd been Seth Atherton, Frank's youngest boy, or store owner, or Johnny's father. But tomorrow, on the dawn train to Galveston, he'd be Seth Atherton, gunman. For the first time he'd be dressed in boots with heels cut for riding and heavy twill Levi's. His shirt would be chambray and his hat a wide-brimmed Stetson he'd never worn in public. Little would remind anyone glancing in his direction of the Atherton businessman who ran the hardware store.

Sliding long fingers over the gun's handle, Seth remembered back almost ten years. He'd sworn when his brother's gun returned draped over a coffin, that if he ever got the chance, he'd even the score with Hawk Sloan.

Slowly he walked past the display of White lead paints and Minnesota sewing machines. When he locked the front door, he closed away a life he'd always known. He had two weeks to find his brother's killer . . . or die trying.

ONE

DALLAS, TEXAS
JULY 10, 1898

Trouble had a way of riding double in True McCormick's life. Blessed with an imagination that had never been fenced, and cursed with a slipknot grasp on reality, she'd grown up wild and free with the West as her playground and the head of the Texas Rangers her adoptive father. Thanks to three Harvey women who'd taken her to raise, she'd had love without knowing roots. But the frontier was taming. Now the only gunfights and Indian battles were in the stories told by the old-timers.

True McCormick ripped the paper from her typewriter when she realized she'd been writing her own thoughts.

It was a waste of time at this point to think about telling the publishers who she really was. They'd never believe their famous writer Granite Westwind was in reality a young woman not out of her twenties. She'd painted the picture of him too clearly. Half the folks in America could describe what Granite Westwind looked like. Tall, dark hair in need of a cut. Stormy eyes that told the bad guys they were about to die a moment before the bullet struck them. Hands lightning fast with twin Colts molded beneath them, and a voice low with deadly calm.

Standing, True began to pace the small hotel sitting room she used as an office when in Dallas. She could picture the shock if New York ever found out the writer of the Westwind novels was short, almost tiny, with curly brown hair and deceptively innocent blue eyes.

"I've been writing the books for years and no one's ever questioned my use of a pen name. Now there's only one thing I can do," she said to the shadow of an old gentleman sitting next to the window.

An aging man in well-worn white linen pointed with his cold pipe. "You can't tell them who you are, True, darlin'. You'd destroy the Westwind legend. You're not just selling stories about the old West in them dime novels; you're selling a fantasy everyone wants to believe is real. Folks don't just buy your books, they buy a hero as well. A hero named Westwind. I didn't spend my life as a writer without learning a few things about readers."

"But, Micah, the editors are demanding Granite Westwind appear in public in one week. They have a whole tour planned starting in Galveston and moving across the state."

She thumbed through the mail, avoiding the letters already opened on her desk. It was the usual correspondence. Several fan letters from folks telling Westwind how much they loved his novels, a few organizations asking for money, a strange note signed 'a friend' warning of a plan to kidnap Westwind.

"I wish someone *would* kidnap Granite Westwind. I'd gladly pay a ransom just to get my hands on him. He's become so real, he even gets marriage proposals and death threats."

"That's it!" the old man shouted as he moved into the light of the room and lifted his pipe high.

True looked up. "What's it? We kidnap a man and call

him Westwind? Or maybe I could say I was married to Westwind?"

"No, no." Micah waved an ancient palm in front of her, erasing her suggestions. "If they want a Granite Westwind, we give them a Granite Westwind. All we have to do is find a man who looks like this hero you've created and prop him up for pictures. You can handle all the talking and press."

True didn't look very excited about the idea. "Where are we going to find such a hero? And even if we find him, he'll never be crazy enough to do it."

True turned as if she were talking to an invisible man beside her. "Excuse me, mister, but would you like to leave your job and family for a month and ride all over Texas playing like you're a dime-novel hero? Oh, pay no attention to the death threats and kidnapping attempts. After all, with the money I have in my bank account, I can afford to pay you maybe half what any cowhand would make."

Micah laughed. "Well, I didn't say it was a great idea. But it's an idea." He rubbed the scattery whiskers on his chin. "But I know *how* we could find him. There are men in places they'd do anything to get out of."

True removed her wire-rimmed glasses and waited. The aging writer might not have a penny to his name, but she'd learned to trust his judgment.

"We could send a wire to every jail in the state looking for a man who fits Westwind's description. Then, starting tomorrow we check every lead from here to Galveston. By the time we're on the coast, we should have our man."

"It'll never work. What kind of man are we going to find in jail?"

The old man smiled. "One dumb enough or desperate enough to go along with this crazy notion."

A slow devilish grin brushed True's lips. "It might just

work, and if we're lucky no one will ever know that our Granite Westwind is a counterfeit hero."

Micah agreed. "If we're lucky, he won't kill us in our sleep before the month is out."

TWO

Seth Atherton rolled slowly over and pressed his forehead against the cold stone wall of the jail cell. His head felt as if a Fourth of July celebration were going on inside his brain complete with exploding rockets, fireworks and cannon blasts.

The taste of sour whiskey lingered in his mouth, reminding him of what a fool he'd been. How could he ever have believed he could come to Galveston and find his brother's killer? He'd spent a week hunting through every saloon and whorehouse in town, and all he'd managed to do was get himself thrown in jail. There was no Hawk Sloan to be found.

Opening his eyes, Seth flinched. It was time he realized a ten-year-old lead was no lead at all. If there had been anything to Hawk Sloan's claim, the Rangers would have followed it up. After all, Seth's brother, Jesse, had been a Ranger when he died.

Seth flattened onto his back and stared at the dripping ceiling. Dear God, how he wished he was back at his desk at the hardware store! Every bone in his body ached from the fight he'd been in, and he couldn't even remember how it had started.

He tried to smile, then recoiled at the pain caused by a busted lip. He'd played the role of gunman all week. Maybe he believed he was a fighter last night. But all the years of riding out to the country to practice his draw had done him little good in the bar when chairs started flying. He considered himself in good shape because he often worked alongside his men unloading goods, but he was a newborn at street fighting.

Seth closed his eyes. Hell, he wasn't a fighter or a lover or anything else exciting. He was a hardware store owner, nothing more. His brother, Jesse, had been the adventurer, the warrior, the seeker. Jesse had left home at eighteen and served in the army during the Indian Wars then joined the Texas Rangers. He'd done everything Seth had always wanted to do but had never tried. He'd taken big bites out of life, as though the feast wouldn't last long. Seth had always stood to the side, afraid even to taste.

"Well, you've tasted adventure now," Seth mumbled, "and at what price." He covered his eyes with his arm, not even wanting to think about what this was going to cost him. For starters, the jailer had said thirty days in this place. How could he spend thirty days here, when he had to be back to reopen the store in one week?

Also, he didn't even have the money for a train ticket back home. Someone had helped themselves to his cash when he'd been knocked out during the fight.

"How am I goin' to get out of this one?" he mumbled to himself, thinking all of Timber Creek would probably turn out to see him arrive home if he had to wire Nell or the banker for money. He'd be the checkerboard gossip around town for weeks.

Thunder rattled the walls of the cell, and lightning brightened the jail for an instant.

"Atherton!" the jailor, whom someone had referred to as Rank, shouted in a voice that would have woken the dead and sent Seth's hangover into fiery spasms across his cloudy mind. "Atherton!" Rank yelled again. "You awake?"

Seth thought of turning back on his bunk and acting as if he were still unconscious, but he guessed men like Rank wouldn't fool easily. The jailor probably used his position to inflict as much pain as possible on any man unlucky enough to cross his path. If Seth didn't answer, Rank would be in the cell pulling him up by his hair, with a couple of extra jabs of the nightstick to make sure he had Seth's attention.

"Atherton!" The jailor ran his stick across the bars and laughed as Seth swore. "Clean your mouth up or there won't be any teeth left in it. There's a lady here to see you."

Rolling from the cot, Seth ignored the aches in his body. He felt as if someone had dropped him from windmill height a few times just to see if he'd bounce. But physical pain was no different from the ache he'd felt when he'd buried his wife five years ago. He was a longtime acquaintance of pain, and he'd finally learned almost to welcome its numbness. If nothing else, it kept him from becoming involved with anyone and opening himself up for more hurt. Seth had his life the way he liked it, and if he ever got back to the peace of Timber Creek, he was never leaving again.

But Atherton had to live through the here and now first. He'd show no sign of pain as he faced any man. And, despite the liquor, there was enough Southern gentleman in him that he'd never neglect to stand before a lady, no matter who she was.

Slowly, Seth turned to face Rank, forcing his back straight and widening his stance. He'd learned the hard way in Galveston that all doors lead to hell, and all strangers were merely enemies he had yet to fight. In one week he'd turned his civilized world over and seen the underbelly of mankind. In seven days Seth Atherton had learned to fight for his life.

But the stranger who stood before him now was a slender little woman in her mid-twenties with dark hair and eyes hidden behind glasses. Beside the jailor, she looked as out of place as fine linen on a trail drive. Her face was almost completely hidden inside a black-hooded cape that glistened silver with rain. As Seth stared, she straightened slightly and seemed to grow taller as she lowered the cape off her shoulders. She handed the wet garment to Rank, dismissing him with a slight nod, but the jailor seemed reluctant to move more than a few feet away.

For a moment all Seth saw was a tiny gold watch pinned over the woman's left breast pocket. The watch and her midnight-colored dress told him all he needed to know about this stranger. She was a lady, as fine and tightly wound as the timepiece she wore. Despite her slight height, she seemed to be looking down at him.

She reminded him of all the women who'd come to call when his Marcy died. Women who hadn't had time to visit with her a month earlier when she'd been ill now wanted to comfort him. As the husband of a bedridden wife he'd hardly been worth a nod, but as a widower with one of the largest businesses in town, his stock seemed to have gone up as the coffin went down.

Seth had turned them all away, knowing he had all he needed—a son, a business, and the memory of Marcy.

Defiantly his fists clenched as the lady outside his cell appraised him like a buyer at a slave auction. Ignoring the scabs across his knuckles that cracked and bled, he tried to make his eyes focus. He wanted to see the woman before him without a hangover blurring his vision. Seth wanted to tell her that he didn't need her anymore than he had needed the black-clad vultures at Marcy's funeral.

Seth studied her pale face and large blue eyes, watching him from behind tiny wire glasses. Despite her youth, she had "old maid" molded into the lift of her chin and the whiteness of her tightly held fingers. A virgin of not only love, but life. What could she possibly want from him?

Having been raised by only his father and brother, he'd never felt comfortable around most women, and some, like this one, managed to make him feel like he was about to break out with the hives.

"Well, miss?" The jailor looked doubtful. "Is this your brother? The description you sent out sure fits, but I don't see how he could be any kin of yours."

The lady lifted her lace handkerchief to her nose and stepped closer to the bars. "I'm not sure. I haven't seen my brother in years. Is his hair black or brown?"

Seth raised an eyebrow and ran his fingers through his hair. He could feel dried blood and tiny chips of glass where a half-empty bottle had slammed into him during last night's fight. He didn't remember anything after that, but judging from the look and smell of his clothes, his body must have mopped the bar floor on his way to jail.

He smiled, thinking Nell would have a heart attack if she saw him like this.

"I think it'll clean up black, miss," Rank answered. "Want me to fetch a bucket?"

"No," the lady replied softly while she studied the prisoner. "His eyes are the right color. Blue-gray like a winter sky."

"I'm sorry, miss." Seth had to speak so they'd stop talking about him as though he couldn't hear. He suddenly wished he could help her, for she had that sad "come to view the body" look about her. Maybe he'd guessed her wrong. She, like himself, was only thinking of a lost brother.

"I've no sister," Seth whispered almost to himself. He tried to dust some of the filth from his shirt, but only spread it into the once white cloth as he took a step toward her.

The lady outside his cell closed her eyes and looked as if she might faint when he neared. Though he had to tell her the truth, he didn't want to yell it out in front of the jailor. "I'm not your brother, miss," Seth whispered, wishing he were presentable enough to step even closer and comfort her.

Rank frowned as though Atherton had just made him out a liar, not to mention making one fine lady unhappy. "The telegram said you were looking for a man about thirty, that stood six feet with black hair and blue eyes." The jailor glared at Seth. "I was sure he had to be the one, even if his eyes right now are more red than blue."

To Seth's amazement, the woman smiled. "Could I have a few moments alone with him? I haven't seen my brother for many years, but I'm sure if I could talk with him, he might wish to acknowledge his family."

"Well?" Rank scratched his ample stomach, hating to leave the night's only interesting diversion.

"Micah will be with me," she added as an old man stepped from the shadows.

The jailor grunted at the aging gentleman, but honored the woman's request and shuffled back into the main office. As soon as he'd disappeared, the old man straightened his jacket as if he'd been ready for a fight and now had to force his body to relax.

"I told you he'd be the one," Micah whispered as he stared through the bars at Seth. "I knew it the minute I set eyes on him."

"He's perfect," the woman whispered back from behind the lacy cloth she held to her face. "I can see the hard, dangerous life he's lived written in his every movement. Look at the way he stands as if ready for a fight at any moment."

Seth gave the woman his meanest frown, the one he always reserved for his son when Johnny wouldn't stop wiggling in church.

The lady seemed unaffected.

"Will the jailor drop the charges?" she whispered to the old man.

"Rank will if you turn on the charm." Micah waved his hands as if drying rags. "And, of course, let a few tears fall, being so glad to see your brother and all. If I'd thought, I'd have wore black, undertaker black. Then I'd have been a perfect background for your crying. Lawmen always take undertakers seriously."

The woman didn't seem to be listening. She stared at Seth as though taking in every detail about him. He'd seen folks buy lumber with about the same amount of interest.

"I'm sorry, miss." These two were starting to make Seth's pounding head hurt even worse. "You can talk to each other all day, but I'm not your brother and the life I've led is none of your concern."

To his surprise the woman lowered her handkerchief, and Seth realized he'd been suckered into her act as easily as the jailor. She was laughing! As he peered closer, he knew without question that she wasn't some frail lady who needed protecting or who fainted easily. Her glasses couldn't hide the determined sparkle in her blue eyes. This was a woman with a mission! Her frosty stare left no doubt it would take more than the smell of a jail to frighten her away.

She twisted her gloved hand around one of the bars separating them and whispered, "I know you're not my brother; I'm an only child."

Seth rubbed his forehead and wondered if he could be dreaming. A proper woman with a mission was worse than the nightmare of the bar fight last night. But when he looked

back, she still stood on the other side of the bars, her
handbag clenched at her side and her face as pale as ever.
This time, she was looking at the old man, whose suit had
been worn one too many days without a cleaning.

"I think he'll do fine, Micah."

Micah nodded once, as if they'd trapped their limit of kill
for the day. "I was about to give up. I swear I've been in
every jail from Dallas to here this week."

The woman turned back to Seth and awarded him the
same quick smile she'd given the jailor. The kind of smile
that warms a man for a moment, then leaves him feeling
colder, for it vanishes so quickly he questions if it were ever
there in the first place.

"I read your arrest report." She pulled a small notepad
from her bag. "You were in a fight early this morning.
According to the report, you listed your occupation as
gunman."

Seth nodded, beginning to clear the fog in his brain. He'd
been sober enough by the time they reached the jail not to
put down his real profession. "You need my gun?" She
didn't look like the type that would hire a gun, but how
would he know? He'd only had the occupation for a week.

"Look, lady, I just listed that as my job because it causes
less problems when I'm checking into one of these fine
rooms for a few days." He smiled at his quick thinking.

"I don't want just your gun," the woman corrected. "I
wish to hire you. I'm willing to pay your bail and damages,
plus a good wage. It's important that you know how to ride
and shoot, however. You can do both?"

She'd caught his curiosity, plus she seemed really to
believe he could be a gunman. "Who do you want killed?"
He was at the point where he'd do about anything to get out
of this place, even pretend to be a hired killer for a few
hours.

She laughed aloud. A quick, easy laugh he'd always thought came to women who didn't lace their stays as tightly as she did. "Oh, no, Mr. Atherton. I don't want you to kill anyone. I want you to bring someone to life."

An hour later Seth was out of jail and strapping on his brother's gun belt.

The aging fellow the lady had called Micah was at Seth's side as they walked out of the sheriff's office. The rain had stopped, but moisture hung in the air like a thin veil brushing everything damp that moved through the night.

"Name's Micah Webb, son." Though the old-timer offered his hand, there was no smile on his face. "I want you to know up front that Miss True McCormick, your new boss, is mighty special to me so I'll be watching you to see you don't step out of line."

Seth raised an eyebrow. No one had given him an order since he was eighteen, and Seth wasn't too sure he liked the idea. It did, however, feel great to be out of jail. He'd play along for a few days then vanish, sending Miss McCormick back any money she'd been out on him.

"Now, I reckon you're fond of the bottle. Hell, son, it smells like half a gallon's been poured over you," Micah said as he sloshed down the muddy streets of Galveston as if it were a sunny day. "But you'd best stay sober while you're working for Miss McCormick, or there'll be me to answer to."

Seth fought down a laugh. The old guy seemed to have forgotten that he was half Seth's weight and twice his age. "Aren't you going to warn me about taking advantage of the lady as well?"

To Seth's surprise Micah laughed. "That weren't something I was worried about. True McCormick can take care of herself."

Without warning the man turned into the doorway of a barber and bathhouse. Before Seth had time to ask any questions, Micah handed the proprietor a few bills and said he'd be back with clean clothes.

Micah waved to Seth. "I'll see you in an hour."

Amid protests, Seth was stripped and thrown in a tub with water hot enough to cook noodles. An old Chinese woman began scrubbing the hide off him, while her husband started dunking his head up and down with no regard for his need to breathe.

By the time Micah returned, Seth was ready to call the entire thing off and go back to jail. He'd suffered less bodily damage in the bar fight than he had being cleaned and shaved. Micah added the final insult by handing him clothes that only a dude would wear. They fit well enough, but they were overstated. The boots even had bright metal tips. The clothes were as far from Seth's everyday work suits as lace from leather.

He stepped out of the dressing area. "I'm not wearing these. Where are my other clothes?" He'd have rather worn the ones soaked in whiskey than these.

Micah chuckled. "Your new boss ordered the others burned." He lifted his eyebrows up and down several times. "You have a dinner engagement with Miss McCormick, and one thing you'd best learn right now, she's the boss."

"Lead the way," Seth said, thinking two days was probably too long a time to give her. Maybe twenty-four hours. Then he'd be gone.

When the old man handed Seth a hat with a wide brim and silver braiding around the crown, he fought down any comment. It was the kind of hat that would be laughed out of any saloon, but Seth only nodded and pointed for Micah to lead the way.

Now, more sober, Seth wondered why True McCormick would trust such an old man to do her bidding. Micah looked like he should be standing in front of a painted wagon selling tonic for a cure-all. "You work for Miss McCormick?"

"No. I've made a living since the War Between the States by writing and other jobs when the mood strikes me. Done everything from acting to preaching. Mostly, though, I write articles, but who knows, someday I may start a book." Micah held his shoulders back proudly. "I'm True's friend, as are most of the folks around the state, so you'd best watch your step, mister."

Another warning, Seth thought. Maybe he'd wire his banker tomorrow morning. Twelve hours seemed a long enough time.

As Seth followed, they passed a large hat stand by the door. In a blink Seth dropped the hat he was holding and picked up a worn Stetson with plain leather trim. Some other cowhand would wear the fancy hat home tonight.

They were at a hotel across from the train station before Micah looked back. He made no comment about the Stetson as he opened the door. "Please step this way, Mr. Westwind."

Seth raised an eyebrow. "Westwind?"

Micah smiled, his almost colorless eyes twinkling like damp snow. "Yessir, Mr. Granite Westwind."

Slowly, Seth remembered his stolen hat and twirled it in his hands. "There must be some mistake," he whispered. "Granite Westwind is one of those dime novelists who writes like he's never been west of Grand Central Station in New York City. I've never been confused with him in my life."

As he stepped through the doorway and into the hotel lobby, a herd of plaid-suited reporters ran toward Seth, almost knocking him back outside in their hurry to ask questions. They all pulled at him, each demanding answers to questions Seth couldn't even hear for the roar of voices. He glanced behind him, but Micah had vanished. An explosion from a flash bar blinded Seth, and for a moment he saw nothing.

When his vision cleared, he noticed Micah near the reception counter and pushed his way forward.

"I thought you'd want your room key!" Micah shouted as he shoved the key into Seth's hand. "You're staying here. Miss McCormick will be sleeping across the street, upstairs with the Harvey girls." What Micah didn't say came through loud and clear. Seth was to keep his distance.

The aging showman raised his hand with the authority of a ringmaster. To Seth's amazement, the crowd quieted down.

"Mr. Westwind will answer all your questions tomorrow, gentlemen!" Micah's voice bellowed above all others. "He has a steak and a lady waiting for him tonight across the street at the Harvey House. And, of course, his reputation cannot allow either to wait long."

Seth glared at him in question, but the old man only turned and led him down the hotel hallway to the side door. Though reporters called after them, they didn't follow as Micah opened the door for Seth and pointed toward the Harvey House. "Enjoy your supper," he said.

Seth glanced back at the mob and wondered what he'd just stepped into. Somehow this mix-up had to do with Miss McCormick. He'd straighten out the reporters in the morning then thank Miss McCormick for her help. Seth had no plans of riding on another man's name.

But right now a steak and seeing the proper lady who hid the sparkle of life behind wire-rims sounded too good to

pass up. There hadn't been a woman since Marcy who'd
made him even think about being alive. What harm could it
do to watch True McCormick across a table for an evening?
Then, next week when he went back to being just plain Seth
Atherton, store owner, he'd have a face to daydream about
and a night of being a hired gun to remember.

THREE

True McCormick watched the man she'd bailed out of jail walk across the crowded restaurant toward her. He was tall, broad shouldered, lean hipped. His midnight hair had been trimmed but still seemed to have a will of its own. His eyes were the smoky blue of a winter sky. When she'd first seen him in jail, she'd thought he'd do for her needs, but now, looking at him cleaned up and sober, she felt as if the real Granite Westwind were moving toward her.

True half expected Seth to walk up to her and introduce himself as her character. She felt she knew Granite Westwind so well, and now he'd come alive. Granite had been a part of her life for years, but he'd always been in her head . . . until tonight. Tonight, thanks to Seth Atherton, Westwind was flesh and blood.

Quickly inspecting her very proper dress, True smiled to herself. Even if the imaginary Granite she had pretended to talk to when she was young did come alive, he'd never recognize her. She was a long way from the little girl who ran away to a new adventure every time her three adoptive mothers weren't looking. Seth Atherton would have no way of knowing the life she'd lived or how easy it had been to make up a character like Westwind. To Seth she must look like an old maid, not a street child who had ridden every train in the West and spent her teen years listening to the wild stories of old-timers. It had taken her Northern school years to mold her into a lady on the outside, but inside True remained a scrappy street urchin longing to listen to the old-timers talking beneath railroad bridges between trains.

"Miss McCormick?" Seth Atherton removed his hat and waited for her to ask him to sit down.

True motioned for him to take the place across from her. "Mr. Atherton." She liked this gentlemanliness about him. During the past few years in New York, she'd missed the almost shy politeness of Southern men. Somehow she'd always thought her Granite Westwind character would have such a trait . . . a strong kind of shyness around ladies. "I took the liberty of ordering you a rare steak with potatoes and onions cooked on the side."

"That's the way I like it." Seth looked at her more closely. "How did you know?"

"You're from Texas, right?" She didn't need an answer. If ever there was a Texan born and bred, surely it had to be the man before her. She studied him closely, noticing things about him she'd never thought to include in Westwind. The sun had brushed tiny lines around his eyes. His hands were not calloused, yet they were strong hands. When his grip lightly brushed the coffee cup, she wondered if his touch could be as gentle as it was ruthless when he held a weapon. Her ideal of a hero sat across from her now, as he had so many times in her imagination.

"Yes, I'm from Texas," Seth answered, watching her as closely as she did him. She looked even more beautiful than she had in the jail but still every bit as proper. A kind of Sunday-morning proper who would never understand why a successful businessman would pretend to be a gunman. He found himself wishing he'd met her at church and could ask to walk her home. But that was crazy; the last thing he needed in his life was a woman.

"I appreciate the meal," Seth pulled himself up straight, "but I don't take handouts. I'd like to know more about the job first, Miss McCormick, before we eat." He didn't care about the employment. He had no intention of accepting work, but he wanted to know more about her.

True agreed as she poured her coffee cup half-full of milk. "The job is quite simple, really. I'd like you to be Granite Westwind for one month. If you agree, the pay is one hundred dollars." If she hadn't been a constant watcher of people, she might have missed the slight lift in his eyebrows at the offer. "We have several public appearances scheduled for Mr. Westwind. You may be asked to ride or shoot but only as a show of skill. I'm Mr. Westwind's secretary and will help you in any way I can."

"Granite Westwind." Seth leaned forward and paused as a Harvey girl passed their table with a pot of coffee. After filling his cup, the waitress flavored Miss McCormick's milk with coffee. "He's the famous dime novelist everyone in the country reads. Why doesn't he do his own public appearances? Why would he want to hire a man to take the bow for work he's done?"

True stirred her diluted coffee as if it were a real drink. "Granite Westwind never, never appears in public! As his typist I can assure you, I'm authorized to employ you to act the part. All you have to do is play a real Wild West hero for thirty days."

"But judging from what I've heard of his books, Westwind is a man who fears nothing. Don't tell me he's afraid of a camera and a few reporters?"

"No," she answered, lifting her chin as if in challenge.

Seth laughed. "I know. He's one of those city cowboys who's never left his desk in Manhattan, or Pittsburgh, or some other overpopulated place. He's probably afraid of horses and has never fired a weapon except in his dreams. Going public would destroy his image."

True looked uncomfortable. "Mr. Atherton, Granite Westwind chooses to be a recluse, and his reasons behind such a decision are none of your business. I've typed all his novels, and I'll be accompanying you on tour. All you'll have to do is assume his identity. I'll answer all the questions." She removed her glasses and folded them, as if putting an end to the conversation as well.

Seth couldn't fight down a grin. He admired her loyalty to her boss. She reminded him of Nell; only the effect True McCormick had on him was far different. The more he stared at her, the more he wanted to continue to look at her. "Your coming along is the first good thing I've heard about this job." Maybe he'd give it a twenty-four-hour try. After all he owed her that much for getting him out of jail. "How about I try this handle on for size for a few days? I make no promises after that."

True lifted her cup in agreement. A month might prove too long for her as well. Atherton could look the part, but he might not be able to carry it off. "Twenty-five a week then?"

"Will Micah be with us?"

"Micah is a friend. He sees himself as a writer but hasn't published anything in years except a few articles. He enjoys popping in and out of my life. He won't be needed on this trip, though. I can take care. . . ."

A sudden shattering of glass stopped her conversation. Screams and shouts rattled the crystal as a thundering of hooves echoed through the dining room. Everyone in the restaurant turned to watch a man on horseback enter the foyer of the Harvey House. The rider was as wild-eyed as the mustang he rode. They twirled and smashed into the walls with the carelessness of a drunk at Sunday tea.

The cowboy pulled his gun and yelled, "Where's the bar in this place?" His weapon blasted, sending everyone in the room into panic.

Operating on pure instincts, Seth leaned around the small

table and jerked Miss McCormick to the floor, tumbling atop her in the fall. Shots rang out as he pulled her beneath the table. He reached for his brother's weapon before remembering he'd checked it at the door.

"Damn!" he whispered, knowing he'd be trapped here until someone silenced the drunk. He turned to offer what protection and comfort he could to Miss McCormick. An apology for having frightened her already formed on his lips as he straightened a few inches away from her.

If he'd expected to see fear or even gratitude, he was sorely mistaken, for beneath him erupted an angry spitfire of a woman.

"Get off of me!" she ordered and pushed against him.

Seth didn't move, deciding the poor lady was frightened out of her senses. "We're safe here," he whispered as his hand stroked her shoulder. He couldn't remember the last time he'd touched a woman to give comfort. "Someone will stop the drunk in a minute and you'll be safe."

True shoved with all her might, and Seth rolled another inch away from her. "Not someone, Mr. Granite Westwind. You!"

"Me?"

The lady pulled a small Lightning Colt from her pocket and handed it to him. "The press would never stop laughing if the great Granite Westwind was found hiding under a table when there was trouble."

As Seth rose on one knee to argue with her that only a fool would go up against a crazy cowhand hunting for liquor, she planted her foot in his chest and shoved.

Seth tumbled backward from under the table with a shout of surprise. He stumbled to his feet with her gun still in his hand. The proper Miss McCormick had just tossed him to the wolves. Everyone in the room had taken cover. He stood alone to face the intruder.

The drunk on horseback shouted something then rode toward Seth with as much speed as the frightened horse could muster.

In the blink of an eye Seth weighed his options. There was nowhere to hide or run—which did away with his first two choices. That left only option three: fight.

The drunk leaned in the saddle and tried to rein the horse in as he took a swing toward Seth.

"Whoa!" Seth shouted. He raised his hands in front of the intruder to block any blow.

The horse reared at the command, slinging the drunk onto a table loaded down with food. Fine Harvey china and crystal shattered beneath him.

Seth shoved the Colt he carried into his belt and grabbed for the horse's reins. The mustang was far more dangerous than the cowhand. Seth had been handling horses since he could walk. His first job at the store had been to harness all the wagons on Saturdays and make deliveries. The animal responded to his sure, commanding grip. The horse shook his mane and without further protest followed him out the door.

When Seth returned only moments later, the restaurant looked like a stirred-up ant bed. The drunken cowhand had disappeared. Everyone was busy moving around putting furniture back in order. The famous Harvey House policy was, as always, to serve the meals no matter what. A cowhand riding through the dining room would only delay the next course.

Harvey Houses had been the West's first fine dining establishments. They hadn't survived from Kansas to California for almost twenty years without being efficient and flexible.

Seth took in the movements around him as he headed straight toward True.

"That's him," someone whispered as Seth passed a table.

"I knew it the moment he walked in," whispered another. "Look at the way he carries himself. A born warrior."

Seth didn't look at anyone but the very proper Miss McCormick. She sat at their table as if nothing had happened. Her pleated sea-green skirt and matching shirt-waist of linen appeared undisturbed by the tumble she'd taken only moments earlier. She carefully unfolded her glasses and cleaned them with the table napkin.

Standing before her, Seth dusted the imprint of her boot off the front of his shirt. She looked like one of those women who couldn't stand even to step on a spider, but she'd had no trouble throwing him to the dragons like he was the only pure heart in the room. "Your Colt, Miss McCormick." He laid the weapon on the table, noticing for the first time that it had a polished ivory handle.

"Thank you," she answered and slid the gun back into the huge pocket of her jacket. "I'm glad to be of assistance. After all, it would never do for the great Granite Westwind to be without a six-shooter."

Seth couldn't believe she wasn't apologizing. She'd almost gotten him killed. Anger sparked in him unlike any he'd ever known. Was everyone in this town in a conspiracy to see him dead? He leaned closer to Miss McCormick. "The next time you kick me, I'll—"

"Don't you dare threaten me!" Her big blue eyes were so innocent, but her words were hard with practiced strength. She was so close Seth could feel her breath brush his ear. "Or I'll slice you up into bite-size hunks and serve you in the Friday night stew here at the Harvey House." Her smile was almost friendly when she leaned back and added, "No one ever threatens me. Not even a gunfighter."

The woman left him speechless. She might be Georgia

sweet lace on the outside, but there was fire-blasted steel on the inside. Suddenly he would have given all he owned to hear that low voice whispering in passion and not in anger. He knew he was standing before her like some mindless oaf who didn't seem capable of following the conversation, but he couldn't help himself. As he stared at True McCormick, his tongue felt as if it had been roped and branded. All air vacated his lungs, and damned if his heart didn't start to beat again after claiming death for five years. This woman had done what no other could—she'd made him want to start living again. The kind of living that only happened between lovers. Maybe he'd stay more than a few days, just to cure himself of this curse she seemed to have put on him simply by looking at him with those wonderful eyes.

The mixture of fire and ice in her fascinated him. He'd always thought women needed protecting. For the first time in his life, Seth decided he might be the one in need of protection, for she left no doubt that she'd carry out her threat if provoked. As others neared their table, she replaced her glasses.

"Congratulations, Mr. Westwind," someone said from behind him. "We're lucky you were in the restaurant."

"Mr. Westwind," a woman pulled at his arm. "I've been an admirer for years, but I never dreamed I'd get to see the master himself in action."

"Mr. Westwind!" another shouted. "I think we may be related. My grandmother was a Westwind."

Suddenly everyone in the room was crowding around him. They pushed and shoved one another for the nearest space. Some shouted questions Seth had no idea how to answer, while others seemed content to pull on his clothing or pat him on the back.

Seth watched over the heads of the crowd as True stood

and spoke to the waitress. She pointed to Seth's steak and then upstairs, indicating she wanted him to follow.

He'd follow, he thought, but not for the food. He wanted to know more about this woman. However, his first priority was fighting his way through the sea of people. They were far more frightening than the drunken cowhand on a horse.

Seth tried to move, but like stink on a mop head, the mob moved with him. He answered their endless inquiries with nods, which only seemed to encourage them to ask louder questions.

When he'd agreed to play Westwind, he never realized how complicated it might be. Finally, after several minutes he managed to reach the bottom of the stairs.

Following Micah's actions from earlier, he raised his hand. To his amazement, the crowd silenced.

"Thank you, folks, for your concern, but I didn't do anything any of you wouldn't have done if you'd had the same encouragement I had." Seth fought the urge to dust the memory of Miss McCormick's boot print from his chest once more.

The crowd seemed to like his speech, even though several shook their heads in doubt. "I'd like to talk to you more," Seth continued, "but I've a lady who needs my attention."

The women blushed and the men snickered, but everyone in the crowd nodded in understanding. To Seth's astonishment, they backed away.

He bounded up the stairs three at a time, thinking he'd better read one of those Westwind books. Only right now, he had to have a few words with one special, frustrating, ill-tempered, lovely lady. She might not believe it from the way she'd met him in the jail, but he seemed to value his life a little more than she did.

As he looked down the hallway, a Harvey girl stepped from one of the private dining rooms. Her black high-necked dress and crisp white apron were in sharp contrast to her warm smile as she passed him, leaving the door slightly ajar.

Seth tipped his hat to her and moved through the open doorway. The smell of food greeted him from a tiny table in the center of the room. As hungry as he was, it was Miss McCormick he wanted to see. Scanning the room, he allowed a moment for his eyes to adjust to the shadowy interior.

The sight before him slammed against his mind. Miss McCormick stood in the shadows by the window. She was smiling up at the drunken cowboy who had caused all the trouble downstairs.

Before Seth could say a word, she handed the trouble-maker a roll of bills. The cowhand shoved the money in the pocket of his food-stained Levi's, stepped through the window, and vanished before Seth could move. The curtains swayed slightly, erasing even the man's memory from the shadows.

Seth ran to the window, almost shoving Miss McCormick aside in his haste, but there was no sign of the cowboy. Only the wet roof of a porch slanting down toward the alley greeted him.

"What did he want?" Seth demanded. "Was he trying to blackmail or rob you, miss?"

"Who?" True moved calmly to the table and took a seat.

"The drunk who caused all the trouble downstairs?"

"What drunk?" Huge innocent blue eyes stared up at Seth while she calmly unfolded her napkin.

"The man who was just standing at the window!"

"What man?" she answered as sweetly as a honey-dipped angel.

Seth dug his fingers into his hair and let out a long breath.

"The man you just handed money to. The one who climbed out the window when I came in."

True looked up at him with a face he'd have been willing to swear could never lie. "Why, Mr. Westwind, if you're going to play the part of a writer, you need to be able to separate fact from fiction."

FOUR

Seth ate his steak in silence, trying to figure out how a woman who looked so pure could lie so easily. It had to be one of two things. One, every person in this town was crazy and he was starting to catch the disease, or two, he'd been hit too hard with a chair last night and he no longer saw what he thought he saw.

Yet Seth couldn't have dreamed up a woman like True McCormick. He'd never been near someone who made him feel as she did. It seemed he'd been an adult all his life, but she had this way of making him feel he was a greenhorn kid at his first barn dance.

When he finished his meal, she spread out an arm full of dime novels in front of him. The titles read: *Granite Westwind Fights the Savages*, *Granite Westwind Saves the Wagon Train*, *Granite Westwind, A Man Who Fights Alone*.

"These are only a few of the novels that have been written over the past seven years. Westwind averages an adventure every three months." True McCormick thumbed through one of the books looking slightly embarrassed. "I forgot to ask if you can read and write."

Seth smiled. "I can do both, and I manage to know most of my numbers, too."

"Good."

The blush on her face was very becoming. Seth remained silent.

"I'd like you to practice signing Westwind's name." She handed him a pad with what must have been Westwind's signature at the top. On Seth's third try his Westwind script could have been a carbon impression of the real one.

While True examined his work, Seth flipped one of the book covers toward him. "Luckily, Westwind and I are about the same basic build and coloring."

Seth looked at the picture on the cover more closely. A bigger-than-life cowboy stood with his feet wide apart and a Colt on each hip. He was tall and rawhide lean. Judging from where his hands rested, an inch away from his gun handles, he was ready for a fight. His face was almost completely shadowed by his hat, but Seth could have posed for the picture.

When he glanced up, True was looking at him from across the table. He had the feeling she was thinking the same thing. He could master the identity as easily as he mastered the signature. While she stared, he looked into her wonderful blue depths, wishing he had an excuse to touch her. He'd have liked the simple pleasure of feeling her hand on his arm, or his fingers sliding along the small of her waist. He wanted to hold her gently in a hug as friends did when greeting.

Looking away suddenly, Seth tried to clear his mind. He was going mad, that was it. He couldn't remember the last time he'd touched a woman, and now something in him had snapped. Never had he felt such a need to hold someone. True McCormick was shattering his peace. He'd best get back home. Maybe he could take inventory next week while everyone was still gone. Maybe he could stay busy enough to forget this lady from Galveston with her proper little glasses, her proper clothes, and her haunting eyes.

She stood, and he tried to concentrate on what she was saying.

"Tomorrow when you leave your hotel, I'll want you wearing a double holster. You'll find both holster and guns in your room. I'll see that all your personal belongings, including the gun you checked downstairs, are stored." True's stance was all business. "Any questions, Mr. Atherton?"

"Call me Seth," he answered, fascinated once more by the beauty in her eyes. A man could fall into those depths and drown without caring. He'd admired his share of women, but he couldn't remember ever being so struck with a lady's looks that he couldn't follow a conversation. He tried to remind himself that this was just a business arrangement and the lady obviously wanted nothing more.

And neither did he, he lied to himself.

True tossed her glasses on the table. "I'll call you Mr. Westwind from this point on, for the public's sake."

"And in private?" He had to ask, his voice husky as it lowered. He wasn't flirting with her, but hoping he'd have a chance. She was the kind of woman men like him only dreamt of holding. A lady through and through, with fire in her eyes.

"There'll be no private time," she answered. "We'll be with the press all day, and at night you'll have rooms at a Harvey House or local hotel in whatever town we're in. I'll always have a room at the Harvey House. When there are no rooms for rent at the Harvey House, I'll stay in the wing where the Harvey employees lodge."

He could almost see her back straightening into the porcelain woman he'd first met. She wasn't going to allow them even to be friends. "You must like this chain of hotels along the railroad," he said, wondering if she were afraid of people in general or him in particular. "I'll give one compliment to the Harvey chain—they cook the best steak in the country."

"I grew up in these hotels and restaurants. Wherever the railroad went, Fred Harvey opened a lunch counter or an entire hotel. And wherever he started a place, my family followed. Because of the Westwind books, I still spend most of my time traveling from one town to another. No matter where I am, I always feel at home where I can hear the dinner gong and sleep to the rhythm of passing trains."

A Harvey waitress tapped on the door, then entered without waiting for them to direct her. "I thought I'd clear the dishes if you're through eating, True."

"That would be fine, Sally." True's smile was genuine, but when Sally turned to reach for the tray, True slipped the leftover roll from the table into her pocket. Her action was too practiced not to have been a habit.

Seth watched her closely. He found it hard to believe that a woman who could afford a private dining room would need to hoard bread. But he'd seen her take the roll with his own eyes.

When the waitress closed the door, he stood and moved to the open window. True hadn't offered to allow him to use her first name, yet for some reason he wanted to say it. "True's an unusual name for a woman."

She followed him to the window. "I was born on a wagon train heading west through the Oklahoma Territory. My folks stopped at a tiny Indian village when it was time for my birth. The old Indian woman who helped deliver me said I was born smiling and therefore true of heart. My mom died that night, and I guess my dad didn't have much imagination because he named me True after what the old midwife said. That was the last thing he did for me, before he took his own life out of grief over my mother."

Seth leaned against the window sill and watched the way the lamplight made her warm brown hair shine. He didn't know the words to comfort her. "It's a nice name." How could he tell her that his wife had also died in childbirth?

But unlike her father, he had never considered ending his life. There was too much to be done.

Staring out into the evening fog left from the rain, Seth realized he could hardly remember what the two years with Marcy had been like. Somehow time had dulled the memory. When she died, he'd grieved silently. She'd been so young. They'd grown up next door to each other, and it had always been almost understood that they'd marry. But he couldn't remember her laughter, or ever seeing her cry, or even one time when she'd been angry. It was almost as if she'd been there, then disappeared, as formless as the fog before him.

"The fog's so thick tonight, it'll be like walking in liquid air," True whispered beside him.

Seth looked down at her. She appeared so tiny and fragile, barely coming to his shoulder. "Will you be leaving the hotel tonight?"

"No." She moved her hand out the open window, feeling the gray mist. Her fingers disappeared into the night. "Your room's just across the street and mine is upstairs. You'd best call it a night for our workday will start before dawn."

Seth knew he should go, but he couldn't help reaching into the fog and touching her hand. Somehow the mist made the action seem less forward. Their fingers touched, yet were curtained in gray. Slowly, he slid his open hand beneath hers. Her touch was so light, it seemed a part of the night. Yet alive, inviting.

He'd expected her to pull away, but her fingers curled slightly and rested on his open hand. He had the feeling that if he tried to grip her hand, she'd fly away like a wild bird.

"Your touch is cold," he whispered, wondering how something so cold could build such a warmth in his gut.

"And yours is warm," she answered as her fingers lightly brushed over his palm. She stared into the mist, as if there were no man beside her connected to the flesh she touched. "I guess that proves you're real."

Seth fought the urge to prove to her just how real he was. He suddenly longed to feel her body against his, with more than their hands touching. There was such a mystery about this Miss True McCormick, with her pearl-handled Lightning Colt in one pocket and a leftover biscuit in the other. For the first time in his life, he wanted to know a woman completely. He wanted to know what she dreamed about, and what she feared, and how she tasted.

"I'm real." He curved his fingers slightly and brushed the side of her hand. "I'll take your job offer, Miss McCormick, but you have to promise to stay beside me"—he paused for a moment too long before finishing the sentence—"to answer questions of course."

"I'll be beside you if trouble comes riding." She smiled up at him with the trust of a child. "I'll back you up with my gun and my life."

Seth couldn't help but laugh. "That sounds like it came right out of one of those Westwind novels."

True pulled her hand away. "It did," she answered as she moved across the room and opened the door for him to leave.

Seth didn't want the evening to end, but they'd have tomorrow together. Hell, he might even stay the entire week. Inventory could wait.

He touched two fingers to his forehead in a silent salute and moved down the hall. Everyone seemed to have settled in for the night as he took the stairs two at a time and passed the foyer.

When he stepped out into the street, the fog greeted him. He opened his hand as he walked across to his hotel, wanting to feel the fog once more. He could still sense the touch of her hand resting on his. Instinct told him it would

take far more than a week to get any closer to the proper
Miss McCormick, but he planned to give it his best try. He
wanted to see what her hair looked like down and free, and
watch how her eyes warmed with passion.

Laughing to himself, Seth glanced back at the Harvey
House. He must be dreaming if he thought he'd ever get
close to her. Just because he could fool her into thinking he
was a gunfighter didn't mean he could play the part of a
lover. The only thing he'd ever see the proper Miss
McCormick take off was those damn glasses she kept
playing with, as though they protected her from the world.

"Evening, Mr. Westwind," the desk clerk said as Seth
stepped into the small entry to his hotel.

"Evening," Seth answered when he realized whom the
man was greeting.

"Your room is just up the stairs, third one on the right."
The clerk smiled as if he'd been practicing his speech.
"We're might glad to have you with us, sir."

"Thank you," Seth answered, fighting down a laugh.
He'd stayed at this hotel twice last week, and he couldn't
remember the clerk ever bothering to look at him, much less
learn his name. It might be fun playing this Westwind
character for a while.

As he opened the door to his room, he noticed that the
light on the nightstand was burning low. The fog from
outside seemed to linger in his room, almost tangible. A man
sat reading in the chair by Seth's bed. The stranger was so
still, he looked like a portrait.

"Sorry," Seth stammered. "I thought this was my room."

The man looked up. Though his hair was graying, his
eyes wrinkled with an intelligence that was far from doting.
The mark of his clothes and the wear on his holster left no
doubt in Seth's mind that this was a man to be given a wide
lane or trouble would come a tumbling. "No." The man lay

his book aside. "It's I who should apologize. Are you Seth Atherton?"

Seth didn't turn loose of the doorknob. "Yes."

"Then you're in the right room, son." The stranger unfolded his long frame from the chair. "I'm Colonel Austin McCormick. Sorry to have barged in on you like this, but I couldn't very well wait in the hallway across the street with those Harvey girls running past every five minutes, asking me if I needed anything."

Seth straightened to attention and offered his hand. "Colonel McCormick of the Texas Rangers? I'm honored to meet you, sir. You're a legend."

Austin laughed. "I don't know about legend, but I've been around long enough to be a relic anyway." He pumped Seth's hand with a strong grip. "I knew an Atherton who rode with the Rangers several years back. Jesse Atherton."

Seth smiled. "That was my brother. He was killed trying to bring in a gang headed by a killer named Hawk Sloan."

"I remember that," Austin said. "Sorry about your brother. We've tried to link Sloan with his murder for years, but none of the gang will talk. Seems they're more afraid of Sloan than the law. But Jesse Atherton was a good Ranger, one of the best."

"Thank you, sir," Seth answered. There were few men Seth could truly say he admired, and one of them stood before him. Jesse always had stories to tell about the great Ranger. Austin McCormick was a brave, fair-minded lawman who'd been lucky enough to stay alive through more scraps than any dime novelist could think of. "How can I be of service to you, sir?"

Austin took a long breath. "I've come about True McCormick."

Seth felt as if someone had just hit him behind the knees

with a two-by-four. The words dribbled out before he could stop them, "You're Miss McCormick's father?"

Austin laughed. "People been telling me that for years. I'd deny it, but her mother would have my hide when I get back to the capitol. My Jenny takes her mothering seriously. If we hadn't had four sons to keep her busy, she'd have smothered True."

Seth didn't breathe as he asked, "And how is True's *mother*?"

"She's fine. Some folks claim the reason I stay alive is that there's not a man in the state whose brave enough to tell Mrs. McCormick I've been killed."

She'd done it again, Seth thought. True McCormick had told him a tale without so much as blinking and he'd been suckered in, feeling awful about her mother dying of childbirth in an Indian camp and her father taking his own life in grief. Seth should have never let her get away with not explaining about the cowboy at her window.

Austin retrieved his hat from the bedpost. "I just dropped by after Micah told me about this Granite Westwind you're impersonating. Micah likes to keep folks up on what True's doing—seems to be his favorite pastime. I wanted to ask you to keep an eye on True." Austin laughed again. "Which isn't easy to do, son, believe me."

"I'll try," Seth answered. "I never dreamed she'd be your daughter."

"That she is, and I love her dearly." Austin frowned. "I didn't want to worry her, but there've been rumors that someone might be wanting to stop this Westwind tour from ever happening. That combined with what Micah tells about Westwind receiving threatening letters is enough to take a few precautions."

The lawman watched Seth closely, not wanting the younger man to take offense. "So, I'll have a Ranger or two posted at every town you and she visit. But if I were you, I'd keep my guard up. There's trouble coming and it'll be double-barreled, I'm guessing. I'm glad she picked a man like you to play Westwind. Any brother of Jesse Atherton is bound to be a good man."

"Don't worry about her," Seth answered as he lifted one of the guns on his bed and checked the chamber. He only wished he could be half the man his brother had been.

Austin moved to the door. "It wasn't her I was worried about, son. It's you." He smiled. "If you live through a tour with True, you'll earn every dime you make. Half the no-accounts in the state would like to go up against the great Granite Westwind. I imagine that's why the real Westwind chooses never to appear in public. So you keep your head low and cool."

He was gone before Seth could ask him any questions.

"I'll try," Seth whispered to himself. He wondered just what he'd signed on to do. He had a feeling *one* lady was going to give him more trouble than all the hotheads in Texas.

FIVE

∽

Fog blanketed the night, suffocating the warm Galveston air with dampness. Seth watched the people moving in shadows below his hotel window. He couldn't sleep. Hell, he couldn't even relax. He couldn't get True off his mind. All the years before they met piled up together didn't pull at his emotions as much as she had in only a few hours. The people in his life were stable, solid, dependable. True made him feel as if it made no difference if he'd known her a day or a year, he'd never understand her or her world.

He'd read poetry about desire so overwhelming that it blocked logic, but Seth hadn't thought it possible such a thing could happen to him. Yet he'd signed on to play the part of another man only because he had to be near her again. He didn't need the money. He didn't have the time, yet he couldn't drag himself away from Galveston.

Everything in his life had always been planned and predictable. She'd changed all that with a look. It angered him that the touch of her hand in his had stirred up his heart. He didn't want to feel anything for her or any woman. "I don't need her," Seth mumbled aloud, "and tomorrow I'll prove it."

He seemed a great deal farther from Timber Creek than a few hours by train. The little hill country settlement was a world away from Galveston. He'd come looking for any member of Hawk Sloan's gang, and he'd discovered a woman who blinded him to all else but her eyes.

"You're cracking up," he mumbled to himself. "You've

mixed one too many cans of paint and smelled too much cherry oil stain."

Frustrated, Seth strapped on the double-holstered gun belt he'd found in his room and shoved his hat low. Maybe he could think better if he walked. The streets of this little coastal town fascinated him. The folks who settled here were both the worst and the best of Texas. There were builders and dreamers blended amid the gamblers and smugglers.

He stepped out of the back door of the hotel and crossed over to the Harvey House thinking he'd walk along the tracks and avoid the streets. The moon offered only a hazy glow of light. For a moment he stood in the blackness, listening to the sounds of the night. A dog howled from somewhere past the station yard. The last train was pulling out on its late run to Houston. An out-of-tune piano played "Dixie" from a bar half a block away. He heard the sound of the cleanup crew from an open kitchen door.

When movement caught his eye from the alley entrance, Seth melted completely into the shadows. As a young couple came into view, he tried to force his muscles to relax. The strangers were only late-night lovers, a Harvey girl trying to say good night to her beau while the young man begged her to stay a minute longer.

Seth didn't want to intrude on the private scene, so he moved farther into the alley. Checking his bearings, he glanced up at the window where he'd stood with True. As if from his memory, he saw a shadow of a youth slip from the open window and slide down the roof to the ground floor.

His first thought was that he might catch a thief, but the boy moved too cautiously to be running from a crime. He also seemed to know the path down too well for it to have been his first attempt. The climber didn't have to glance down to know the next hold in his descent.

Interested, Seth followed. He guessed, from the boy's

frame, that he must be around thirteen. His clothes appeared plain, but not ragged. This was no street child.

The shadow of the boy crossed the street and moved into the alley behind a four-story hotel that housed mostly businessmen for the night. Seth stayed well behind in the blackness. He normally wasn't interested in other people's comings and goings, but there was something different about the lad. Something strangely familiar in the way he moved.

Rounding the corner, Seth saw the boy kneeling beside porch steps leading to a kitchen door. Someone had nailed slats into one side of the steps to keep people from putting trash there, but the wood was rotting and broken in several places.

"Come on out," the boy's soft voice whispered. "I know you're in there."

Seth moved closer, trying to see the identity at the other end of the one-way conversation.

"I brought you a biscuit." The boy lifted his offering. "It's as good as the one I brought you last night. I even put two strips of bacon in it for you."

Seth studied the blackness beyond the steps, looking for a pair of animal eyes. The youth must be trying to coax a wild cat or dog from hiding, he thought.

The boy knelt lower. "You don't have to be afraid. I know what it's like to be scared of everyone you meet. I was just like you once. I had people kick me and tell me to get away from their places like I was lower than a rat."

Seth wished he could move closer and hear better. He wanted to help. The boy's voice sounded close to tears. He'd seen youths not fully grown left alone in these coastal towns when their parents died. There were always more children than homes for them, so the older ones were left on the streets.

The boy continued talking. "I know what it's like to fight the dogs for the leftovers the cooks set out. I remember how some of the cooks poured sour milk over the scraps so I wouldn't bother them. I know how frightened you feel when you have to go to sleep, praying you won't be awakened by someone beating you because you're on their property."

Something moved from beneath the steps. Seth fought down an oath against everyone in the town as he watched a tiny child crawl from between the boards. She was almost as tall as his son of six, but wouldn't have weighed half as much. Her hair was matted around her thin face and her clothes wouldn't even have been kept as rags in most households. Her spider-thin arms and legs were covered with dirt, and she had no shoes. A makeshift bandage of rags tied around her left arm looked stiff with dried blood and dirt.

The boy slowly handed the child the biscuit and waited as the orphan crammed the entire thing into her mouth at once.

"What's your name?"

"Emily," the girl mumbled as she chewed. "My folks both died with yellow fever last year, but I wasn't lucky enough to get it."

"Maybe you have a guardian angel," the boy whispered.

"Are you it?" the girl asked, raking the few extra crumbs around her lips into her mouth.

"No," the boy answered. "I'm just his helper. I know a place where you can sleep, though. It's down by the water. They don't have much food, but what they have is good and no one will hurt you. The nuns who run the place kind of look like angels. I'll take you there if you like."

The shadowy helper opened his arms, and the little girl almost jumped into his embrace. Holding her tight, the boy stood. "I'll see that you're safe. I promise no one will hurt you again." The lad didn't seem to notice the filth of the child, for he held her tightly in loving arms.

The little girl cried softly and hugged her savior tighter. When she did, the boy's hat tumbled.

Seth felt his very bones turn to oatmeal as dark brown hair fell in long curls over the shadow's back.

"True?" Seth whispered her name before he could stop himself.

She glanced in his direction, and he blended deeper into the blackness. He couldn't see her face, but as he looked more closely at the pants and jacket, he could see the curves of a woman and not the lean straightness of a boy. Miss McCormick might have thrown off all the fancy clothes, but the body frame was still the same.

True replaced her hat and disappeared into the darkness at the other end of the alley.

Seth ran after her. He had to see her face. He needed to know that the shadow who moved through the night could be the proper lady he'd had dinner with only hours before.

But the lady was now a citizen of the streets and moved swiftly, easily losing him without even bothering to glance back.

He searched the noisy, wicked streets of Galveston, but found no trace of True carrying a little girl. By the time he finally returned to the hotel, he'd convinced himself that he'd only imagined the boy to be True McCormick. After all, what would a proper young lady, who was obviously educated back East, be doing roaming the streets of one of the roughest towns in the West? It didn't make sense, but then nothing about her made sense.

True carried the child through the darkened streets she'd learned by heart years ago. Emily clung to her so tightly True could hardly breathe, but she didn't try to pull the child away. True remembered how long and dearly she'd waited for someone to help her when she was Emily's age. If three young Harvey girls hadn't taken her in and all declared themselves to be her mother, True wasn't sure she could have survived.

"Don't worry," she whispered. "When we get to the home, they'll have cornbread and milk waiting." She wished she could promise more, but the nuns were begging in the market for meat most days.

Emily rubbed her cheek against True's shoulder. "I figure this place we're goin' must be heaven."

"No," True answered. "It's better than that. It's a place you can call home for as long as you like."

The orphanage was on the edge of town, along the beach. It was a big house, but not large enough for the almost ninety children housed within. When the weather was bad, waves almost lapped the porch steps.

Sister Mary answered the door. "Another," she said, crossing herself and looking Heavenward.

True entered the home run by six French nuns. "Her arm's hurt. Send for the doctor while I clean her up."

The sister followed True into the kitchen. "I can send, but no one will come. The doctors are overworked and we've no way to pay."

"I'll pay," True insisted.

The nun didn't look hopeful. "I'll try. But it's late and they'll have to come all this way."

All conversation stopped while they both worked on cleaning Emily. She wouldn't allow them to touch her arm, but they washed her hair and body. While True dried Emily's hair by the stove, the child downed three glasses of buttermilk stuffed with hunks of cornbread. By the time True pulled a nightgown over her, Emily was falling asleep while still standing.

True lay the sleeping child down on a blanket in the corner of the kitchen. "Let her sleep now. If the doctor hasn't come by morning, let me know. I'll ask Audrey Gates to come."

"She gave up doctoring a long time ago. The last I heard she was packing to leave for the gold fields in Alaska."

"She'll come if I ask her." True sounded sure. Audrey Gates's mind might be a cupboard of abandoned professions and old sayings, but she'd never let True down since they'd met when True was six and Audrey was the pastry cook for one of the first Harvey Houses. "She'll come if she knows a child is hurting."

The nun nodded and smiled. She covered Emily with a cotton kitchen towel.

True looked worried. "You will take her in?" She knew without asking that there wasn't even a blanket to spare in the home.

The sister understood True's question. "We haven't turned a child away yet." She touched True's shoulder as if extending the hospitality to her.

"Thank you," True whispered, then vanished back into the night.

True was several yards down the beach when she saw Sister Mary turn off the light in the kitchen. It was very late, but True needed to walk.

Slowly, as she moved along the beach, the water's movement washed over her worries and pulled away her fears. Her mind relaxed, and the memory of the way Seth had touched her hand in the fog returned. His fingers had been strong and warm, almost caressing. When she'd made up Granite Westwind, she'd created on paper the perfect hero. Maybe she'd never found a man who interested her because she had Westwind and none could measure up to him.

The only problem tonight was that Granite Westwind had become flesh and not the hero of his own adventures in fiction. He'd walked off the pages of her stories and into her life. Seth Atherton was everything she thought a hero would be and more . . . far more.

She could see honor and truth in his eyes. She could almost believe that Seth, like Westwind, would hold good over bad, right over wrong, and honesty no matter the cost. He was a fighter, a survivor—she could feel it with even his slight touch. He was a man who lived in the real world, not fiction.

True knelt in the sand and lifted both halves of an empty shell. The milky inside shone pale in the moonlight.

"Funny thing is," she whispered to herself, "even playing a part, Seth is the more whole person. I'm the one who is only the shell of what I pretend to be."

SIX

∽

An hour later True slipped back through the open window of the private dining room on the second floor of the Harvey House. She'd walked until she'd forced herself to see reality. Seth Atherton was just a drifter, a gunman. True couldn't allow him to matter to her; there was too much at stake. She'd keep their relationship all business, and as soon as the tour was over, she'd pay him and say good-bye. There were books waiting to be written and money already promised.

The room where she and Seth dined earlier was black now, but still warm from the dying fire. This was one of the safest rooms to climb into at the hotel, for here she had no fear of frightening someone who was sleeping. True had left her clothes on a chair and would dress before she moved up another two flights to where the Harvey girls stayed. The waitress, Sally, had promised to have a bed turned down for her. She'd be lucky to get four hours sleep before daybreak.

As True moved across the room, she felt the presence of someone before she saw him. Turning her head slightly, she made out the outline of a man leaning next to the fireplace. His arms were crossed, and along his shadow she noticed the handle of a gun at each hip.

Her first instinct was to run for the window, but she was too far into the room to get away before he caught her.

With the skill of a seasoned soldier, she slipped her hand over the pearl-handled weapon at her waist and raised it toward the outline.

"Who's there?" she demanded.

A low laugh startled her more than a scream would have. "Put down the gun, True," Seth Atherton answered. "I mean you no harm."

"What are you doing here?" True asked between clenched teeth. Never in her years of climbing in and out of windows had she been caught.

"I might ask you the same question." He moved a step closer. "As far as I know this window is not listed as one of the entrances to the hotel, but it certainly has a lot of traffic."

"I'm not in the habit of explaining my comings and goings, Mr. Atherton." True didn't lower her gun even though she slid her finger from the trigger. She'd learned the hard way that it was better to tell nothing than to try and explain her whereabouts. Folks either didn't understand or they felt the need to change her ways.

"And I'm not in the habit of having someone point a gun at me, Miss McCormick." He moved closer. "Which reminds me. That story you told me at dinner about your parents dying was very touching, especially when I met your father a few minutes after I left you."

True removed her hat and allowed her hair to tumble free. "I can explain that, though it's really none of your business." Seth was so close she could feel his words against her cheek.

"Then how about starting with the drunken cowhand at this window earlier and ending with where you went tonight?" He was a creature of order, and there seemed little order in Miss McCormick's life after sunset.

True tilted her head slightly. "I went to meet a lover, as you've probably guessed. Isn't that why all people sneak off in the darkness?" She tossed her hair back, unaware of how becoming she looked. "If he discovers I've told you, he'll come gunning for you. So if I were you, I'd keep my opinion of midnight affairs silent."

"You don't look like the kind of woman who keeps a lover in the shadows."

"And you don't look like the kind of man who sticks his nose into someone else's business. I would have guessed you wiser than that."

Seth couldn't help but tempt death by leaning closer. He could feel the barrel of the gun brush his chest, but this woman had an effect on him worse than liquor. "Does this lover have a name?"

True straightened. "Of course he has a name. My lover's a huge beast of a man named Wiley. He's also the fastest man in Texas with a sidearm and a knife. He'd shoot you twice and claw your eyes out for frightening me tonight."

Seth moved and, with a sudden jerk, pulled the gun from her hand. He'd seen some of what she did in the darkness and wished he could tell her he admired her for it, but her stories got in the way. How could they talk of a child named Emily when she'd made up a ridiculous story about having a lover?

"You left out how fast he'd be with a whip and rifle," Seth teased.

He'd expected her to back away, but she slammed forward with a rage that shocked him. She caught him off balance, and he toppled with her violent shove. Falling, he gripped the gun in one hand and her arm in the other. She tumbled atop him with a yell. Before she could pull away, he rolled and pinned her to the floor.

"Don't make up a story, True," he whispered, wishing she'd open her arms to him as she had the child. "You sound like your boss, Westwind. Maybe you should try writing."

The feel of her beneath him was maddening. Seth's wife had been quiet and gentle, never wild and fiery like True.

Even though he tried to use enough pressure to restrain her, he could feel her moving beneath him. He wanted to hold her so dearly he wasn't sure he could think of anything else. Never, never had a woman's nearness intoxicated him so.

"What makes you think I don't have a lover?" she said, continuing to try and free her self.

He lowered his body over her, pinning her hard against the floor. "This," he whispered as his lips touched hers.

Seth hadn't meant to kiss her. He'd only wanted to make sense out of her life. What kind of woman could be all porcelain cold at dinner and roam the streets at night? He felt as if he'd discovered a being from the stars and had to taste her just once before she vanished. The taste of her only added to the mystery.

Her lips were as soft as he'd thought they might be. Her mouth opened slightly in protest when his kiss grew more insistent.

A kiss meant to be a taste turned deep with the hunger of a lifetime.

"True," he said against her lips, wishing he could put his thoughts into words. She was the most exciting, frustrating woman he'd ever met. She tasted of a passion he'd never craved. Part of him longed to drink deeply of her, another part wanted to run, for she polluted his sterile world with desire.

True went very still in his embrace while she accumulated her anger. A fire burned through her. No man had ever dared kiss her as Seth was kissing her. His mouth was hard, demanding, giving. He was like a man who'd hungered forever for the taste of her lips. She didn't want to admit that the fire of rage inside her was sparked by a passion for more. She'd been kissed before, but never, never like this. Never so wild and strong with raw need.

Seth released his grip on her gun and dug his fingers into

her hair. Cradling her head in his hand, he lifted her slightly to meet his lips. She tasted of magic and wonder and life. More life than he'd ever held. True was soft and strong, sweet and newborn. He'd stake his own life she hadn't just left a lover.

For the first time since his wife died, he wanted another woman in his bed. He wanted her with every ounce of his being and soul. But he was taking what she hadn't freely given. He wanted True in his arms, but willingly.

Seth raised his head and ended the embrace. He couldn't believe he'd kissed her so wild and passionately when she'd done nothing to encourage such an action. She must think him insane. He wasn't sure how it had happened. Maybe this town *was* driving him mad.

"I'm—" he began.

The pearl handle of her Colt slammed into the side of his face, and the room blazed with stars as he rolled off her in pain.

True jumped up and twisted on the light, then stood like a warring savage above him. Her rich hair was wild and free around her flushed cheeks and bruised lips. He wiped the blood from his forehead and looked up at her. She'd never been as beautiful to him as she was now. There was no doubt, he thought, he was going completely mad.

"If you ever try to kiss me again, Mr. Atherton," she stormed at him, "I swear I'll shoot you!"

Seth felt as if he'd been on a three-day drunk and sobered in a blink. "Don't worry, lady. If I ever try to touch you again, you can hand me the gun and I'll shoot myself."

She strode past the dress she'd left folded across a chair and opened the door. "Be ready at six, Mr. Granite Westwind, and try to think of a reason for your injury that the press will accept."

Seth pulled a folded napkin from the table and pressed it

against the wound she'd inflicted. "If I don't bleed to death before daylight."

"If you do, Granite Westwind will write your epitaph!" True showed no sympathy for his pounding head as she slammed the door behind her.

SEVEN

> The moon mourned the loss of an entire settle-
> ment as Granite Westwind rode among the
> ruins, swearing that he'd avenge every man,
> woman, and child slaughtered by the outlaws.
> He lifted a half-burned ribbon from the bloody
> ground and crushed it against his heart, the
> same ribbon little Savanna Smith had worn only
> the night before.

Seth closed the book and wished he could get his hands
on Granite Westwind. The man was milking the audience
for all they were worth. He must be paid by the number of
people he killed off in each book. If as many people had
really died in Texas as Granite seemed to have run across
during his time, there'd have been no one left to repopulate.
It was a wonder someone didn't want to kill him. He painted
the West as a wild and violent place, full of daily gunfights
and hourly Indian raids. Half the folks back East probably
thought it was still that way in Texas.

As he dressed, Seth wondered how such books could get
to be big sellers. He'd seen railroad workers reading them
on breaks, cowhands trading them around a roundup camp-
fire, and boys buying them to fold inside schoolbooks.
Everyone wanted to live the adventurous life between the
pages of a Westwind novel.

Everyone except Seth, that is. He liked his quiet life just
fine. He worked hard all week and enjoyed riding out to the

family farm a few miles from town. His father seemed content to plant a few acres, in garden and tend the fruit trees, but Seth liked to sit with Johnny on his knee and plan how they'd someday run cattle and raise horses on the land. The time was always bittersweet, for he'd remember how Johnny's mother used to dream the same dream with him. She'd always promised they'd have a dozen children who'd need a ranch to roam. But she died about the time the house was finished. Now, with Johnny his only child, Seth's plans were placed in storage. Maybe his grandchildren would fill the house with noise.

A pounding at the door shook him from his daydream. "Are you ready, Mr. Westwind?" came the sound of Micah's raspy voice.

"I'm ready." Seth opened the door and smiled at the old man. He was wearing the same wrinkled white suit, only he'd dressed it up with a new tie. A James A. Garfield campaign button was pinned to one lapel, and a wilted white carnation hung from the other.

Micah bowed low. "Mr. Westwind."

"I guess it's time for the charade to begin." Seth strapped on his holster.

"Yes, sir," Micah answered as he strolled into the room.

"Well, am I presentable?" Seth had gone down to the men's clothing store in the lobby of the hotel and traded all the clothes True had sent him for cash. Then he'd stepped across the street to a huge mercantile and bought his clothes like everyone else. Or at least everyone except Micah, who looked like he'd been wearing the same suit for some time.

Seth's pants were a durable black weave meant to last. His shirt was white, with a string tie added to dress his outfit up a bit. The jacket was leather and molded to his strong shoulders as if it had been tailor-made. The boots were plain and polished. The double-holstered Colts on his hips were the only fancy thing he wore.

"Hope she likes the outfit 'cause I got three more just like this." Seth wanted to add that he'd feel more comfortable in a suit and suspenders, but he guessed that would be too far from how Mr. Westwind would dress.

"I offered to pick out your clothes," Micah said, "but for some reason True doesn't seem to have much faith in my judgment. I told her I'm real good at picking a style that'll last." His eyebrows danced up and down while he lifted a cane in the air.

As Seth passed him, Micah took a close look at the younger man. "But look at you. If I didn't know better, I'd swear you were Granite Westwind in the flesh."

Seth picked up a plain dove-colored Stetson and placed it on his still-damp hair. "Thank you, Micah. I only hope she approves."

While they moved down the hallway, Seth added, "You didn't tell me last night that you knew the real Granite Westwind. I got the impression Miss McCormick was the only one who ever talked with him."

"I don't know him as well as she does. Just pass-and-wave friends you might say." Micah looked uncomfortable with the question. "True is the only one who talks with him."

"Are they courting?" Seth wasn't sure why, but he had to ask. "Or engaged?"

"Heavens no," Micah answered with a laugh.

"Well, what does the man look like? True didn't want to talk about him."

"The Granite Westwind everyone wants to meet looks very much as you do now," Micah said when they started down the stairs. He lowered his voice. "Has Colonel McCormick told you of the problems you may encounter?"

Seth couldn't tell if he'd changed the subject on purpose or because of time. "He mentioned something about someone wanting to stop the tour from taking place." Seth studied Micah carefully. The man was definitely not telling him all he knew. Seth could almost see the words rattling around in his mouth trying to break out. If both the Colonel and Micah were worried about him, maybe there was something to the threats Austin McCormick mentioned.

"Why would anyone want to stop a writer from giving a few public appearances?"

Micah shook his head. "If you ask me, it's not the writer they're gunning for, it's the man. Some folks don't see Westwind as a fictional character from a historical novel, but a real-life man who lives all the adventures he writes about. If they could have a showdown with the great Granite Westwind, that would make them, in a way, equally as great."

Micah shook his head so fast it seemed to take his wrinkled skin a moment to catch up. "The letters Westwind gets frighten me so much I'm thinking of putting off starting my novel. There could be bad trouble if any of those threats materialize."

Seth thumbed his hat back a few inches. "That doesn't make sense. Anyone who reads those novels ought to be able to figure out that no man could really live like that. Hell, the West he lives in never existed. Most days were dull and routine."

"Dull and routine doesn't sell books." Micah reached the bottom of the stairs. "Speaking of selling books, the show is about to begin."

Seth looked around the lobby and saw twenty men in plaid suits waiting for him. They had all been given coffee and huge plates of tiny cinnamon rolls, so they couldn't very well rush him today. He had a feeling the refreshments served just before his arrival were planned.

Miss McCormick sat at a table in the center of the room with a stack of Westwind books beside her. Her hair was pulled into a tight little bun, her lace collar worn high around her neck. She looked so proper, Seth found it impossible to believe this could be the same woman he'd kissed. He stared at the wire-rimmed glasses perched on her nose and wished he could shatter the wall between them as easily as he could crush the glasses in his fist. But he knew there were two things that would never happen. He'd never be as close to True as he'd like to be, and he'd never break her glasses, no matter how much he hated the way they hid her eyes.

Seth noticed the empty chair beside her and headed straight toward it.

"Morning, Miss McCormick," he said, removing his hat and sliding into place. He didn't look her in the eyes, for he knew that if he did, the attraction he felt would still be there. Since he'd never had such strong feelings toward a woman, he figured it would take a while to learn to hide them, but he'd manage. She'd made it plain how she felt toward him, and he'd respect her wishes. He'd never beg a woman to care for him. And if he tried to kiss her again, he had the feeling she'd use the other end of the gun next time.

"Good morning, Mr. Westwind." She glanced at the bruise on the side of his forehead. "You look well today." Her voice was so formal it could have belonged to one of the Harvey girls serving coffee.

Seth didn't want to think about the fool he'd made of himself the night before. She must think him so starved for a touch that he attacked women. She wouldn't have to hit him twice with her Colt to make her point. "Shall we begin?" he said as formally as he could.

"Yes," she whispered as she stood and straightened into the porcelain lady he'd first met. "Gentlemen of the press," her voice grew louder and became all business, "Mr. Westwind would like to autograph a book for each of you at this time. I'm his secretary. Please address all questions to me while he's writing. When he's finished, he'll be happy to take as many questions as time will allow."

The reporters stepped before the table one after the other. Each asked True a few questions while Seth signed the books. By the time they were halfway through with the autographs, Seth could have answered the questions himself, for they were the same ones over and over again. He also noticed that when Miss McCormick didn't seem to know an answer, she said she couldn't reveal such a fact at this time because it was part of the subject of the book Mr. Westwind was working on.

The story of Granite Westwind was totally different from Seth's life. Granite's parents had been killed by Indians soon after he was born. He was raised by an older relative who was a frontiersman. He'd cut his teeth on adventure by joining the Texas Rangers and served as both an Indian scout and a railroad troubleshooter.

The life stories were so far apart it was almost laughable. Seth had spent the past twelve years of his life building a business while Granite had killed hundreds of cattle rustlers and renegade Indians. Granite might not stop until every bad guy was caught, but Seth didn't leave the office until the books balanced for the day.

Seth couldn't hide a smile. His life was so boring compared to Westwind's.

If True knew how dull his life was, Seth thought, she'd probably be bored to death, after knowing Westwind. He had to let her believe he was a gunfighter; at least that sounded more interesting than being a small town hardware store owner trying to raise a son.

True smiled politely at a reporter as she handed out the last book. "Thank you for coming, gentlemen. I'm sure Mr. Westwind would like to stay and visit, but he has a train to catch."

Seth followed her lead and stood. He was careful not to touch her. "Thanks for coming by, fellows," he said, knowing they expected him to say something. "You'll be hearing about what I'm up to in my next book."

As the men moved closer, Micah stepped between Seth and the reporters. Suddenly, they all seemed to have one more question to ask before he left, and Seth had a feeling it would be the same way even if he stayed another hour.

Micah knew his job. He separated Seth and True from the reporters and hurried them into a hallway.

Seth thanked the old man with a slight pat on the shoulder. "Did you used to be in the circus or on the stage? You do that pretty well, old-timer."

Micah grinned. "I was a preacher for a time. Ain't no better way to learn about moving the masses." He barred the door when a reporter tried to open it. "Y'all go on. I'll catch up to you in a day or two."

"Follow me through the kitchen," True whispered as she pulled on her jacket and lifted her case. "We can avoid any others."

Seth placed his arm at the small of her back and followed. As they crossed through the narrow employee entrance, he was aware of how very small she was. He would have sworn she was one hundred–proof lady if he hadn't seen her last night. In the darkness he'd felt a woman full of fire and passions. That warm, feeling woman was somewhere inside this cold china casing.

Several Harvey employees waved good-bye as Seth and

True crossed the street and passed through the Harvey House to the train station. It was more than a polite gesture. Seth had the feeling these people really cared about True, as though she were one of the family.

One of the cooks handed True a note when they passed. "This came from the orphanage," the woman whispered.

True nodded her thanks and stepped out of the hotel.

They walked across the loading dock to a private car. Several families stood along the dock, stretching their legs before climbing back onto the train. "I booked a private car so you wouldn't have to answer questions from town to town. Mr. Westwind's publisher agreed to cover the cost for the month," True explained. "If you'll go on inside, I had the Harvey House deliver breakfast for you. Your luggage has already been packed and sent down, including the gun you checked at the restaurant last night."

"Aren't you coming?" Seth fought the urge to touch her. He didn't want the tour to be like this—them close in public, then separating as soon as she could get away. He had to prove to her that she had nothing to fear from being near him.

"I'll be back later. I've somewhere to go before we leave Galveston."

Seth glanced at the steps of the passenger car, knowing his breakfast was getting cold. "I'm going with you."

"No," True said simply. "That's unnecessary."

"But I need to ask you a few questions before I run into any more reporters." True glanced around as if debating running while Seth continued, "I'm going with you, Miss McCormick."

True didn't have time to argue. She knew there was trouble at the home or the nuns wouldn't have sent her a note. She didn't have to read the message. The train was due to leave in one hour and she needed every minute. There was no time to make up a story Seth would believe about her destination.

"Then come along." She shoved her writing satchel onto the top step of their private car. "I haven't got time to argue."

Seth followed her along the platform to where several hacks waited for hire. She climbed into the first one and gave the driver directions before Seth was seated. The driver slapped the horse into action, knocking Seth backward in the seat. He almost fell across True.

"Get off of me!" She shoved him, angry that he'd barged into her private life. "Are you sure you've had nothing to drink today? I've heard people say that once a man takes to the bottle it's very hard for him to quit."

Seth sat closer than necessary. "Despite what you may think of me from the way we met, I'm not the town drunk. I do manage to stay sober during most daylight hours."

"Oh," True twisted in the seat to stare at him, "am I to understand that your being in jail was a once-in-a-lifetime experience?"

Seth laughed. "Would you believe me if I said it was?"

"No."

"Then I might as well admit it's my second home," Seth lied.

"And what do you do when you're not residing at the local jail?" True didn't want to admit that she cared. She'd meant to keep her distance from this handsome man who would be out of her life in days, but he was too close to ignore. His shoulder was touching hers, and when the buggy rocked, his leg brushed lightly against her. He was too real for her to be comfortable. She felt much safer with her men living only on the pages of books.

"I've got a place in the country," Seth said honestly. "It's not much more than land and trees, but it's real pretty. My father retired out there to follow his dream of farming, but I'm afraid I spend little time there."

She had to ask. "Are you married?"

"I was." Seth looked away. He never talked about Marcy with anyone. Everyone in his life already knew about her, except Johnny, who'd been too young to remember. "My wife died over five years ago."

"Is that when you took to gunfighting and drinking?" True could never resist asking questions.

Seth looked at her and raised an eyebrow. "Among other things," he said, making it plain that he didn't want to talk about his wife's death. Knowing True, she'd probably think overwork was a vice equal to the first two she'd mentioned.

"Sometimes loneliness is easier to handle than the pain that comes along with people or love." True had meant the words to be kind, but they came out preachy.

Seth held to the bar handle on the buggy. He didn't want to talk about his life; he wanted to just enjoy this day. "Where are we going, anyway?"

True watched him closely. He didn't sound all that interested in anything but changing the subject.

"To a huge house on the beach. It's used by a group of nuns from France who have set up an orphanage."

Seth groaned. "I don't care much for kids." He didn't want to tell her that the little girl she'd helped last night had almost broken his heart with her suffering.

True laughed. "That's what my father used to say."

Looking at her with a mocking smile, Seth added, "Yeah, but I can see why he might have had reason to make such a statement."

True's fist balled to defend herself without any thought that she was acting the part of a lady this morning. It wouldn't be the first time she had fought dressed in lace.

Seth raised his hands in surrender before she could level

a blow. "I see that fire sparking in those beautiful blue eyes of yours, and I might as well give up before I get whipped again."

Lowering her fist, True replied, "I noticed you were only slightly bruised by the lesson."

"I'm a fast learner."

The buggy slammed to a stop, almost throwing the travelers out. True straightened her coat and jumped down without accepting the hand he offered. "Wait here," she said to the driver. "We won't be long."

"But . . . ," the driver started to argue.

"Follow the lady's wishes," Seth said. "I'll make it worth your time."

He took hold of True's elbow and started up the sandy path leading to the orphanage. "Which reminds me. I had some money in my pocket the night I went to jail. Old Rank didn't happen to give it to you when you paid me out, did he?"

"Not a dime," True answered.

Seth wasn't surprised. "Then I'll need an advance on my salary. It wouldn't be proper for you to pay the hack or buy my dinner."

"But that's part of the deal."

"I don't care." Seth tried to keep his voice low. "I don't like a woman picking up my bills."

True wasn't sure she understood, but she pulled two new twenty-dollar gold pieces from her bag. "Here. This should make you feel better. Now you can pay your own way, but I'm taking this advance out of your pay."

Seth crammed the money in his pocket. He didn't like taking money from her even if she was his boss. There was something that felt wrong about it. Then he realized he'd never worked for anyone but himself.

When they reached the bottom of the steps, children came running to greet them. They all seemed to know True, and

Seth heard several thank her for the cinnamon rolls she'd sent over from the Harvey House. The children were worse than the reporters as they surrounded her.

Only one child stood back away from the others. She'd been cleaned up, but Seth knew she was the one True had coaxed from under the steps last night. Her curly hair, minus the dirt, was light blond. She looked like a little angel all dressed in the white uniform of the home. Only the bloodstained bandage on her arm and the tear rolling down her face reminded him of the life she'd lived.

"Emily?" Seth folded down to her level, having no idea how to talk to her. Yet she looked so alone, he had to give it a try.

She stared at him with frightened eyes. "Who are you?"

"I'm Se—" He'd better keep the game up even out here. "I'm Granite Westwind, a friend of True's."

Emily's eyes widened. "You're a hero. The nuns read me one of your stories late last night when I woke up afraid."

Without any warning, she lifted her arms to him.

For a moment he didn't know what to do. She looked within a year of Johnny's age by height, but the pain in her eyes had to have taken more than six years to accumulate. She must have been eight, maybe nine, though very small for her age. Slowly, carefully, he lifted her in his embrace and stood. She clung to him as tightly as she could.

"I'm scared," she whispered and began to cry softly against his shoulder. "I wish I could be brave like you, but I can't."

Seth spread his big hand over her back and wished he could protect her against the world. He didn't know what else to do but let her cry. "It's going to be all right," he whispered, wishing he believed it.

"No," Emily sobbed. "The doc says she has to operate on my cut or a gang might set in and I'd lose my arm."

"A gang?" Seth asked.

A tall woman in a black-and-white pin-striped suit stepped from inside and answered, "Gangrene." She offered her hand, but everything about her, from her rigid back to her frown, was less than friendly. "I'm Audrey Gates, and you are?"

Seth shifted the child in his arms. "I'm Granite Westwind."

"Of course you are. The hero come to life." Her dislike seemed to jell instantly into hatred. "How could I have not recognized you?"

Seth knew he'd best change the subject. From the look she was giving him, it seemed she was no fan of Westwind. "Tell me about Emily."

With his comment, Audrey smiled at the child, and he realized what a beautiful woman she could be.

"I've just tried to explain to her that the arm is badly infected. I brought along a fine doctor from the medical school to operate on it in order to remove some of the dead skin. With the operation, she'll only have a scar. Without it, she'll lose her arm and maybe her life."

Seth lifted one of the child's sunshine curls in his palm. "You've got to let the doctor help you, Emily. It's the only way."

"I can't!" Emily cried. "I'm scared!"

He said the only thing that he could think of, "I'll be right here with you."

The little girl's crying stopped abruptly. She looked up at Seth and wiped her nose on her sleeve. "You'll stay with me till it's over?"

"Of course," Seth answered with determination while he watched True moving in his direction. Today was the first day of their tour, and he was already planning to cancel.

True nodded as if she understood, and they all walked into the house. "I'll let the people in Houston know we'll be in later,"

True whispered as she brushed Seth's shoulder with her fingers.

The action was small, almost unnoticed, but Seth felt the warmth of her hand long after she'd left the room. Somehow, of all the things he'd done since he'd known her, he'd finally done something right.

Three hours later the surgery was over and Emily was resting quietly. Seth stood on the porch of the orphanage watching the ocean roll in and out. He'd sat beside her bed during the surgery and felt her pain even as she lay unconscious. Now it was difficult to let go and move away from this child he hadn't know existed until last night.

The thought kept crossing his mind—if he hadn't been around to take care of Johnny, would someone have sat with his son as Seth had with Emily? If Johnny were alone in the world, would a woman like True find him? Seth feared that would be a long shot.

"Want some coffee?" True asked from behind him.

"Thanks," Seth took the cup from her hand, noticing she'd let her hair down. The moist breeze made it curl and wave in a wonderful cloud around her shoulders, making her look almost childlike. Seth swallowed the coffee and tried to think of something to say besides how her beauty took his breath away. "I thought the doc would never finish. That Audrey woman was right by his side telling him what to do half the time."

"Audrey is almost as good a doctor as she is a cook. When I was a kid, I stayed with her one summer when she taught at the medical school here in Galveston. I think that was the summer before she opened a hat shop in Dallas."

"Quite a woman. Has she ever married?"

"No," True answered. "She loved a man once, but he disappeared. I doubt she'd be any happier with one man than she would be with one career. We're lucky to have caught her. I think she leaves for the gold strike in Alaska in a few days. But she'll be back. Micah says no one ever says good-bye to Audrey. It's a waste of words."

Seth watched True closely, wondering if she were very much like Audrey Gates. Neither was the type of woman who would want to settle in a little place like Timber Creek.

He looked out at the water, trying to decide why it even mattered to him one way or the other. "Do you think Emily is going to be all right?"

"She'll be fine, thanks to you." True walked past him and stared out into the Gulf. "The nuns said she wouldn't think about allowing the doctor to cut on her before you came along this morning. You may have very well saved her life."

"I'm glad I could help. It makes me sad to think that a kid so small could have an accident that would leave a wound like that, and no one around to notice she was hurting."

True turned to face him. "It wasn't an accident." Each word seemed hard for her to say. "A butcher named Alex, who delivers meat to the hotels, cut her arm with his knife because she was stealing a few ounces of his delivery. Sort of taking his pound of flesh for her theft."

"That couldn't be true." He didn't want to believe such a thing. "Why didn't she tell someone?"

"He's cut others, only not so deeply. I can show you more scars on arms here at the home. Besides, who would she tell? If she couldn't get anyone to notice her bleeding, who would help her? Even without the cut, she's so thin she wouldn't have lived another winter on the streets."

In sudden anger Seth threw his coffee cup as hard as he could onto the beach. Before True could say more, he was off the porch in one bound and running toward the waiting hack.

"Where do you think you're going?" True yelled.

"Never mind," Seth answered. "I'll be back in a half hour." He turned and pointed a finger at her in warning. "And don't follow me, lady."

True tilted her head slightly to the left and smiled. "I wouldn't dream of it."

EIGHT

True ran back into the house, certain she knew where Seth was going. He planned to teach the butcher a lesson. She'd thought of the same thing herself, but hadn't acted as fast as he had.

She should have realized a fighter like Seth Atherton would take action first and talk later. Hadn't he kissed her without asking? Hadn't they met in jail after he'd been in a fight? What more proof did she need?

"Send one of the boys to saddle a horse!" True yelled as she took the steps in double time, heading for the attic. "Do you still have a change of clothes for me upstairs?" She didn't wait for the nun to answer.

Audrey Gates was right behind True. "You're not planning to do something foolish like go after that butcher, are you?"

"No!" True shouted. "I'm going after the fool who's already gone after the butcher."

Audrey paused. "Not your Granite Westwind?"

"Yes." True was half a flight ahead. "Without me, he'll get himself killed the first day I hired him." She knew he was fiery, but she figured she could handle him at least during the tour.

"He's libel to get you both killed." Audrey started back down the stairs. "I'll go see if Austin McCormick is still in town and tell him to stop this insanity. My Granny Gates used to say half the men in Texas should be shot for being crazy. Near as I can tell Granny was only half right."

"It'll be too late," True said as she vanished into the attic. Hurriedly she rummaged through the bundle of clothes she'd left at the home in case she ever needed them. "No gun!" she whispered in frustration as she realized she'd be of little help to Seth without a weapon. True had placed her Lightning Colts in her case this morning, thinking the most dangerous thing she'd be doing was boarding the train. Now they were halfway to Houston and she was here.

The nuns wouldn't have anything smaller than a shotgun, and Audrey never carried a pistol. True's only choice was to ride back to the Harvey House and talk Micah out of one of those old relics he called weapons, then pray she wasn't too late to stop Seth from being killed. The butcher was not a man to challenge alone. He had a reputation in town for using his knife for more than business, and more than one man who faced him had been stabbed before he could clear leather.

Tying back her hair with a ribbon, True started down the stairs with the same haste with which she'd climbed them. Audrey and the nuns were nowhere in sight as she ran out the front door and onto the porch.

"I saddled our horse," a boy said while he held the reins of the oldest mustang True had ever seen. "He ain't much, but you don't have to worry about him bolting and running off on you."

True thanked the boy and climbed into the saddle. She'd learned to ride years ago when one of her adoptive mothers had married a rancher.

Slapping the horse into a walk, True promised herself she'd buy the children's home a new horse as soon as she had the money.

It seemed to take her hours to get to Micah's small office on the third floor of the Sante Fe Building, which also contained the Harvey House.

His writer's room there was a duplicate of the one he kept in Dallas. Books and yellowed paper were stacked in a room more suited for a closet than an office. Aging articles he'd written years ago for the local newspaper covered one wall. The only order was in the tall stack of Westwind novels carefully placed on a shelf behind his desk. Each one had been autographed to him personally by Westwind.

True talked him out of an old Patterson Colt in minutes, but the thing barely fit into the oversized pocket of her skirt. Micah knew she was a fine shot, but he'd never been one who cared much for weapons. He said he'd seen enough killing during the War Between the States to last him ten lifetimes.

"I'm going with you." Micah stood from behind his desk and pulled a dusty white Panama hat from atop a pile of books. It was a size too big, but it seemed to go with his baggy white suit. "After all, it's my fault. I'm the one who talked you into writing the damned Westwind books in the first place. If it wasn't for me, you'd have probably married some farmer and have five kids by now."

"Not likely," True answered, remembering the night Micah had sat up until dawn listening to her tell one story after another about the adventures she'd heard. He'd talked her into writing them down, and she'd had a friend in New York submit the manuscripts for her.

"We're wasting daylight." True hurried out the door, knowing Micah would follow. "Trouble's on the wind."

"You're starting to sound like one of your books, again." Micah laughed. "Wouldn't it be a hoot if Seth Atherton became your Granite Westwind? He's handsome enough, I'll give him that, and did you see those shoulders? I swear it looks like he's been lifting heavy supplies all his life and not gun fighting."

"More likely, he'll be buried as Granite Westwind. I

believed him when he told me he had no desire to be a hero."

Micah followed her through the building. "He's a nice enough fellow, but he's got the eyes of a man who was born to wander. Mark my words, girl, that man never slept in the same bed long enough to worry about changing the sheets."

True didn't answer as she crossed the street to the side road leading to the butcher's shop. Alex the Butcher didn't sell to the public, only to restaurants and hotels, so there was no need for a fancy storefront entrance.

Micah kept mumbling as they walked. "But I'll tell you, darlin', he's sure as hell acting like a hero. Running off to save a little girl. Sounds like something Westwind would do. But then I always thought the character a little too good. I'll hold my judgment on Seth until the type's set."

The air was strangely silent as they moved toward the open door of Alex's shop. True could smell the blood that coated the floor of all such establishments. She could also smell the odor of rotting meat as she stepped slowly from the side street into the darkness of the business.

"Mr. Alex!" she shouted. "Is anyone here?"

The room was littered with beef. It looked as though a food fight had just happened and all the ammunition had been raw meat. Micah shadowed the doorway as True moved farther inside.

"Mr. Alex!" she called again as she stepped around the counter.

The air smelled like a battlefield, thanks to the blood and dust. Several knives were scattered across the floor, and one was stuck in the window frame.

Something moved from behind the curtain dividing the workroom from what looked to be back living quarters. True raised her borrowed gun and stepped closer. She knew she'd have only enough time to get off one shot if a knife came flying from between the curtains, so she must make it count.

"Who's there?" True held her breath. "Come out or I'll shoot you through the cloth."

The curtain seemed to tremble for a moment before a slight man in his fifties slowly moved out. His clothes were covered in blood, and his face was as white as bleached linen. "Don't shoot, miss. We've had enough trouble this morning."

True lowered the gun slightly. "What happened?"

"Some crazy man came in here about fifteen minutes ago. He wanted to talk to Mr. Alex. At first he acted real nice, like he was opening a new restaurant and might need some meat." The man was still so frightened his words came out almost like hiccups. "Then he asked Mr. Alex how he handled folks stealing deliveries."

True closed her eyes. She could see how Seth had set the man up, making sure he was the right one before striking. She had to admire Seth for that, even though part of the blood on the floor was probably his.

The little man continued, "I didn't hear what Mr. Alex said, but the next thing I knew the stranger was using the boss for a punching bag."

The man's arms began to fly around him like twin windmills. "The stranger was hitting Alex from every direction. Throwing him across the counters. Shoving him up against the displays." He stopped suddenly and whispered, "Then Alex pulled the knife he keeps on the back of his belt. The stranger saw the blow coming and blocked it with both hands. He didn't see the other knife Alex pulled from his boot."

True fought down a scream. "Is he hurt?"

The slight man nodded. "Pretty bad, I'm afraid. Both his

eyes are almost swollen shut, and his face looks like it was hit with a cleaver. His wife was giving him hell for fighting when I left him."

"Wife?" She forced herself to take a deep breath of the smelly air. "No, not Mr. Alex. Was the stranger hurt?"

The man nodded. "The boss slit him across the gut, but I don't think it was too bad because he was still yelling when three deputies carried him off a few minutes ago."

True stumbled into Micah in her haste to leave.

"Now, slow down," Micah warned. "Don't go off half-cocked. At least we know where he is and that he's alive."

"We've got to get to him." True shoved her way past Micah. "He may be dying."

She lifted her skirts and ran in a most unladylike way down the side road. When she reached the street, True slowed to a more proper pace. The jail was only a block away. She couldn't bear to think what the jailor might do to Seth this time. Everyone who'd met the man knew the Rank's fondness for giving his customers a few extra licks. With Seth bleeding, the blows might kill him.

True whirled into the sheriff's office like a tiny dust devil crossing the open plains. She addressed the jailor. "Mr. Rank, are you holding my brother here again?"

Rank's feet hit the floor at the same time his chair fell upright. "Getting here mighty fast, aren't you, miss?" He glanced at the three deputies who'd brought Seth in. They were standing around a cold Franklin stove trying to wipe blood off their clothes.

"I need to see him. Now!" True tried to make her voice sound calm.

"I ain't sure I've even finished with the charges yet on that so-called brother of yours. He darn near killed a man this morning for no reason at all. I suggest you come back tomorrow. These things take time to look into. It's going to cost you more to get him out this time. He's a real bad one."

True was in no mood to argue. She brushed the handle of the gun in her skirt pocket and debated busting Seth out of this two-bit jail. Her hesitation was more from having to explain her actions to her father than any fear of the jailor.

"But I understand he was hurt in the fight. I need to see him. He may need medical attention."

"If he'll quieten down, he won't bleed to death." Rank crossed his arms as if dynamite would be needed to blast him from his chair. "Men like him don't die in some jail, they die in a gunfight in the street. One look in those gray eyes and you can tell he's a born killer."

True could hear Seth yelling an oath against Rank from somewhere behind the barred door. She almost smiled with relief. At least she knew he was still alive.

Rank placed his feet back on his desk and let out a long yawn. "You ain't seeing him today, lady, unless fish start flying."

"I'll get a lawyer!" True threatened.

Rank laughed. "There ain't an honest lawyer on this island who'd run up against me. I suggest you take that old companion with you and come back tomorrow."

"But . . ."

"Now!" Rank yelled. "Before I throw you two in jail as well."

True fingered the handle of the gun in her pocket once more. Just before she lifted it from the folds, they heard boots stomping across the porch.

With a sudden slam, Colonel Austin McCormick entered the room. On a calm afternoon, sitting in a rocker, he was an impressive man, but armed and angry he was downright magnificent. He was flanked on either side by men who looked as only Texas Rangers looked—tough and rock-hard to the bone.

Rank's chair hit the floor for the second time. He jumped up as if he knew he was about to see fish fly. The jailor stood open-mouthed as a tall woman in a pin-striped jacket hurried around the Colonel.

"I'm here to treat Mr. Westwind." The woman was full of purpose. "I'm Dr. Audrey Gates." She glanced down as if to show a doctor's bag, then put her hands behind her, hoping no one else would notice she'd come unprepared.

"Mr. Westwind?" Rank tried to hang on to a thread of his dignity. "We ain't got no Mr. Westwind in this jail, Doc."

The Colonel's voice was only a whisper, but everyone froze listening. "The man you just brought in for fighting at the butcher shop is, to my understanding, Granite Westwind. I'm Colonel McCormick with the Texas Rangers, and we're here to ensure his safety."

Rank felt as if all his blood was dribbling out his toes. He didn't even have the energy to order his men to open the cell. The famous Granite Westwind was in his jail, and he hadn't even known it. Hell, he'd said the man had killer eyes.

"Well, don't just stand there!" Dr. Gates ordered. "Open the cell."

Rank did as he was told. He stood like a doorman as True and the old man passed him, then the doctor, then more Rangers than he'd ever seen gathered together at once.

Before everyone could get in the cell, Audrey Gates exclaimed that she wouldn't make mud pies in this filth much less doctor a man. Two of the young Rangers picked up a protesting Granite Westwind and carried him out.

"I'll take responsibility for this man," Colonel McCormick said as he passed Rank. "Is he being charged with anything?"

"He beat up the butcher," Rank mumbled.

"Then," Austin grumbled, "I suggest you investigate the butcher."

Rank nodded. He suspected what the butcher had been doing, but he had no evidence. However, the word of Granite Westwind might be proof enough for him to try and get the butcher to change his ways.

Seth swore as the Rangers lugged him none-too-gently through the office and out the door. His shirt was bloody and his lip looked as if it were bleeding, but that didn't seem to lessen the yelling.

"Take him to the Harvey House!" Audrey ordered. "It's the only place close I know will be clean enough."

As True passed Rank, she said, "I'll take Mr. Westwind's guns."

Rank noticed that the Colonel waited for her at the door. "Yes, miss."

True looked slightly guilty. "I'm sorry I had to lie to you last night about Mr. Westwind's identity, but he likes to travel just as an ordinary cowhand sometimes. It helps in the research."

"I understand," Rank said, already thinking of the stories he'd tell his friends at the bar tonight. "I knew he wasn't no regular cowhand the minute I brought him in after the bar fight."

"You did?"

"Sure. Ordinary cowhands don't have four hundred dollars cash in their pocket."

"Of course." True smiled. "Not much gets past you, does it, Officer Rank?"

"No, miss." Rank grinned, figuring he'd saved a little of his pride by making the point.

True lifted her palm, remembering the two twenty-dollar

gold pieces she'd handed Seth this morning. "By the way, I'll take Mr. Westwind's four hundred and forty dollars."

Rank reddened and glanced at the door to see if McCormick was still watching. He was.

He pulled the money from the desk and counted it out to True, silently cursing himself for being so smart.

True took the money and walked out, with Micah and McCormick flanking her.

NINE

True waited with Micah and her father outside Seth's door. She'd listened several times to the Colonel's lecture about how her wild schemes always got someone hurt. She knew it was just Austin's way of telling her how much he loved her, but if it hadn't been for her need to see Seth alive, she would have escaped hours ago.

All her life, she'd handled her problems by running. Luckily, her three mothers had never tried to hold her too tightly. She'd learned when she was younger than Emily that the only person she could depend on was herself. Her adoptive father had saved her from commiting a crime today, but tomorrow he might be in the state capital and Micah might be writing some story from his past and not know what month he was in.

A hero like Seth had always been with her in spirit. Late at night when she'd roamed the streets of half the towns in the West, she'd often pretended someone like him, her own private Granite Westwind, walked beside her. In her fantasies, he'd always understood and gone along with her schemes. But in her dreams he'd never gotten hurt!

"Hiring a man to play Granite Westwind has got to be at the top on your list of crazy ideas," McCormick said as he finished his lecture. "If anyone finds out he's a fake, the real Granite Westwind will be fired and you'll be out of a job, True."

"No, she's had wilder ideas." Micah twirled his hat with the skill of a dandy as he eased the conversation away from

Westwind and onto safer ground. "I remember a time when True and I were living at the Beasley Boarding House in Dallas."

McCormick frowned at Micah, but the old writer didn't take the hint. "She was tired of hearing all the snoring going on around her every night and decided to make everyone believe the place was haunted by old man Beasley's first wife."

True giggled. "I almost pulled it off."

"I think it was leaving the footprint on the cake icing that gave you away."

McCormick didn't want to admit he was interested, but one eyebrow rose as he waited for the story to unfold. He'd learned after meeting Micah years ago that old writers never die, they just rewrite the stories in their lives until no one knows where fact leaves off and fiction begins.

Laughter seemed to be fighting to break out all over Micah. "You see, the first Mrs. Beasley had been almost six feet tall in her not-so-tiny stockinged feet. When Beasley saw the dainty footprint, he lost his faith in ghosts."

True defended herself. "How was I to know? From her picture, I thought the woman was simply homely. I didn't know she was also a pine."

"To make matters worse, you tracked icing all the way back to your room," Micah added. "When Beasley kicked you out, I was dumb enough to speak up and he had my things packed and beside yours on the porch before you finished buttoning your shoes."

McCormick laughed. "That's not as bad as when you put privy signs on the new church's confessionals." He exploded with laughter.

True stood and paced. "I'm glad I could bring you two such enjoyment in your old age." She looked toward the door. "But this time I got someone hurt."

Austin McCormick shook his head. "You didn't do anything to him, True. Seth did what he thought he had to do. To tell the truth, when Audrey told me what the butcher had done, I had a mind to do much the same as your man. I can't fault him for wanting to help a child. It happened to me once myself." He looked at True, remembering how she'd captured his heart the day she'd met him.

"But what if he dies?"

"He's made of tougher stuff than you give him credit for, kid." Austin took her hand. "I heard he was asking questions about one of the meanest men in Texas before he signed up with you to play this little game. If Seth is lucky, he won't find this guy they call Hawk Sloan."

She started to ask more, but the door opened.

"True," Audrey whispered from Seth's room. "You can come in now."

"How is he?" True asked.

"He's fine," Audrey answered. "Most of the blood I cleaned off him belonged to someone else. If he takes it easy tomorrow, I don't see any reason he can't travel by train. To someone as hardheaded as your Mr. Westwind seems, this is only a scratch."

"Thanks."

"Don't thank me or send for me again." Her voice was stern, but Audrey's smile was as warm as always toward True. "I had to bribe Mary, my housekeeper, to unpack my doctor's kit this morning when the nuns sent a note. I told you before, I gave up doctoring a long time ago. I'm on my way to Alaska to pan for gold in a few days, and when I get back, I plan on opening my own bakery." She didn't give True any time to question her. "I've decided giving up cooking is harder than giving up doctoring. Folks get hungry a lot more often than they need a doctor, and no one ever calls a baker out in the middle of the night."

Audrey seemed to ignore Austin and Micah's grumbling from the hallway. They'd both known her long enough to guess this wasn't her final career choice.

True passed the doctor and entered Seth's room. He was propped up in bed against the headboard with his eyes closed. The afternoon sun danced in his hair, like diamonds in midnight. His shirt lay piled on the floor and a white bandage was wrapped around his waist. His bare chest looked as if it had been carved from solid muscle.

"Hello, cowboy," True whispered. "Rough day on the range?"

"I've had better," he answered as he slowly opened blue-gray eyes to watch her. He wanted to add that he'd never had worse. He hadn't been in a fight in all his adult life before he came to Galveston, and this was his second in less than a week. At this rate his son wouldn't recognize him when he got back to Timber Creek.

True sat cross-legged on the bed beside him. "I'm sorry. Somehow, I figure it was my fault."

"No." Seth didn't move; this was the closest she'd come to him willingly since he'd met her, and he didn't want to frighten her away. "I guess I lost my temper." He could never remember being so angry, or losing control so completely.

"I understand." True leaned closer and lay her hand gently on his arm. "We'll take the train tomorrow. I should have guessed that a man who lives the life you do is used to taking swift and violent action."

Seth didn't answer. He couldn't without telling her the truth about himself. Somehow he guessed she would understand a gunfighter's life far easier than she would a small town store owner's. She'd grown up around men like Colonel McCormick and the Texas Rangers. Adventure must be True's middle name. How would she understand the pleasure he felt when his inventory balanced at the end of the quarter? How could he explain that this man before her, that she seemed to be trying to understand so well, was opposite from him?

Her touch was light, but it might as well have been a boulder weighing down his heart. He tried to remember the last time a woman had touched him, with kindness. He'd gladly beat up the butcher again if she'd stay so near. It crossed his mind that what might make men crave adventure was the women waiting to hear their stories. Somehow just being near True was changing him. He felt as though someone were spinning him hard and all his emotions were flying out to the surface, exposed and raw.

"Are you all right?" True placed her fingers on his forehead, softly brushing his hair to one side. "You look pale. Should I get the doc?"

"No." Seth closed his eyes and gritted his teeth. He wasn't sure when it had started, this need to touch her. Maybe it had been growing since last night when he'd tried to protect her by pulling her under the table. "I'm fine," he lied, for how could he ever tell her about the pain she caused in his heart? It had been far easier to confront Alex with his knives, than to reach out and capture True's hand in his.

"Can I get you something?"

Seth was silent for so long she wasn't sure he planned to answer. Then, finally, he whispered, "Could we start over?" He knew he was leaving her in a few days. She wasn't of his real world. But he'd like to have a memory to take home.

"Over?"

"Seems like since we first met you've been getting a bad impression of me. Not that some of it isn't true, but I'd like a chance to put the right foot forward for a change. Maybe I'm not as bad or as wild as you think."

"What would you like to do? Go back to the jail and begin again?"

"No. I've tried that already today." Seth feared it was impossible. He'd spent most of the time they'd been together making a fool of himself. "I'd like to invite you to dinner. That is if Rank left me any of the advance money you gave me this morning."

True pulled the roll of bills from her pocket. "It seems when he realized who you were, he remembered the money from last night as well."

Seth took the cash in disbelief. He'd never thought he'd see his four hundred dollars again. He'd brought far more money than needed to Galveston when he'd decided to look for Jesse's killer, with the thought that he might have to buy a great many drinks to loosen a few tongues.

"You're not the drifter you claimed to be," True reasoned aloud. "Drifters don't carry hundred-dollar bills."

"I never said I was a drifter," Seth answered, realizing that with the money he could square his debt with her and go back home. He could hand her half the cash for her trouble and be on the next train to Timber Creek.

"You listed your occupation as gunman. Men who wear a gun for hire don't usually hang around in one place too long."

"Maybe I had a run of luck with cards?"

True laughed. "Sure. You looked like you were the lucky type when I first saw you in jail."

Seth's hand covered his bandage as he laughed.

True took a wild guess. "You had a reason for coming to Galveston besides getting drunk and into some bar fight. My father hinted at it just now in the hallway, but I knew there was no use asking more because he tends to close up when it comes to telling too much about someone else's business."

Seth's dark eyes hardened, and she knew she'd guessed right. "You were here on business," she whispered.

Letting out a long breath, he wondered how much he should tell her. He could see the excitement in her eyes. She thought she was going to uncover a story.

"Yes," he answered, slowly leaning close enough to smell the honey soap she must wash her hair in. "Private business."

Her eyes widened with interest as she waited.

Seth knew he should pull away, but her nearness was like watching a lightning storm. He should take cover, but the beauty of it fascinated him.

Silent seconds passed. Her face reddened slightly. "You're not going to tell me, are you?"

"No." He fought the urge to brush his cheek against hers. If they were going to start over, he needed to be very careful. He could go home tomorrow, he told himself. Tonight he'd be with True.

She moved from the bed. "It doesn't matter. I'm not really interested anyway."

He knew she was pretending. She had the kind of mind that never stopped questioning, but he wasn't ready for his life to be opened up and inspected by her. Though it sounded insane even to his own mind, he wanted her to believe, if only for one more night, that he was the wild fighter she'd pulled from a jail.

As she moved toward the door, he said, "See you at dinner?"

"At dinner," she answered, studying him closely, as if trying to make all the pieces of a puzzle fit together. "I'm looking forward to it."

Hours later, the dinner went surprisingly well, with only short lapses where neither could think of anything to say. True was at her proper best, and this made Seth nervous. He far preferred her less formal. But he knew how to play the perfect gentleman. He'd played the role all his life.

As the waitress served dessert in the same private dining room they'd eaten in last night, he decided to try and crack the shell she seemed so fond of forming around herself. "Mind my asking something a bit personal, Miss McCormick?"

"Not if I can also."

He could tell by her dancing blue eyes that she was already thinking of her question.

"Why is it a beautiful woman like you hasn't married?" Most women by their mid-twenties already had a house filled with children.

True didn't look the least embarrassed. Her father asked the question almost every time she saw him. "Men want to own a woman, body and soul, like she's a piece of land they have to stake a claim on. I guess I never met a man worth the price."

Seth looked away, remembering a time marriage had been a part of his world. "Maybe only the very young are willing to risk the price."

"Were you very young when you married?"

"Young enough to believe in forever," he answered, remembering the plans he and Marcy used to talk over when they were children, about growing old together. They had hardly had time to grow up before she died.

When he looked back at True, her blue eyes were filled with concern. "Did you love her dearly?"

"You mean for property?" He hadn't meant the words to come out quite as hard as they did.

Without thinking, True lay her hand over his fingers resting on the table. "I hadn't meant to be cruel."

Seth pulled his hand away. He didn't want her pity. He'd accepted none when Marcy died and he'd accept none now.

"Forget it. The truth is I didn't own her body and soul. In fact, when she died, I realized how little I knew her at all." He closed his eyes and let out a long breath. "I can't remember a single conversation we had that was totally open, or a secret we ever shared, or even an argument. We were like two private people playing grown-up in our roles of husband and wife."

"How did she die?"

"In childbirth," he answered. "So did the baby, a girl."

"Now I understand why you roam."

He could see her mind working. He'd given her enough facts to build the story of his life in her mind. He thought for the second time since he'd known her that she should be the writer, not Granite Westwind.

When the Harvey girl cleared away the dishes, True once again slipped a roll into her coat pocket.

"Going hunting again tonight?" Seth asked as he finished off his coffee.

"An old habit," she answered. "Would you believe I was one of eleven kids and there was never enough food to go around?"

"No," Seth answered honestly. "But it sounds like a grand tale, Miss McCormick."

True shrugged. "I like coloring the facts. It makes life more interesting. I learned that from an old railroader named Don Robertson. If you came into the station telling of a boring day, you ate alone, but if you had a story, there was always company to share it with."

Seth stood and moved to the window. "I've never thought of it much, but I guess there's very little color in my life." He thought maybe he should at least finish out the week with her. She'd already given him a great deal to think about. "I like the way you see things, True McCormick. I'd like you to teach me."

The night was clear for Galveston. He could even see the fuzzy lights of the stars.

True joined him at the window, careful to stay the width of the curtain away. "I feel like I've known you for a very long time. Like I know what you'd do even before you think it."

"You're confusing me with the character Westwind you keep typing up. He's the one who's brave and true. I have no desire to be a hero."

"Then why didn't you leave this afternoon? You had four hundred dollars. You don't need the money you'll make this week."

Seth almost said, "Because of you," but he held his tongue. How could he explain to someone so innocent that she was the first woman he'd wanted since his wife? Maybe True was the first woman he'd ever *really* wanted. How could he answer her question when he didn't even know the answer himself?

She watched him so closely he felt she was reading his thoughts. True seemed to look inside of him to where he never allowed anyone else to see. He wished he could believe that just for one moment True would care about him as no one had before. Seth wanted to believe that part of the reason he'd always been so hard was that he'd never had anyone to hold him up if he started to fall. He'd been rigid for so long, maybe he'd petrified clean through and there was no softness left inside him. How could she teach him to color his world when his fists were filled with charcoal?

Seth moved toward the door. "I guess I'd best say good night. Thank you for having dinner with me, Miss McCormick." He needed to get out of the room before he made a fool of himself again.

"You're not going to answer my question about why you stayed?"

"No," he said, wishing he could think of something else to talk about.

True smiled suddenly as if she understood. "If you're not too tired, then why don't we play a game?" She removed her glasses and placed them on the table.

"What kind?" Seth couldn't remember ever playing a game in his life except poker, and he'd only done that a few times.

"It's called, 'If only for tonight.'" The magic of a wild imagination danced in her eyes. "We pretend that what we do tonight is only a few pages of a book and those pages will be forever closed come morning. So whatever we say or do happens only for tonight and will never be mentioned or thought of again by either of us."

Seth smiled. He never thought much of playing games, but this one sounded interesting. "Have you ever played this before?"

"I don't know because even if I did, I tore up the pages when morning came."

Seth laughed. "All right, what shall we do?"

True placed her finger to her lips. "Wait here."

He waited only a moment until she returned. She'd covered her dress with a floor-length black cape. "Shall we go?"

"Now?"

"Now," True answered as she stepped through the window.

Seth hesitated. "Don't you want to use the door?"

"No, only for tonight, we use the window. I'll show you the way down. I've made this climb a few times before." True giggled. "Don't worry, if you fall, I'll catch you."

Seth grumbled. He was too old to be doing this. If he fell, he'd crush her, but he didn't seem to be able to stop True. If she was going to insist on doing something crazy, the least he could do was join her for tonight.

If only for tonight!

He was halfway down the side of the building when a pain jabbed into his side and he realized that Dr. Gates probably didn't include this on her list of light activity.

TEN

They crept through the dark streets of Galveston like warriors passing through enemy lines. Without a word True reached for Seth's hand and pulled him close to her side. He knew it would be wiser to walk with both hands unencumbered, but he couldn't pull away. There was something so wild and untamed about this True McCormick of the night. He was afraid to let go of her lest she disappear.

After his wife died, he'd longed to have someone just to be with. A hand to hold. Another person to share the day. Well-meaning folks had asked what they could do to help, and he'd wanted to say, "Sleep beside me, sit across the table at dawn, touch me." But his pride would never have allowed him to ask. Now, as True held his fingers tightly, it seemed a cruel joke to remind him of how good another's warmth felt, when iron control had already scabbed over his heart.

"Tell me what you wish to do only for tonight." She moved closer to him while she spoke, brushing her shoulder against his arm.

Seth smiled, loving the easy nearness of her. This game might prove interesting. "I'd like to call you by your first name."

"Granted," she replied. "Now my turn. I want to walk down Post Office Street and have you buy me a shot of whiskey."

"But that's the worst street in town. This time of night it'll be full of drunks, gamblers, and whores."

True pulled him forward. "And us."

As they stepped onto one of the wildest streets in the West, Seth rested his hand on his gun. He didn't like this part of her game at all. All it would take was one drunken sailor getting a look at True's face, and Seth would be fighting half the street. He really didn't like the idea of ending up in Rank's hands again.

To his amazement, True seemed at home in this environment. She walked without fear, and a few times he thought he caught a prostitute or two about to greet her, before the women of the night saw Seth standing beside True.

"You know these people?"

True smiled up at him innocently. "Is the answer your next request?"

"Yes," Seth said, frustrated that he had to play a game to get her to answer a simple question.

"I know a few of the women," True answered. "I've been down here with Dr. Gates on calls. Audrey may have given up her practice, but she still loves being on the spot when needed." True looked up at him, unshed tears making her eyes sparkle in the saloon lights as she tilted her head slightly. "Plus my real mother was a whore on a street in Chicago that was worse than this one. She ran off and left me when I was six, thinking I could take care of myself better than she could. My earliest memories are of having to sleep on the steps while she worked at night."

Seth could hear the sadness in her words. "But you survived," he said, trying to make her feel better.

"No," True answered. "Actually, I died in the winter of '86."

Seth reached for her, but only her laughter remained. True darted up an alley and into the blackness of the night. He fought down an oath and followed, hoping no one else in the narrow pathway could see any better than he could.

"True!" he shouted as loud as he dared. "True!" He stumbled over a pile of trash and thought again of taking up swearing as a full-time hobby. This was only a game to her, but it could turn deadly at any moment if one of the drunks nearby thought that either of them had money.

He knew she was near. He could smell the perfume she'd worn at dinner. A light fragrance that reminded him of spring. Suddenly he knew she wouldn't have left him here. It wasn't part of the game she played.

Slowly, with great effort, he forced himself to raise his hands from his Colt's handle and reach out into the blackness. He closed his useless eyes and listened for her breathing.

After a few minutes of silence, his hand brushed the side of her cape. She remained still, as if thinking he wouldn't recognize the feel of her and would move on. He touched the softness of the light wool, expecting her to bolt again at any second, but she remained planted in one spot.

Without a word he moved closer. Using the tips of his fingers, he brushed her shoulder and moved down her arm. When she didn't pull away, he allowed his hands to return up her arms, over her shoulders to the hood of her cape. Slowly, hesitantly, he lowered the hood and lightly stroked her hair. It was silk to his fingers. He'd wanted to touch it since he'd seen it down this morning, looking like a cloud of chocolate velvet floating around her.

The total blackness made the feel of her far more exciting than if he'd been able to see. Timidly he moved his hands to cup her face. Her skin was soft, and he could feel the smile on her lips. Her nose was slightly cold, and her eyelashes fluttered when his fingers explored.

He fought the urge to pull her near. He'd have liked nothing more than to crush her softness against his chest and taste deeply of her mouth, yet this blind touching, in its way, was just as intoxicating. She could have easily stepped away from him into the night, but she remained like a statue. He could feel her warmth, hear her light intake of breath, smell the nearness of her, but she made no move.

"True," he whispered, wondering where she wanted him to go from here.

As before, she seemed to read his thoughts. "Continue," she answered in a whisper that was so low he wasn't sure if it was her words or his prayer. "Touch me, again."

His fingers lightly moved over her face, loving the feel of her skin beneath his hand. Sometimes in the loneliness of his dreams he'd thought he could almost feel a woman beside him, but never this real, never this wonderful.

He gently moved his fingers through her hair, allowing the silky strands to slide away from his open grip. Tenderly his hand circled her throat. He could feel her pulse throbbing against his palm, a pounding as if knocking at the entrance to his heart.

It's a waste of time, he thought as his thumb traced the outline of bone beneath the flesh of her throat. I'm dead inside. The illusion of tonight is all I can offer, no more.

The sudden sound of voices rattled through the darkness when one of the back doors opened and shattered their heaven. A bartender swore as he tossed a drunk into the alley.

True grabbed Seth's hand and they were running once more. He was so shaken by the moment they'd shared in the darkness, he didn't pay attention to what direction they traveled until they reached a brick building everyone in Galveston called "Old Red." It housed the medical school that had been on the island for years. Anyone who'd ever visited Galveston marveled at the quality of the structure's workmanship.

True pulled Seth up the stairs to the darkened porch. "I want to shake hands with one of the cadavers."

"What!"

"I want to—"

"I heard you, but I'm not going in there." He'd never done such a wild thing as to even think about breaking into a building.

"Try the door."

"No." Seth pulled her a foot away. "I'm not going in there. How about we go to the jail and you can shake hands with the near dead? Or we could go back to the alley. About now that drunk who got tossed out on his head is wishing he was dead."

"Try the door." True stood stiff with determination. Her fists were on her hips as though she were ready for a fight.

Seth lay his hand on the knob. "It's locked."

"Then we climb to the second floor and break in."

"No." Seth wouldn't budge on the point. He could be just as hardheaded as she. "I'm not shaking hands with a dead man."

True pulled her skirt above her knees and began climbing up the side of the building. She was out of his reach before he realized what she was doing.

"Come down from there! Ladies don't go climbing up the sides of public buildings."

True swore in a most unladylike fashion. "Don't tell me what to do. You sound like my father. If you like, you can wait here until I get back, or you can come with me." Her words sounded angry. "Ordering me around, however, is not one of your options. I've never followed orders in my life, and I don't intend to start with yours."

Seth closed his fist. She had a way of making him wish he believed in jailing women just because they drove a man to the point of insanity. "How will I know if you shake hands with a dead man?"

"I'll come back and tell you," she answered. "I'd never lie about something like that."

Seth laughed suddenly. "It'd be the only thing you wouldn't lie about." She was too far up the side of the building to hear him. "If there ever was a woman reality tiptoed around, it has to be her," he mumbled to himself.

He waited only another moment before turning the knob on the unlocked door.

True climbed the uneven brickwork to the second floor of the medical school. She'd explored the building several years before. The first medical school west of the Mississippi had been her playground one summer when she'd come to visit Audrey. While Dr. Audrey Gates lectured to the med students, True had pretended the huge red brick building was a castle and spent hours looking for secret passages.

She folded beneath one of the brick overhangs and silently slipped into a window that had been unlocked since the day she'd found it seven years ago. The air inside the building always smelled clean and sterile, as if the floors were scrubbed daily. The walls felt cool to her touch as she fumbled along the wide hall to the stairs. She'd never seen a body in Old Red, but she figured they must keep them here to practice on.

Part of her wanted to go back and return to Seth. She'd liked the way he'd touched her in the darkness. No one had ever touched her so gently. It was almost as if he were afraid of her, as though he thought her a great treasure to be handled with care. She'd never dreamed a gunman like Seth Atherton would have gentle hands, so gentle they made her long for more.

True tiptoed down the stairs to the main floor. She had to

finish what she'd set out to do. Adventure was not adrenaline to her, but life's blood.

As she turned down the main hallway, she saw that a table on wheels blocked part of the entrance to one of the classrooms.

True moved closer.

A long sheet covered something lying atop the table. As she neared, she detected the outline of a body beneath the sheet. From the length, she figured it had to be a man, or a woman as tall as old man Beasley's dead wife. The hallway was so silent, True could hear her own heart pounding.

Of all the times she'd crawled into the building looking for a dead man to shake hands with, she'd never seen such a sight. It looked as if someone had left the body just outside the classroom so that at first light it would be ready for the medical students to examine.

Fighting down fear in her throat, she moved closer. The fingers of a hand stuck out from beneath the sheet. Fingers that looked white in the pale light coming from the front windows by the door.

True forced herself to take a step closer. Slowly, very slowly, she reached out her hand and took two of the dead man's fingers. They felt strangely warm to her touch, as though the blood had not quite stopped flowing. She'd done it, she thought to herself, and let out a long held breath. She'd shaken hands with a dead man.

In the fraction of time that she released the hand, the dead man's fingers curled to entrap her.

True drew in air to scream as the white sheet moved. She fought to pull away, but the two fingers had hooked her and were pulling her closer to the body.

Just as she screamed, Seth threw the sheet back and smiled at her from the portable table.

Fear, relief, and anger exploded within her. True's mind

told her it had only been a trick, but her feet hadn't got the message. She jerked her hand from his grip and ran out the door as fast as she could, knowing that he'd be right behind her.

Running down the alley and past the hospital, True headed for the docks. She ran until she could run no longer, and still she could hear Seth only a step behind her. They crossed the tracks between the huge warehouses that held cotton ready for shipment. When she stopped suddenly, he halted only a few feet behind.

Folding forward, he took several long breaths. "I'm sorry I frightened you, True. I thought it would make you laugh." Gripping his side, Seth tried to ignore the pain from the butcher's knife wound.

"You scared a year's life out of me!" she said, fighting for breath as she moved to one of the overturned cotton bales close to the dock. It smelled as only cotton can, warm with earth, rich with growth, and seedy in decay.

He followed and helped her up onto the burlap-covered softness. "I couldn't resist when I realized the door to the school was unlocked."

Taking deep breaths, True turned her back to him while she untied her cape.

He wanted to say he was sorry again, but he didn't know if it would help. Here he was making a fool of himself with her again as if it were a part in a play he was destined to act out until the final curtain call.

Lying back on the cotton, he locked his hands beneath his head and stared at the stars.

A giggle caught on the wind and reached him. When he turned toward her, True held her mouth, trying to keep from laughing. "I was so frightened," she whispered between giggles. "It was wonderful. When you grabbed my fingers, I thought the devil himself had hold of me."

As if they'd been friends for a lifetime, she rolled beside him and lay her head on his arm. "This has been a great 'only for tonight' game."

Seth slowly straightened his arm and pulled her close to him. She fitted against him with an easy breath. "What do we do next?" he whispered into her hair.

"It's your turn. What have you always wanted to do and never done?"

"I'd like to lay here and watch the stars with you beside me," he answered honestly before he could stop himself.

"You've never watched the stars?"

"Not with you. Not even alone for a long time." He couldn't remember the last time he'd relaxed and watched the night sky.

True rolled toward him and placed her chin on his chest. "Only on one condition."

"Name it," he whispered, thinking that she'd probably make him promise to be a gentleman. Somehow he couldn't imagine any of the women in Timber Creek even considering lying beside him to watch the stars. They'd think it outrageous.

"You have to touch me again," True whispered. "I liked what you started in the alley when we were in total darkness."

For a long time, Seth didn't answer. He thought back over all his life, and he couldn't remember anyone ever asking to be touched by him. He couldn't believe True was asking it as simply as if it were only a slight favor.

"What else?" He had to know the depth of the fall before he toppled into the canyon.

"Nothing else. Just touch me." She rolled to her back and lay so still next to him, he wasn't sure what she wanted him to do. "I like the way your hands feel as they brush my skin. I'd like you to do it some more. I'll ask nothing else of you, if you'll only repeat what you did in the alley—nothing more, nothing less."

"You'll stop me when you don't enjoy it?"

True smiled at him. "Please, patience isn't my strong characteristic. I don't want to talk. I want to feel you touching me again."

Seth rolled to his side and propped his head up one elbow. "Fold your arms behind your back," he ordered softly.

"Why?" True asked, already following the order.

"Because, I don't want you to be tempted to touch me in return." He slowly pulled the cape away from her shoulders. "I'll touch you, but this is my game. If you want nothing more and nothing less, you must remain as still as you did in the alley."

The grin that lifted her full lips was etched in mischief. "All right, but remember, the next request is mine."

"Close your eyes, True," he whispered as his hand lightly brushed over her cheek. Her mouth opened slightly in pleasure, and he ran his finger along her lips. He stroked her face tenderly, letting his fingers move into her hair with each crossing, loving the softness of her flesh and the magical way her curls circled around his fingers, caressing him with velvet.

Slowly, she relaxed and his hand slid along her shoulder and arm. When he reached her waist, he unbuttoned the two huge buttons holding her jacket together. Hesitantly, he opened it to uncover the soft silk blouse beneath. In the moonlight he could see the rise and fall of her breasts as she rested so trustingly beside him.

He wanted to kiss her, but that hadn't been part of the game they played. Slowly, so timidly at first he was only feeling the warmth of her, he lay his hand between the skirt's waistband and her breasts.

With a soft cry of pleasure, she moved her head to one side, but didn't open her eyes.

He returned to her face, moving slowly over her skin, brushing his knuckles along her cheek and circling her neck feather-light in his grip.

When he moved down her arm to her waist once more, she moaned softly again as his hand spread across her abdomen. He increased the pressure of his palm until he could feel his hand warm her skin through the silk.

One button at a time he began to unfasten her blouse. As he spread the fabric open, his fingers slid beneath the silk and brushed her skin.

Again she moved in pleasure, but made no protest. He studied her face in the moonlight. She smiled slightly when he continued, and he knew she'd just deepened the scar of loneliness inside him, for after tonight he'd never stop longing for a woman as wonderful as her.

The need to hold her was a fire in his mind burning out all reason. If he died tomorrow or lived to be a hundred, he'd never forget the wonder of her. His hands moved over her shoulders, along her arms, across her waist, touching silk and skin with each crossing.

As he passed the valley between her breasts, he rolled his knuckles between the mounds. She cried softly, and he smiled, loving the thought that she welcomed his caress. There was something so childlike in her pleasure, so womanly in her sigh.

Gently, he tugged at the material until her blouse fell open to reveal a camisole of lace that barely covered full breasts.

Though he'd always thought his hands were rough and hard, tonight he tried to make his touch tender. Very carefully so he wouldn't startle her, he brushed her face with his fingers. He shoved the material from her shoulders and spread his hands over her smooth skin.

When he carefully pushed the straps of her camisole down her arms, the lace slid dangerously low over her breasts.

He wanted to shove the material away and view the perfection he saw outlined in the lace, but he forced himself to go slow. Passion might run wild in her someday, but it must be awakened slowly, one pleasure at a time so that each stage could be cherished.

He brushed his knuckles between her breasts, and she cried in pure joy. Silently begging him for more, she arched her back as he slowly moved his fingers over the warm flesh just above the lace. The very core of his being was loving the softness, needing the feel of her breath against his throat, wanting the way she moved slightly in pleasure to last forever. The first taste of desire washed away all other longings and needs in his life, addicting him forever to its fulfilling.

Feather-light, his fingers moved back and forth over each breast, pushing the lace a hair lower with each passing. Slowly, he leaned closer until his lips touched her throat. He had to taste her or go mad with longing. Her flesh was soft, lightly salty from running, and honey-dipped with desire. As his mouth opened over her throat, he felt her pulse with the tip of his tongue.

She cried softly with pleasure when he slid his mouth lower onto her shoulder. As he kissed the hollow between her neck and shoulder, his hand molded over the ripe fullness of one breast. She seemed to swell in his grip, a perfection to hold. He could feel the hard point pressed against the center of his palm.

She struggled slightly, and he released her, realizing he'd gone too far. But she didn't pull away. She remained beside him. Hesitantly, he placed his hand below her breasts and spread his fingers wide across her waist.

He waited for her to object, but True remained still. Go slow, Seth reminded himself. Don't frighten her again. His fingers slid over the silk of her camisole. Very gently, with each passing, he brushed the bottom of her breasts, letting their weight rest only slightly against his fingers.

When she didn't object, he tasted the flesh beneath her ear as his fist passed up and down the hollow between her mounds. Her cry of pleasure almost shattered all restraint he'd mustered.

Seth lay his face in her hair and whispered, "I don't think I can go any farther without going all the way to loving you." He was almost mindless with the sensations flooding over him. "True, what do you want?"

She moved until her cheek rested against his. "I want to sleep right here in your arms," she whispered as though the request were a small one. "One of the reasons I go out at night is I'm afraid to sleep. I used to crawl into the wardrobe every time I was afraid, because I could touch all the walls and knew I was surrounded and safe. I want to be surrounded by your arms tonight."

Seth pulled her tightly against his heart. "Is that all?"

"No," she whispered as she pushed him to the point of insanity by pressing her breasts against his chest. "I want your promise that we'll play the touching part of this game again. I've never had anyone make me feel the way I feel when you're near."

"Whenever you like," he answered as he kissed her forehead. There would be time to show her more of loving later. He wouldn't frighten her, for he wasn't sure he could bear to see fear in her eyes when she looked at him. He needed time to accept this wonder in his life as well. A man doesn't go from the desert to the ocean without needing time to adjust.

"I'd like to do this again." Her plea was a sleepy request.

"There'll be other nights." He pulled her cape over them both and closed his eyes to all the world. There would be no thought of going home tomorrow, he decided.

They fell asleep in the roughest town in Texas with a bale of cotton as their bed, the stars as a roof, and a promise on Seth's lips.

ELEVEN

Seth awoke with only the memory of True beside him. He could hear the fishing boats getting an early start out to sea and the noisy gulls calling after them for food. The humidity that weighed the cotton bales down and made them more valuable after a few months on the docks seemed to rest heavy even on his clothes after a night by the water.

For a moment he didn't want to open his eyes, as though he could refuse to leave a dream after waking. He wanted to hold to the memory of her in his arms. But he could hear movement on the docks and knew it would be only a matter of time before he was discovered.

Looking up at the gray dawn, he smiled. What a night! He'd run with a wildcat all over Galveston and slept with an angel in his arms. An angel who'd made him promise to touch her again. If he could die right now, he would be dying at the happiest moment in his life. Never had anything felt so wonderful as True beside him. If she cried with pleasure from a single touch, he could hardly wait to see what she'd do if they made love.

Seth stood and laughed aloud. If that night ever came, he'd best rent the rooms on either side of them or folks would be complaining about the noise. He ran his fingers through his damp hair, not believing he was even thinking such a thing. He'd never have a woman like True for even one night, and she'd never care for someone like him.

He dusted off his clothes. Nell would be shocked to see him walk into the office this way. She'd probably faint. He might forget a haircut, or rarely buy new clothes, yet he believed in being neat and pressed. But then he'd never spent the night with a woman like True before.

Unable to wipe the smile from his lips, he stretched and walked to the Harvey House. A feeling of emptiness that had covered him like a thin web most of his life seemed to be evaporating. Several times during the night he'd awoken and slowly moved his hand along her arm or back. She'd cuddled against him like a trusting child, making his heart feel as if it might explode. The wonder of a woman sleeping beside him was a pleasure he'd decided a long time ago would always be denied him.

He had a feeling True would be at the Harvey House by now. She seemed to consider the place home. He thought of stopping by his hotel to change clothes and shave, but then he remembered his things had been packed on a train that left without him yesterday morning.

When he stepped into the private dining room they'd used before, True was sitting at the table writing. She didn't look up as he entered, giving him time to drink in her beauty. She was dressed all porcelain-tight again, in an ivory traveling suit with a long skirt and sleeves that puffed out from her shoulders. But he'd felt what lay beneath, and the feel of her would weave into his dreams every night he lived. There was nothing porcelain in the warmth of her skin or the softness of her curves.

"Mr. Westwind," she said as she finished writing and turned the page of her notebook. "There're coffee and rolls on the sideboard. I'll fill you in on the schedule while you eat."

He poured a cup and sat down across from her. "True?" he whispered, waiting for her to look up. God, how he loved her name.

Icy blue eyes stared up at him. "It's Miss McCormick, Mr. Westwind. Please don't forget again."

"About last night . . . ," he started.

"There was no last night, Mr. Westwind."

Her statement, issued so directly, made him question his own sanity. Could he have dreamed it? Could another woman who looked just like her have been the one who ran wild in the streets with him last night? Anger overshadowed his doubt. "There was no last night," he repeated with bitterness, remembering the rules of the game.

She nodded slightly and turned another page of her notebook, as if the matter were of little importance. "You'd best drink that coffee, because we're due to leave in thirty minutes. I've had a shaving kit put on the train so you can clean up en route to Houston."

Seth swallowed the scalding coffee, almost welcoming the pain. Maybe if he burned his tongue and throat he would be able to keep from talking. She'd told him the game was only for the night and she'd meant it. In the shadows, he'd agreed to the short span of time, but now he wanted to argue for more.

"I'm ready," he said as he stood. He offered his arm. "Miss McCormick." She didn't touch him as she passed and moved out the door.

"Welcome back to the real world," he mumbled as he shoved his hat low.

The train ride to Houston seemed endless. Except along the gulf, the land looked parched and bleached by the July sun. True sat at a large desk in the private car and never stopped writing in her notebook. Seth took one of the chairs by the window and lost himself in thought. He relived every detail of the past evening over and over until he wondered if his mind were playing tricks on him. No, he thought, he couldn't have dreamed something so perfect as True in his arms.

Looking at her now, he found it hard to believe that she was the same woman. She looked so untouchable. She didn't seem even to notice he sat in the car with her. Seth crossed his arms and stretched his long legs out on the seat in front of him. If she wanted to forget last night ever happened, he could play the same game. He closed his eyes, lowered his hat to shade his face, and tried to get some sleep.

True was very much aware that he was so near. He looked out of place with the overdone furnishings and fringe-trimmed windows. Every time he'd walked across the small space, it had taken her several minutes to find her place in her writing again. She'd tried, but she couldn't make herself stop watching him. He looked so strong and handsome . . . and angry in his black suit and polished boots. Each time he looked up at her with stormy eyes, no hero she could ever conjure up could be as powerful as he seemed.

Seth Atherton could be a very dangerous man, she thought, wondering how many men had been caught at the wrong end of his gun. Yet it wasn't his power that frightened her, but his tenderness. Somehow he'd touched her deeply when he'd held little Emily in his arms and later fought for the child like a shining knight. His hands might be deadly with a gun, but they'd been so gentle when they touched her. Even now she could feel her body respond to the memory of his caress.

She knew he'd expected her to be as she'd been last night, but she couldn't. True had let him closer than she should have. It would be hard watching him for the next few days, but she had to keep her distance. She had too many people depending on her to allow one man to change her plans. If she allowed him to get too close, he could destroy every-thing she'd worked to build.

Once, she'd let a man into her life, and his rejection had been almost unbearable. Her adopted father and mothers would accept her for what she was, even Micah understood her, but when a man looked at her with love, he expected her to conform to what he wanted in a wife. And True knew she could never do that. No matter how nice her clothes were, she was a child of the streets and always would be. Whores and orphans were her family and the night her backyard.

The sacrifice of living alone was her only choice. She couldn't risk having Seth turn away from her. It was better never to allow him near, then suffer the loss. However, she'd never dreamed a man's touch could be as intoxicating as Seth's had been last night. Why couldn't he just be happy with the way it was? They could play their parts during the day, and he could hold her at night. Why couldn't he accept what she offered? It made sense to her.

True tried to force herself to think of the story she wrote. It was hard to think of Granite Westwind between the pages of a book when a man every bit as strong and untamed sat only a few feet away, looking more handsome than she could ever describe Granite to be.

With a sudden jerk, he tossed his hat aside and stood, stretching long, powerful muscles. His brows were shoved together as he resumed his seat and frowned at the passing countryside. The day had turned as rainy and gray as his mood. His dark hair needed combing, but it always looked that way. His bottom lip stuck out slightly with a stubborn-ness that True found irresistible. Everything about his manner told her he was a loner, a man who didn't have much to do with people. But from the first night, she'd felt his need to hold her. Or maybe it was his need to have her near? Maybe her accepting him was the most important need this strong man had.

True stood, restless and feeling a little enclosed by the space. She knew many of the railroad men, for Harvey House employees and railroaders considered themselves in the same family. Most of the men along the line treated her like a niece. If she'd been alone, she would have talked them into allowing her to ride up front with the engineer so she could see where they were headed.

She walked across the room and sat in the chair opposite Seth, forcing herself to remain all business.

He didn't look at her, but she knew he was very much aware of her nearness.

"I thought I'd go over the plans for the next few days. I've arranged everything for you, including books to be handed out at each stop." She paused, for he showed no sign of listening to her. "I thought we'd go over the speech I'd like you to give tonight. Because we lost yesterday, we'll do some double time today."

When he didn't answer, she tried again. "I was very pleased at the way you handled yourself yesterday morning at the press meeting."

He looked at her then. A cold, hard stare. "You weren't sure I could write and talk at the same time. You thought I'd make a fool of myself, or, worse, of you."

He'd guessed her worry and she felt embarrassed. "No, really, I figured you could do the job."

Seth straightened and pulled his feet off the seat beside her chair. He stared at her with angry, tired eyes. "If you'll hand the speech to me, I'll read it over and try not to sound too tongue-tied."

True handed him the piece of paper and waited.

"That will be all, Miss McCormick," Seth said without looking back at her.

Anger bubbled in her blood. True couldn't believe he would dismiss her as if she were no more than a secretary. She opened her mouth to say something, then realized he was doing exactly as she'd instructed him to do. He was treating her as though there were only a professional relationship between Westwind and his secretary.

Frustrated, she stood and stormed to her desk, aware as she turned away that he was smiling for the first time since they'd left the station that morning.

All day the same pattern repeated itself. As they moved from press meeting to book club luncheon to bookstore signings, he treated her with polite indifference. With each public appearance he took on more of the leadership role — answering questions, welcoming people, even telling a joke to a small group of men as they waited to go on stage for a lecture.

True was forced to sit in the audience that evening as the monster of her own creation spoke to a house full of excited fans. She wanted to stand up and shout that this was her tour, but he'd stolen it from her so effortlessly she didn't know how to fight. From what she could tell, Seth didn't use a word of the speech she'd given him. Her creation had taken on a life of its own. True feared it might be that of a madman and there was nothing she could do about him.

As the evening ended, the crowd gave Seth a rousing round of applause. If she stood up and told them he was only a man she'd pulled from a jail cell to impersonate Granite Westwind, they'd probably stone her.

As he waved to the audience and stepped backstage, she held her tongue. It had been a long, tiring day, and if she hadn't been so angry at him, she'd have admitted he'd done grand. He'd played the part of Granite Westwind to the hilt, even spinning his Colts a few times for the children.

Now, for the first time today, she noticed his shoulders

slumped slightly in the backstage shadows. He rubbed his hand against his lower ribs, where only she knew a bandage still covered yesterday's knife wound. Though he said nothing, her counterfeit hero was tiring.

"Mr. Westwind!" the stage manager shouted. "You and your lady best hurry. There's a bad storm brewing outside. I told the driver to park at the end of the alley so you can get away fast."

"She's not my lady, sir." Seth winked at the manager. "She's my secretary and she is a lady, but she's not *my* lady."

True wasn't sure what to say. She disliked the two men talking about her as though she were invisible, and she wasn't sure if Seth was paying her a compliment or making fun of her.

Before she could decide, he grabbed her by the arm and pulled her along the passage to the back exit. When the stage manager opened the door, a blast of rain blew in.

"The carriage should already be at the end of the alley, Mr. Westwind. You'd best hurry before every fan in the hall decides he'd like to shake your hand."

Looking at True, Seth asked, "Where's your cape?"

"I left it in the carriage," she answered, wanting to add that she'd had enough to carry with papers and extra books without having to keep up with a cape all evening.

Seth nodded as if he understood. Without hesitation, he pulled off his jacket and placed it over True's head. "This should keep you dry." Before she could argue, he lifted her in his arms and ran into the rain.

As they moved through the downpour, he held her tightly against him, shielding her as much as he could with his body. She felt the pounding of his heart and pressed her cheek against the warmth of his chest. After a day when they seemed to be miles apart, it felt good to relax for a moment in his arms.

Suddenly the rain stopped pounding against the jacket she had over her. True looked up. They were beneath the shelter of an overhanging awning that stood halfway between the stage entrance and the street.

His arms were like iron around her as he moved his mouth close to her ear.

"True," he whispered. "Something's wrong."

She tried to see clearly through the rain. The carriage was nowhere in sight. He lowered her legs slowly to the ground, freeing his hands in case his guns were needed.

She didn't bother to act as if it were only bad luck that the carriage wasn't there. It was a privately hired coach and the driver had been told to be ready. She could feel trouble in the air, just as she knew Seth could. They both studied the street and waited.

Suddenly Seth pushed her against the building and covered her with his body as a bullet shattered the glass in the window only inches away.

They both dropped low and moved around the corner of the window frame back into the shadows. Seth pulled his gun and watched the blackness for movement.

His hand absently caressed the back of her neck. "Do you know Houston like you do Galveston?"

"Not as well, but I can find my way around," True answered, wishing she could get her gun from her case.

"Is there another way out of this alley?"

"No," True answered. "But that must have been a stray bullet. No one would be shooting at us."

"Didn't your father tell you?"

"Tell me what?"

"That someone wants to put an end to the Westwind tour." Seth couldn't believe everyone had warned him and no one had bothered to tell True. If she was the one organizing this for the real Westwind, he should have told her of the danger she could possibly be in. Only a fool would put a woman like her in harm's way.

"No! He only told me to be careful. He tells me that every time he sees me. Westwind is always getting letters from crazy people saying they love or hate him."

Seth leaned against the building. They were so close her shoulder rested against his arm. "At least we've got the rain," he whispered. The water was almost a fall pouring off the roof and curtaining the street from view. "If we're having trouble seeing them, they must have the same problem."

"Who?"

"Whoever wants me dead."

"Why would anyone want to kill you?" True's voice was slightly higher than usual with excitement.

"Not me. Granite Westwind."

Another round of gunfire thundered through the alley, missing them by several feet. True remembered the letters of warning she'd so lightly tossed away. "Oh, no!" she spread her hand against Seth's chest. "I wouldn't have hired you if I'd known! I . . ."

Seth heard fear in her voice for the first time. "Can we talk about this later when we're not being used as a target? How do we get out of here?"

Another round sounded, and Seth realized that whoever was shooting at them was moving closer.

Seth crept up the steps to the stage door. The gaslight provided only enough beam to encircle the back entrance to the hall. "Go inside until this is over, True. It's me they're shooting at. You'll be safe inside."

"No," she answered. "I'm staying with you."

"You'll get us both killed. Go back inside." Another bullet splattered the brick a few feet from them, but neither seemed to notice.

"How many times do I have to tell you, I don't take orders from you or anyone else?"

Seth forgot the gunman completely. "You're about the most maddening woman in the world, True McCormick. For a few bits, I'd give you the spanking you've been needing all your life."

"Just try it and I'll scalp you from head to toe and leave your bones out to dry." The lady had disappeared and the hellcat was back. She shoved at him as if it would be an equal fight and he were not almost twice her size.

They hardly noticed a sound at the alley. Seth pulled her beneath the steps of the stage door and pressed her against the wall. "I don't care if you take orders or not. Stay here or I swear I'll arrest you as the Harvey House biscuit thief."

True opened her mouth to argue as a shadow appeared from the end of the alley. She watched Seth stiffen and pull his other gun as he faced the stranger walking boldly toward them.

"True?" the shadow yelled. "Are you all right?"

Seth hesitated, but True broke into a dead run toward the man. "Link!" she screamed in delight.

Seth watched the shadow holster his pistols and lift her off the ground in a hug.

As the stranger stepped into the light of the stage door, True still had her arms around his neck. He was about the same age as Seth, only a few inches shorter. From his coloring, Seth figured he had to be part Indian, and judging from the scar above his eye, the man had seen his share of battles. The stranger offered his hand. "Mr. Westwind, are you all right?"

Seth shoved his weapons back in place. He wasn't accustomed to having to thank someone for saving his life. "I'm fine. Thanks for your help."

"It's only part of the job. I'm the Ranger McCormick assigned to watch over you while you're in Houston. Name's Lincoln Raine, but most folk just call me Link. I appreciate you two having such a noisy argument just now. The lead gunman was so busy listening to you, he didn't hear me sneaking up on him. The sheriff's men frightened off the rest of his gang."

"We weren't arguing." True straightened. "I was only making Mr. Westwind aware of a few facts."

Link laughed. "If I know you, it doesn't matter what the argument was about. You were willing to fight to the death, right?"

When True didn't answer, he laughed again. "You haven't changed in twelve years, kid."

Seth picked up True's satchel. "Why don't we continue this reunion out of the rain, Officer Lincoln?" He tried to make his words friendly, but Seth couldn't help but be a little jealous of this Ranger who seemed to know True so well.

"Sounds fine," Link answered. "I found your carriage around the corner. The driver's got quite a bump on his head, but I think he's going to be all right."

"Who were these men?" Seth needed to know the enemy.

"Just hired guns. Not even very good ones. Maybe we'll learn something from the man I clubbed when he comes to." He glanced behind them as if he expected them to be followed. "Have you seen Micah?"

"You know Micah," True laced her arm in Link's. "He'll show up when he's good and ready, or when he gets hungry enough. He was planning to follow us up at least as far as

Houston. He thought he might do a story about the Westwind tour and sell it."

"As long as he stays out of my hair," Link said. "The old guy has been telling me how to do my job for years. He thinks just because he was in the war that he knows everything. He's a wealth of useless facts and worn stories. As soon as he finds out you've been shot at, he'll be down at my office thinking he should help with the investigation."

"He's only trying to help," True said, trying to defend Micah.

Link nodded and jerked his head toward the street. "Let's run for the carriage."

Seth rode back to the hotel sitting beside the driver, as True and Link talked about people they both seemed to know and love. True invited Link to share dinner with them, and the Ranger settled in for the evening.

Seth tried his best to be polite, but he had little to say. After only sleeping a few hours the night before and spending the day feeling as if he were at the head of a parade, Seth had difficulty staying awake during the meal. By the time the waitress had served dessert, he was yawning.

"If you two will excuse me," Seth rose as he interrupted their conversation, "I think I'll turn in."

Link stood and offered his hand. "It was nice to meet you. I'll be in the background these next few days if you need me again." He followed Seth to the door and lowered his voice. "Keep an eye on True."

"That's what everyone says," Seth answered. "It's not easy."

"I know. My mother used to say she was like the wind. You can dance with her, but you can't capture her." Link flipped Seth a quarter.

"What's this?" Seth raised an eyebrow.

"That's to cover the spanking. She's been needing one ever since I've known her, but no man's been willing to risk his life and limbs to give her what she deserves."

Seth smiled and tipped his hat to Link. For the first time he decided he really liked the half-breed Ranger.

TWELVE

The storm kept Seth awake long after midnight. He lay on his back listening to the rain pounding against his window. Every now and then thunder rattled the glass until he thought it might crack.

At least the noise blocked out Link and True talking in the next room. He could hear them laughing about things only old friends shared. Seth didn't want to admit that he felt left out and more than a little jealous.

Rolling over, he pulled a pillow atop his head. How could he feel such jealousy over a woman he wasn't even sure he liked and whom he knew would never fit in his world? He could just see her explaining to the lady's reading club at church how she roamed the streets at night or how her friends were a scarred half-breed lawman and an old writer. When she wasn't telling Seth some crazy story, she was treating him like a hired man she'd bought by the pound. Chances were looking good, Seth decided, that she had even slept in his arms last night just to drive him to the breaking point.

If he had any sense at all, he'd leave for Timber Creek tomorrow and never look back. In the past three days he'd been in two fights, in jail twice, shot at, and knifed. He also was no closer to finding his brother's killer than he had been when he'd left home. In five days it would be time to open the store again, and he could pretend this was only a bad dream.

Finally, the light went out in the seating area that served

as a dining room and separated his quarters from True's. Seth assumed she'd gone to bed and was sleeping through this wrath nature pounded on Houston. At least with the rain he thought it reasonable to guess she hadn't gone out.

He lay wide awake, wondering if by standing in the rain he could wash the smell of her from his senses and the feel of her from his hands. No, he decided, it would take a direct lightning hit to shake her memory from him. Even then, he'd probably stand burned to a crisp and still feel the way her head rested on his shoulder when she slept . . . or the softness that had pressed against his fingers when he slid his knuckles between her breasts . . . or the taste of her skin.

What was it about this woman that made him think there was something missing in his solid, satisfying life?

A blast of lightning brightened the inside to daylight, and Seth thought he heard a cry of fright.

He jumped from bed, knowing something must be wrong. Pulling on his pants, he hurried to the door, not bothering to grab a shirt. The trouble they'd had earlier might have decided to make another appearance. Lifting one Colt from its cradle at his bedpost, Seth moved into the parlor.

Flickers from a dying fire were the only movements in the room. The cry came again from the other bedroom. Slowly, he crossed the wooden floor to True's door.

"True?" he whispered as he turned the knob and found her door unlocked. "True?"

In the lightning flashes, he could see that the bed had been slept in for at least a while, but the covers were thrown wide as though True had left in haste.

Another round of lighting shattered the tiny room. Windows along two sides seemed to echo the light back and forth between them. The thin curtains did nothing to buffer the stark glare. A moment later thunder rattled the hotel walls and Seth heard another muffled cry of fright.

The room was empty except for the bed and wardrobe. As lightning flashed again, he remembered what True had told him last night about hiding where she could touch the walls.

He opened the wardrobe door, knowing he'd find her inside.

Curled up in a ball, True had her head down while she hugged her knees. Her dark hair blanketed the white gown she wore. The porcelain lady had been completely replaced by a frightened child.

"True." Seth kept his voice low so he wouldn't startle her. "Are you all right?"

He expected her to look at him and give him a lecture about how she could take care of herself and didn't need anyone, but she looked at him with huge frightened eyes and raised her arms.

Seth couldn't have turned away if it had meant saving his life. Without any thought of what she'd say in the morning, he drew her into his arms.

She held to him tightly as he walked slowly back to his room. Her body seemed cold, and he felt her shivering even though the air wasn't cool enough to need a fire. As she pressed against him, he could feel her heart pounding wildly against his chest.

"It's only a storm," he whispered into her hair. "Your room has too many windows. Why don't we trade quarters for tonight? "

True didn't answer as he placed her on the sheets still warm from his body and pulled a cover over her. She looked so beautiful she took his breath away. In all his life he could not remember ever wanting just to stare at a woman for hours, but he would never get his fill of this woman's blue eyes.

"You'll be all right in here. This room's a little darker so the lightning shouldn't bother you as much." He couldn't resist leaning forward and kissing her forehead. He knew she was a woman, but right now, with her eyes so huge in fright and her hair tossed, she looked like a lost child.

"Stay with me and just hold me," she whispered as he pulled away.

He looked down at her in his bed and knew he wanted nothing more from paradise then to grant her request. "Are you sure?"

"Hold me until the storm is over."

Seth stared at her, wondering if he'd ever have the willpower to deny her anything. She seemed to be begging for what he'd gladly give. "And come morning we'll pretend this never happened?"

Her chin lifted slightly. "Yes. You have to swear you'll tell no one how you found me."

He hesitated, knowing he wanted True in his arms both night and day. He wanted her to speak to him in more than a tone that ordered or demanded. Somehow the porcelain lady and the fiery woman of the night must blend.

She moved as if to leave. "Never mind. I'm sorry I asked. I'll be all right in the wardrobe." She seemed suddenly embarrassed by her weakness. "I'm only afraid of the lightning. It makes me think the building is on fire. I can hardly see it with the wardrobe doors closed."

"No. Don't go." He knelt beside her. "I won't tell anyone how I found you. I'll hold you, tonight. If that's what you want."

Her pride battled her fear. "Don't do me any favors. I can take care of myself. I don't need anyone . . ."

He silenced her with a kiss, while his body pinned her to the bed. As he'd expected, she fought back, swinging her arms and trying to kick at him through the layers of covers and gown between them. As she fought, he lowered his weight over her and captured her wrists with his hands.

When he broke the kiss, her eyes were afire with anger. None of the little girl who'd been afraid remained. He held a strong-minded woman captive beneath him. She struggled, then abandoned the useless fight in favor of a verbal attack.

As she opened her mouth to speak, he said, "Before you start threatening to kill me and serve me to the buzzards, hear me out, True." He relaxed his grip slightly on her wrists. "I'm not going to hurt you in any way. I'd like nothing more than to hold you. But come dawn, I won't be treated like a whore that you wouldn't speak to. You can play all the games you want everywhere but here. When you're in my arms, there will be no games."

True took a deep breath. "What is it you want of me?"

"The impossible. Stability," he answered. "If you want me to hold you or touch you, tell me so. If you hate my kisses, then tell me and I'll never bother you with them again. But don't act as though you hate me one moment and want me to hold you the next." He released her wrists and lay beside her with his eyes closed. He wasn't sure how it had happened, but someone must have left the gate open, and a stampede had run over his emotions.

True was probably going to attack at any moment and try to claw his eyes out, but he didn't care. He'd said what he had to say and now he'd face her wrath. Every time he faced her, he felt as if someone were throwing scalding water on him in a snowstorm.

The storm outside was nothing compared to the explosion of emotions going on inside him.

"I didn't hate your kisses," she answered after a long silence between them. "It's your delivery that needs some work. I'd just like once to know when you're going to kiss me and have it not come like an attack. Where'd you learn to kiss, the Indian wars?" True laughed suddenly. "With a third kiss, do I get scalped?"

Seth opened one eye, shocked by her reaction. He tried not to smile. "You do a pretty good job of acting like you hate it." He knew he was no expert at kissing, but surely he wasn't as bad as she seemed to think. "Tell me, is it just me, or all men, you're determined to drive loco?"

True ignored his last question. "I've been kissed once before, and yours was not as unpleasant as the other."

Seth laughed. "You've been kissed once." He couldn't believe this woman could be well into her twenties and so innocent. "I thought that by your age you'd have been more than kissed by now."

True raised her proud chin. "In fact I have. I've made love to hundreds of men. I can't even remember all their names. Sometimes I was so busy, I had to sleep with so many, there wasn't enough room in the bed."

"Liar." Seth laughed, loving the way she made up stories as fast as her mouth moved.

"I never lie."

"Then if you've had that many lovers, you kiss me this time. Teach me how it's supposed to feel."

He leaned back against the headboard and crossed his arms over his bare chest. "I'm waiting. Prove you're not lying about those hundred lovers."

True rolled to her side and stretched to reach him. "I don't like kissing much, but I'll show you that I can do it."

With determination she pressed her lips lightly to his. "There," she said. "That wasn't such a hard thing to prove. It's not something that matters anyway."

Seth rolled with her until her back sunk deep into the mattress. "Not like that," he whispered, watching her closely for signs of anger. "That wasn't a kiss. How about like this?"

His lips lowered over her mouth with a softness that surprised her. His thumb stroked her cheek as his lips caressèd hers. With a slight tug on her chin, he opened her mouth and showed her what a kiss was like. She learned fast and returned his kiss with playful enthusiasm.

Her hands brushed his bare shoulders, feeling the strength beneath his flesh. His skin was warm, and his muscles hardened as her fingers moved along his arm. His mouth played with hers—kissing, tasting, molding. She let out a long sigh of pleasure and wrapped her arms tightly around his neck.

"More," she whispered against his mouth. "Please."

He lowered his weight over her, warming her completely as his kiss deepened with her request. He shoved the covers to her waist so that only her gown stood between her full breasts and the pounding of his heart.

A hunger deep within him gnawed at his restraint. She had come to his bed not out of passion, but out of fear. If she'd only kissed another once, she couldn't be aware that the rise and fall of her breasts was driving him wild. She couldn't know how close they were to the edge of ending all rational thought.

Finally, using all his reserve, he rolled away. He stared at the window, watching the near-forgotten storm outside. The kiss had affected him deeply. Far more deeply than he'd intended. Somehow every time he touched her, he dug the cavern in his heart deeper, and he knew in the future he'd long for something he'd never even known to miss before. Even now he wanted nothing more than to pull her into a mindless passion neither had ever experienced.

He knew he should stay away from her. Being around her was like juggling nitroglycerin. Eventually, something was going to explode. And even if it didn't, she'd be gone from his life soon and he'd have only memories. After only one kiss, his life wouldn't be the same when he returned. Sure, the store would be there, work, his son, the people he'd known all his life, but True would be missing.

"I've changed my mind," she whispered as she brushed her lips with her fingers. "I think I like kissing."

"I'm glad," he answered without looking at her.

True sat up and twisted until she could see his face. "You didn't like my kiss?"

Seth folded his arms over his chest. "I liked it a great deal."

"Then kiss me again." She leaned against his arm.

"Is that an order, part of the job?" He forced his entire body to freeze as her soft breasts pressed against him.

"No, only a request." Her pride would not allow her to ask again. "Never mind. Forget I asked."

She was off the bed before her words registered in his brain.

"Wait!" he caught her at the door. With a sudden jerk, he twisted her around and into his arms. "I'll kiss you if you like. I'll kiss you so deeply, you'll know you never have to ask anyone again."

Digging his fingers into her hair, he lowered his mouth, full and warm, over hers. He plunged deep inside, bruising her lips with a need to taste her. Her arms encircled his neck, and he lifted her off the ground as the kiss turned tender. Slowly, as she learned, their lips grew playful, teasing.

Finally, he lay her gently back on the bed and stretched out beside her before finally ending the kiss.

True took a long breath and asked, "Where did you learn to do that?"

Seth laughed and turned toward her. Her mouth looked a little puffy and still moist. "Well, let's see, there was Polly in the second grade and Sarah in the third, and oh yes, the twins that summer I was twelve and . . ."

True covered his mouth with her hand. "Never mind. Sometimes I should stop asking questions."

"Agreed." His answer was muffled by her fingers. He wished he could tell her that he'd never kissed a woman the way he'd kissed her. But kissing her seemed as natural as breathing. She saw him as a man of the world; he couldn't destroy that image.

She moved her fingers along his lip then brushed the day's growth of beard covering his cheek.

"What am I going to do with you, True McCormick?"

"Hold me," she whispered as thunder rattled the walls once more. "Hold me until the storm is over and then kiss me one more time."

"I'll hold you," His hand slid beneath the cover and spread across her gown at her waist. "If you'll come into my arms willingly come morning."

"I promise," True answered as she curled beside him and closed her eyes.

His arms were warm bands of protection around her. True rested her head on his chest and listened to his heart pound. She knew he was no more real in her life than the Granite Westwind she'd created. If he knew who she really was, he'd be gone just like the only other man who'd said he cared for her.

But Seth had never said he cared. He'd never talked of love or forever as her first beau had. Maybe Seth Atherton wasn't looking for a wife to cook his meals and clean his house. Maybe he was only looking for someone to hold during a storm . . . as she was.

She lay awake listening to the easy sound of his breathing until the storm ended. Very slowly, she pulled away from Seth and tiptoed back to her room. Without turning on a light, she dressed in the boy's clothes she always carried in her bag.

The wet night air welcomed True as she moved quieter than a ghost down the streets. True loved this time of night after a rain. The world was clean and newborn as it slept.

The shadows welcomed her, and the fuzzy light from dirty windows guided her through the alleys. True was home.

THIRTEEN

A pounding sounded on the parlor door, shaking the walls with each blow. Seth came fully awake all at once like a wild animal ready to fight.

"True!" he shouted, though the effort was unnecessary. She'd disappeared sometime before dawn while he slept. He spread his hand into the covers but could no longer feel the warmth of her body. Her presence had been a grand torture during the night, for he'd wanted more. This one fact frightened him into hesitating. What kind of man was he becoming? Never had he wanted a woman so dearly. Not until three days ago, when True came into his life.

The pounding came again. Seth climbed from bed and looked for his shirt. By the time he'd found it and crossed to the door, the knocking had started its third stanza.

"What!" he opened the door, ready to attack.

Micah took one look at Seth, in an unbuttoned shirt and wrinkled pants, and raised his cane as if it were an honored weapon. The old man's eyes crinkled up so far into his face, Seth couldn't tell if they were open or closed. Extra skin always seemed to hang off his body as though he'd washed his bones and they'd shrunk. Now angry, his face had even more lines.

To Seth's total amazement, the old man squared his shoulders as though preparing to fight. "This better not be True's room or you're in for a thrashing."

"Not that it's any of your business, but no," Seth

answered and watched the aging writer relax, "her room's next door."

"That's lucky for you, son." Micah exhaled a deep breath, as if he'd been holding air for some time.

"Micah!" True shouted from behind Seth. She almost knocked Seth over as she ran from her room to the hallway. "Micah! I'm so glad you're here."

The ancient one hugged her warmly. Seth could tell that in a life of very few treasures Micah considered his greatest find True's friendship. He also guessed her warm greeting had more to do with covering her embarrassment over last night than with any great need to see Micah.

True pushed Seth aside again as she pulled Micah into the parlor. She sat him down at the table and began pampering him as if he were the King of Texas.

Seth was starting to feel like one of those turnstyles used at the big train station in Kansas City. "I'm sorry to be in the way," he mumbled as he moved to the sideboard and poured himself coffee while there was still a clean cup.

"Nonsense." True laughed. "It's just that I've been hoping Micah would come by this morning with news of who shot at us last night."

The old man smiled enough to reveal the few teeth he had left. "I haven't seen Link this morning." He winked at True. "I plan on paying him a visit, though. The young fellow needs my advice now and then."

Seth studied Micah. He still had on the same suit he'd worn in Galveston. Now there was a huge whiskey-colored stain on the once white lapel. "I hope you brought a change of clothes," Seth mumbled.

Micah waved Seth's comment aside. "I haven't had time to change from last night. I went hunting for information after I heard about the shooting."

Seth wanted to add, "or from the night before, or the night before that," but he remained silent.

True stopped pouring her coffee. "And you've been out drinking a little I'd guess."

Micah grinned, admitting guilt. "I reckon I'd done my share of both, when I stumbled across something."

True sat down and gave him her full attention, but Seth withheld his judgment.

All Micah needed to continue was True's smile. "I was outside a saloon this morning when I heard two men talking. One of them was a big fellow who looked like he'd been eating a bit too regular, and the other was a hired gun. I could tell just by the way he kept patting his six-shooter, like it was his only friend. He must have been pretty good at his job because he was struttin' like a rooster who thought the sun just come up every morning so he could crow."

Seth pulled up a chair on the other side of the old man. He figured if Micah happened ever to get around to the story, he might have something to say.

Micah smiled, happy to have another member in his audience. "Well, the big man started swearing at the gunman like he done something wrong. I couldn't tell what they were fighting about until the gunman turned and said something like, 'Westwind will be dead before the end of the week or I'll give the money back.'"

True's face paled, but Seth's showed more interest than fear as he asked, "Can you describe both men? Every detail. Where did they go? What else did they say?"

Micah raised a wrinkled hand that looked as if it had enough lifelines for generations. "I'd had a few drinks by then so I was in no shape to follow them. The big man yelled something like how he was still young enough to do the job himself if the gunman couldn't carry it out. I don't remember what else they said." He looked at Seth and shook his head. "I'd hate it powerful much if you were killed off after all the trouble we went to finding you."

True met Seth's gaze. "We've got to call off the tour. It's not worth risking your life no matter what the publishers say. Not only do we have someone wanting to kill you, but he sounds like he's willing to pay to see you dead."

Seth laughed. He'd only got Westwind's life two days ago, so it didn't seem like too big a risk. "We're not calling off the tour. Not on just what some old drunk says."

"I ain't that old," Micah objected to the adjective. "And I wasn't so drunk I don't remember what I heard. I took only enough time to finish my drinking and then I headed over here."

"It's not just Micah. What about the gunfire last night?" True stood, straightening her tailored blue dress as if she were putting her thoughts in order. "I'm going to the sheriff's office and find out if Link learned anything from the man they captured."

"I'm going with you." Seth noticed that she was fully dressed, and he hadn't even shaved. "Wait for me to get my boots on."

True opened the door. "I haven't got time. Stay here with Micah and have breakfast until I get back."

Micah was the only one who thought that was a grand idea.

By the time True was halfway down the two flights of stairs, Seth had caught up with her, his boots in hand. "I don't take orders," he mumbled as he tried to button his shirt and hold his boots, gun belt, and hat at the same time.

True stopped so quickly, he almost lost his footing. "That is exactly what you were hired to do—follow orders, nothing more."

"Wrong." Seth was eye level with her thanks to the steps. "I thought you hired me to *be* Granite Westwind. And as you so kindly told me the first night, Westwind would never hide from trouble."

True was so angry she couldn't get the words to come out of her mouth. She wanted to shoot the stubborn man herself. Couldn't he see that being in public, even walking the streets, could be dangerous?

"All right, *be* Westwind, but get your boots on first. What kind of hero runs around in his stockinged feet?"

Seth shoved his gun belt and hat at her and pulled on his boots. When he looked up, he had to smile at how anger warmed her cheeks. No matter how mad he was at her, he could never forget how beautiful she looked. Something about her was perfection. He thought of asking for the morning kiss she'd promised, but he had no doubt she'd murder him on the stairs for such a suggestion.

"Thanks, darlin'," he whispered as he took his guns and strapped them on.

"Don't darlin' me, you pigheaded, foolish excuse for a hero. I'll . . ."

"Save it for later," Seth laughed. "Right now, we've got to find Link." He took the steps three at a time, and True ran to keep up with him.

Finding Link didn't prove to be any problem. They almost collided with him as they entered the lobby. The Ranger was doing his job and looked very official in his white shirt with a circle star pinned to the pocket. Like all Rangers, he gave the impression he was a solution waiting for a problem.

"Mornin'." He smiled as he watched them storm toward him. "You two getting along as smooth as ever, I see."

"Mind your own business, Link!" True snapped, sending the Ranger into a full laugh.

Seth ignored them both. This was some teasing game they'd probably played with each other for years. Right now he was trying to figure out how he could keep True busy and out of the line of fire. "Officer Raine, I was wondering if you'd be willing to accompany me on the tour for the next few days, until things quiet down. I thought we could give Miss McCormick some rest."

Link grinned as if he could see war paint on both their faces. "That sounds like a fine plan," he whispered to True and Seth, but neither of them was listening to him.

FOURTEEN

True could not remember ever being so angry with anyone in her life. Seth Atherton had walked in and taken over as if he really were her boss. She'd kept the secret of her occupation so well hidden from even close friends like Link, that now she couldn't turn to him for help. How could anyone believe she wrote as Granite Westwind, when Granite Westwind stood before them in the flesh? Link was so friendly to Seth, one would think the two men had been childhood buddies.

"I need to continue the tour with you, Mr. Westwind," she said, trying to sound calm as she walked down the crowded Houston street between Link and Seth. "After all, Mr. Westwind, I'm the one who booked all the dates."

"Write them on a paper, Miss McCormick." Seth didn't even look at her as he issued the order. He was afraid she'd see how much he wanted her with him, but his desire to keep her beside him wasn't worth her life. If he had to live the next few days looking over his shoulder, he'd do better if she wasn't there to distract him.

With the flare of a gentleman, he held the door for her to enter the newsstand/bookstore. "This will be your last public appearance with me, Miss McCormick."

"I'll set up guard out here." Link tipped his hat when Seth waited for him to enter the store. "After all, Mr. Westwind, you've got True to protect you once you're inside."

The two men looked at each other as if they shared some private joke True had no part in. She stormed into the interior, swearing she'd hate them both for one day longer than eternity.

The only employee in the store was busy at the front and pointed them toward the rear. Seth followed True to the stack of Westwind novels along the back wall.

"I'm only doing this for your own safety," he whispered as he lifted the first book and signed Westwind's name.

"Don't do me any favors." True spoke between clenched teeth. "Just sign the books, and we'll move on to the next place."

"I'll move on," Seth corrected. "You're going back to the hotel."

"Like hell."

Just as he lifted his hands to her shoulders, she delivered a blow to his ribs. Seth folded forward in surprise and pain as he bit back the oath that tried to pass his lips. Normally her small fist would have done him no harm, but the tender skin only inches from her blow had yet to heal from the butcher's knife wound.

The chubby store manager stepped from the back storage room when he heard the groan. "Is something wrong?" The manager was newspaper pale, and his eyes were almost completely colorless behind thick glasses.

True's smile appeared handed down from the angels. "Mr. Westwind isn't feeling very well." Her body straightened to her porcelain doll pose, and her small fist uncoiled. "Do you have a glass of water for him?"

The manager nodded and disappeared.

Atherton pulled her close and whispered against her cheek. "I feel fine, Miss McCormick. Did it ever cross that jumble of matter you call a brain that I'm twice your size, and it might not be to your advantage to start a brawl with me?"

She looked up at him with innocent blue eyes. "Even the

smallest rattlesnakes are deadly." Her voice was honey again.

He had never wanted to kiss a woman so strongly. He'd have given every dime he had to touch her right now. She was standing in a public place threatening him, and all he could think of was holding her. He jerked away, forcing himself not to look at her. Maybe he should let her hit him a few more times. Maybe one of the blows would knock some sense back into his brain.

He picked up a book and signed it. The store owner brought a dipper of water and apologized for having no glasses. Seth didn't care about glasses, but he wished the dipper were from a bucket of liquor.

Ten minutes passed before he dared look at True. She sat several feet away, at a small reading table, writing in her notebook as always. People were starting to come into the store, all wanting to shake Westwind's hand and tell him which one of his books was their favorite.

Seth smelled Micah's whiskey breath before he saw the man. The old writer stood back between the stacks, trying to tell the store owner that he was a personal friend of Granite Westwind. In Micah's present attire, he certainly didn't look the part. Now the whiskey-colored stain had gravy drippings on the other lapel to compete with for space on the once white suit.

"I had breakfast with him this very mornin'!" Micah yelled as the owner grabbed him by the collar and started pushing him through the store. "We're writing colleagues and have been for years." Micah was at the door and still talking. "Of course, my works take some time longer to complete. Research, you know."

Dropping the book he was signing, Seth hurried to Micah's aid. "Wait!" He touched the owner on the shoulder. "He's telling the truth; Micah is my friend." The words stuck in Seth's throat, but he didn't want to face True if he allowed them to throw the old guy out.

Several people in the store mumbled. Half seemed to think it was only fitting that Granite Westwind would have friends from all walks of life, and the other half felt he must be saving the day, as always. If this were a Westwind book, the old man would be someone rich and powerful in disguise.

Seth hurried Micah out the door before the old man could talk to anyone else. No telling what story he'd tell if he had a room full of people to listen. Seth wasn't sure the bag of bones had any closer touch with reality than True seemed to possess.

"You didn't have breakfast with me," Seth whispered.

"Yes, I did," Micah answered. "I ate most of yours and True's meal, but I brought you a few rolls and links of sausage. There ain't no use in wasting good food." He pulled the breakfast remains from his pocket. "Want them?"

Seth had never considered himself a picky eater. But looking down at a biscuit and two sausages, in a hand darkened with filth from a night of drinking, took his appetite. "No, thanks," he managed to say as True followed him into the fresh air.

"How about you, True?"

To Seth's amazement, True looked at the food as if she were trying to decide between appetizers at some fancy party.

"Thanks." She smiled. "But you save them for lunch."

Micah nodded his appreciation as he almost bumped into Link leaning against the brick storefront. "You're that Ranger I've seen hanging about True before." He was back in his self-appointed father role now.

Link touched his hat and started a speech that sounded as if he'd given it to Micah a few times before. "I've been hanging around the kid since she was about six and I was fifteen. I've done my part in raising her. My dad was foreman of a ranch up in Kansas where she often stayed until they sent her back East to school."

Turning back toward the door, Seth only hoped Link could keep the old man occupied. Probably all the Ranger would have to do was ask Micah about the book he planned to write.

Seth saw the sun reflecting off the long barrel of a rifle in the glass store panels only a moment before he heard the blast. He jumped toward True by instinct.

The world changed in the flash of fire and the rumble of one blast. Link pulled his gun and stepped in front of True. True screamed and reached for Micah. The old man fell between them, doubling over as though he'd been punched in the stomach.

Seth cradled Micah in his arms, breaking his fall as they both hit the wooden sidewalk. Before the sound cleared the air, Link was in full run across the street toward the building from where the shot had been fired.

"Get back in the store!" Seth shouted at True.

"Micah!" Tears bubbled onto her cheeks. "Micah, you've been hit!"

Lifting the old man, Seth knew the only way he could get True to safety was to move Micah first. "Open the door!" he shouted as he stood.

Micah's eyes were wide with fright. His hands gripped his middle, but blood still managed to ooze between his knuckles. His bottom lip shook, but he didn't cry out.

True ran around them to open the door. "We have to get him to the hospital."

"First, we have to get him to safety, then the hospital."

Seth lay the man down on the tile floor just inside the

door. "Stay down, True, until Link returns. Keep your hands pressed over the wound to slow the blood."

True looked up at him. "Where are you going?"

"I'm backing up the Ranger." Seth didn't allow any time for discussion. He was out the door before True could stop him. He knew as well as she did that the bullet had been meant for him, but he couldn't hide inside while someone took shots. If he was to die, he'd rather it be face-on in a gunfight and not by ambush. He'd never been shot at before yesterday, and the realization that someone wanted to kill him angered him far more than it frightened him.

Seth pulled his left Colt from its holster. He might need both guns fast, and he wanted the backup on the right side. He crossed the street knowing that he couldn't be more than thirty seconds behind Link.

Shots rang out from the side street. Seth crossed the width of a small hotel before the sound stopped ringing. He rounded the corner and saw Link standing next to a broken-down carriage. The Ranger had both weapons drawn and was firing into the far end of an alley. Seth rolled against the outside wall of the building and came shoulder to shoulder with Link.

"Mornin', Lincoln," he said, as if they'd just encountered each other on the street. "Need any help?"

Link grinned, his brown eyes friendly. "You're the last person I expected to see here, Mr. Westwind. Can you use those polished Colts?"

Sudden firing stopped their conversation. Reason, logic, common sense were all outweighed by the adrenaline throbbing through Seth's veins. He shot back, while Link stopped to reload. He heard a cry from the other end of the street and knew one bullet had hit its mark.

Silence followed—long, weighted silence. The kind of

almost deafening quiet that must follow all battles, Seth
guessed.

"They're gone," Link whispered.

"Or waiting for us to make the next move." Seth glanced
at the carriage. "How about we take our cover with us?"

The two men shouldered the broken carriage and pushed
it slowly down the alley. When they reached the far end, all
they found were several spent shells and a few drops of
blood.

"I hit one of them." Seth knelt and touched the red liquid
puddled in the dirt.

"That makes us even," Link answered, as he turned
toward Seth.

For the first time, Seth saw the stain of crimson on the
sleeve of Link's shirt. He stood and examined the wound.
"Why didn't you say something?"

"It's only a scratch," Link answered, as he pulled a white
handkerchief from his pocket. "I was hit far worse in my
first gunfight, when I wasn't even shaving."

Seth helped him tie off the bandage. "I didn't think
Indians shaved."

Link laughed. "My mother doesn't. Unfortunately, my
father isn't Indian and has a full beard every winter."

The two men stared at each other for only a blink's time,
but in that space an understanding passed between them—an
acceptance, an offer of friendship that would not be easily
withdrawn.

As they walked back to the bookstore, Link retrieved his
jacket from the street where he'd dropped it. "I'd appreciate
it, Mr. Westwind, if you wouldn't mention my arm to True.
Once she starts worrying about something, she'll drive a
fellow nuts."

"Agreed," Seth answered, knowing that True was driving

him insane already, and he had a feeling she hadn't worked herself up to full speed.

When they reached the bookstore, the place was empty except for the chubby owner. "They've gone," he announced, throwing his arms wide as if tossing his future away. "A man shot in front of my store. What am I going to do?"

"Is Micah dead?" Seth stopped the man's raving.

"Where have they gone?" Link added.

"Three blocks down to the hospital. As soon as you disappeared, your secretary got some men to help her carry the old man out the back door. She kept crying that there was no time to lose."

Though Link was a few inches shorter, his strides matched Seth's as they stormed down the walk. The pounding of the boots echoed, warning everyone to step aside. A man would have to have had a death wish to cross two such men, for they were powerful and full of purpose.

No one stepped in their way until they reached the hospital corridor; then only one person dared stand up against them.

Amid the sterile whiteness, they were stopped by a slender lady with sadness in her bottomless blue eyes.

FIFTEEN

"This will never work." Link helped True onto the train. "The old man will be dead before you can get him to Audrey in Galveston."

True looked to Seth for support, but he was having no part of her argument with Link. "What other chance do we have?" she repeated for the tenth time since they'd left the hospital. "The doctors have give him only a matter of hours to live. I can't just sit in the hospital holding his hand until he bleeds to death. Audrey knows all the doctors at the medical school. Maybe one of them can do something?"

Link tried to look as if he understood, but to him it seemed that True was only making the old man miserable during his last few hours of life, because she couldn't let him go. "All right. We'll take him to Audrey, but a nurse goes with us all the way. Maybe she can help him to rest easier."

Link watched the hospital staff load Micah. "At least I'll be getting Westwind away from a hired assassin. Maybe with half the Houston police working on finding the man who shot at us, the tour will be safer to continue in a few days."

"Thanks for your support," True said sarcastically as she moved through the private car to where they'd put Micah. "I'm staying with Micah during the trip. You worry about Westwind."

Link swore softly as she disappeared. "That girl has been nothing but a pain since she stormed into my life." He nodded his thanks as Seth handed him a drink. "I only see her every few years, but I'm not over being mad at her about something until she's back in my life again stirring up all kinds of hell. When she was a kid, everyone thought I should be the one to ride herd on her when they were busy."

"Everyone?" Seth took his seat as the train rattled into motion. He'd been amazed at how True had talked the men in the train yard into hooking her car onto the first engine heading down to Galveston.

"Didn't she tell you she has three mothers? It takes that many people to keep up with her." Link drained his glass. "Three young Harvey girls adopted True when she was about six. Half the time they thought one of the others was watching her. Sometimes she'd be gone for a week before they'd figure out she wasn't with any of them. Not that she didn't love her new folks. She's crazy about all of them, but True's a wild thing that has to run free." Link looked slightly embarrassed. "But I guess you know that. She's worked for you for several years now."

"We mostly handle our correspondence through the mail." Seth didn't know what else to say. He wanted to tell Link the truth about how he was hired to play Granite Westwind, but he figured if Colonel McCormick didn't tell his Rangers, maybe there was a reason. "I'll say one thing for her. She doesn't surrender anyone to death easily. If I'm ever near dying, I think I'd want True in my corner."

"It's just stubbornness," Link answered.

The door leading to the berths opened. "Mr. Westwind," True said. "Micah wants to talk to you."

Seth stood. "How is he?"

"He's coughing up blood, but I think the wrappings they applied at the hospital helped."

Seth moved past her in the narrow hallway. They couldn't help but touch as the train made them sway. He wanted to pull her into his arms and make all the sadness in her eyes go away, but he knew that was impossible.

Slowly, he stepped into the walkway next to the only open berth. Micah looked very old and pale curled into the space. A nurse, loaned from the hospital for the trip, sat in a chair only a few feet away.

"Westwind?" Micah whispered. "That you?"

"Yes." Seth touched the old man's arm. "How are you holding up?"

Micah coughed. "I've had better days. Fact is, most days following Jackson through the war were better than today."

"You fought with General Jackson?" Somehow Seth didn't see a soldier beneath the writer's mask.

"With honor. In more battles than I've nightmares to remember. I got so I could sense a bullet coming. Guess I've still got the touch. Only before you go thinking I saved your life, I'd best confess I just made a mistake and jumped the wrong way. My sense of it coming was as good as ever, but my hearing must be off."

Seth smiled. Maybe he did see a soldier in the old man, after all. Even in pain he didn't want to take the glory when none was due.

Micah coughed, and some of the life was gone from his eyes when he looked back at Seth. "I have to tell you something just in case I don't make it."

Seth didn't insult the man by arguing. He knelt beside the bed. "What is it?"

Micah smiled slightly. "I've known True longer than anyone alive. She thinks real highly of you. Speaks well of you."

"Thanks," Seth answered.

"I seen the way you look at her when you're not mad. Don't ruin what you two have together by falling in love with her. If you do, she'll run like a jackrabbit trying to cross Main Street."

"But—"

Micah closed his eyes. "She may look a fine lady now, but she's a street kid, and she thinks she don't deserve love. You try to give love to her, and she'll kick it away like it was no more than pity."

"You love her dearly, don't you?" Seth gripped Micah's arm, willing his strength into the man.

"Course I do. So does everyone she touches. She needs a good man like you, but she'll run if you ever tell her you love her."

"Why are you telling me this?"

Micah gripped his middle. "'Cause I know I ain't goin' be around to see after her. One winter, years ago, I was so sick with a cold all I wanted to do was curl up and freeze to death. True wouldn't let me. She yelled and badgered until I stayed alive just to keep her quiet. I figure I owe her one, so I'm telling you. If you want to hold True, you have to do it with an open hand."

A sudden coughing fit ended their conversation. The nurse waved Seth away. As he moved through the door to the main room, he heard Micah mumbling something about it being very cold for July.

When they reached Galveston, True was silent as they loaded the old man onto an ambulance wagon and rushed him to the hospital. Dr. Audrey Gates had been wired and was ready with a full staff in the operating room when they arrived. Hours passed slowly as they waited in silence. True paced while Seth kept reliving the scene, trying to think of anything he could have done to stop the shooting.

Link stood guard like a statue at the entrance, his eyes searching every face.

Finally, Audrey came out to meet them. She looked tired

and her hair was damp from being covered, but the woman's beauty still remained. Her smile was warm for both True and Link and only slightly cooler for Seth.

"We've done all we can." She touched True's shoulder. "We'll know something before the night's through." Silently she touched Link also, as if the two were still children. "There's nothing we can do here. Let's go home and have some supper. I sent word for Marie to cook something up just in case." She glanced at Seth. "You're invited, too, of course."

Seth realized he hadn't eaten all day. The memory of the biscuit Micah had offered this morning didn't seem that unappealing at the moment.

An hour later they all sat around the table of Audrey's kitchen eating everything Marie pulled from the icebox and pie safe. Boxes marked "Alaska" lined one wall and some of the furniture had been covered, but it was obvious to Seth that Audrey's travels would someday wind up back here.

When Link pulled off his coat to help with the dishes, Seth saw Audrey notice his arm, but she didn't comment. She was a good doctor, he thought. The kind that blended caring with skill. He guessed Audrey knew she'd only be bringing on more trouble if she mentioned Link's wound in front of everyone.

Audrey stood to all her six foot height and looked at Link. "True, if you and Mr. Westwind don't mind, I need to talk to Ranger Raine in my office for a few minutes."

True smiled for the first time in hours. "If it's Ranger Raine, it must be business, because you've known him since he was fifteen."

"Maybe she's just paying me a little respect, which you might think about sometime, brat." Link winked. No matter how old he and True grew, there would always be some of the childhood badgering between them.

Audrey didn't comment as she led Link out of the kitchen as though he were a boy and not a man of more than thirty.

True moved to the sink and dumped a load of dishes into a dry tub. She gripped the sides of the counter and stared at the dirty plates as if she had no idea what to do next.

Seth had been waiting all day for a moment alone with her. He'd watched her silently hide every emotion except anger for hours. Standing, he joined her, placing his hands on either side of hers. He could feel the warmth of her back only an inch from his chest.

"True," he whispered, wishing he could think of the right words. He knew better than to ask her if she was all right. Link had made that mistake once too often today, and she'd snapped at him.

"Let go of the hurt, True." He gently placed his hands on her shoulders. Her muscles were so tight he could almost believe she was made of porcelain and not flesh.

"I can't," she whispered as she leaned back against his chest. "Micah may be dying and all I can think of is how I'll miss him. I want to shake him and ask why he's doing this to me. As if he had some choice. I've never even told him how much I love him."

He felt her go stiff in his arms. "Let down the wall, True. I'm here." He said the words he wished someone had said to him the night his wife and baby girl died.

She snapped like a frozen branch against a wind, crumbling against Seth's chest as if all the energy had left her body at once. Lifting her in his arms, he carried her into the darkness of the living room. He sat down in one of Audrey's huge overstuffed chairs and pulled True to him.

"He knows you love him," Seth whispered, as he brushed a wayward strand of hair out of her eyes. "He told me you saved his life. How could he not know you love him?"

Tears ran unchecked down her cheeks as she rested in his

arms. "But it wasn't for him," she admitted. "It was because I was afraid of being alone. I made him live that time, but I can do nothing now."

"Hush." Seth rubbed his chin against her hair. "You've done all you can."

He wasn't sure what he whispered to her while he held her, but slowly she relaxed and fell asleep in his lap. As she let go of her pain, Seth allowed the grief he'd never confronted, from Marcy's death, to pass away. All these years, he realized, he'd been mad at Marcy for not fighting to live. Anger had kept him from mourning her. She'd died and left him without ever really loving him, and that knowledge had hurt more than her death. He'd been a good husband and father, but in the end she hadn't even asked to see him. Since then he'd thought he'd gotten what he deserved, but now, holding True, he knew there was more to caring, far more.

Pulling her against his heart, Seth whispered to himself, "I know how Micah feels. You've made me live also."

Seth could hear the mumble of Link and Audrey in the other room, but he didn't really care what they were saying. He closed his eyes and joined True in sleep.

Audrey washed her hands as she ordered Link to take off his shirt.

"It's only a scratch," he protested as he started unbuttoning. "Stop trying to mother me, Doc."

"Don't tell me it's a scratch. I've been patching you up since the time you were shorter than me."

Link laughed. "I've always been taller than you. It just took me a few years to stand up straight around you. I was just a kid, and you were a starched and proper Harvey girl. Lord, you took my breath away in that black-and-white uniform."

Audrey brought the supplies to the examining table Link leaned against. "And now you're a grand Ranger."

Link's voice slowed. "And you're a doctor. Still as untouchable as ever." His voice was very low, almost a thought. "And still as beautiful."

She cleaned the wound as if she hadn't heard his words. He was right; the bullet had only grazed him. It was little to worry about this time, but she'd known that if it had been ten times worse, he'd have still ignored it and bit back the pain. Link flexed his powerful arm as she wrapped the bandage. "Don't go flattering me, boy. I'm long past having my head turned by a few pretty words."

While she worked, he played with an auburn curl that had escaped her bun. "I've always thought your hair was the color of an early summer sunrise—red and fiery." He'd never been a man to flatter anyone. His words now sounded practiced, as though he'd thought them a hundred times or maybe said them when alone.

She moved away. "Stop acting like I'm someone you don't know and would like to call on. Flattery may work on the barmaids on Post Office Street, but not here. I've not only known you most your life, but I know where every scar is on your body."

Link moved his arm, making sure the bandage wasn't too tight. "Maybe not all scars show."

Audrey's laughter had no humor in it. "I've had longer in life to learn that than you have, kid."

"Not all that much longer," he answered.

"You've gotten by." She patted his arm in the same comforting gesture she'd used at the hospital. "I've very proud of the way you turned out. I know you're one of the best Rangers in the state."

He pulled away from her touch as though it had been a slap. "There's a lot you don't know about me, Doc."

Audrey was busy putting up supplies. "Is that a fact, Officer Raine? Well, why don't you fill me in on some of the things I don't know?"

Link moved as silently as his Indian ancestors. He was behind her before she was even aware of it. He reached toward her, but when he was within a few inches, his hand dropped as if it were too heavy to hold. "Nothing," he whispered. "I guess there's nothing."

He didn't see Audrey close her eyes and let out a long breath. Link moved away and added, "You've got to stop thinking of me as a kid. I was a boy when you met me almost eighteen years ago. I've been a man for a long time."

She crossed to the windows and looked out into the black night. He was right, of course. She'd been in her early twenties when they'd met, and he'd been in his teens. Yet all these years she'd always thought of him as a boy. Where had the years gone? When had she turned around and seen an old maid looking back at her in the mirror?

Slowly, as if forcing herself to see clearly, she faced him and stared for the first time in years. His body had the hard leanness of a fighter and not a youth. Thin lines wrinkled into his eyes, and a touch of gray brushed just above his ears. There was a hardness about him. A hardness she didn't remember. "You're right, of course. From this night on I'll not think of you as younger. We start on even ground."

"Agreed," Link answered. It was a beginning to a race he had no hope of ever winning or even getting to complete.

Audrey studied Link in the shadowy bay window's reflection. He was nothing like her, she decided. Maybe that's why they could never seem to say more than a few words to each other. He was a fighter, a warrior who made his living killing folks the law thought needed killing. She was a peacemaker, a healer, who wanted to help others.

A tapping sounded on the back office door, ending any more discussion.

"Evening, Doc." A young man stepped into the light. "I came over to let you know the old fellow you worked on today doesn't look like he'll make it another hour. He's fighting hard. Came around about a half hour ago and been calling for someone named True."

"Thank you," Audrey whispered. The youth nodded and hurried back into the night.

As she closed the door, Link moved to her side and awkwardly placed his arm around her shoulder. "I'm sorry," he said.

Audrey patted his hand. When she stepped away to lift her coat from the rack, she thought she saw a whisper of passion in his warm brown eyes. But that couldn't be. More likely it was a slight crack in the mask of authority he always seemed to hold so dear. Much as the Ranger might hate to admit it, he cared for Micah.

Link let out a long breath and ran his tan fingers through his black hair. "I'm not surprised he's calling for True. He knows it's the end and he needs to say his good-byes. Not that you didn't do all you could, Doc." His voice was back to that of the polite stranger he'd always been to her, but his gaze seemed warmer toward her. "I've just seen that look of death on one too many faces over the past few years."

"I know," Audrey agreed. She straightened slowly, pulling herself together as a baker gathers scraps for another roll of dough.

Wordlessly she handed her coat to Link to hold. Their hands touched beneath the material.

For a moment neither pulled away. They stood, eye level to each other, and stared as if each were looking for the first time at an old friend.

There will never be anything between us, Audrey thought

as she refused to lower her gaze. The slow smile that touched the Ranger's lips told her he wasn't thinking in terms of never, but of someday.

"I'd best tell True it's time to go back to the hospital." Audrey turned away, but she could feel Lincoln watching her leave the room.

SIXTEEN

Seth stood in the shadows and watched True kneeling beside Micah's bed. She held his hand tightly in both hers as if he were drowning and she could somehow pull him back from deep water.

The old man's voice was so weak Seth could barely hear the words he whispered.

"Now, don't go crying like some silly girl. You and me, we've been around and we know there ain't nothing hard about dying. It's the staying alive that gives you fits in this world."

Tears sparkled down True's face, but she didn't make a sound.

"I'm sorry I didn't have time to write that book. I was thinking it was about time to start. The stories been in my head for years." He closed his eyes and rested awhile before whispering. "I'm never gonna write it, am I, girl?"

"No," True answered. In all the years she'd known him, she'd never seen a page of the book he was always going to write someday. For years he'd been rewriting and changing plots in his mind, until now there was no more time.

True lowered her cheek against Micah's palm. Somehow he'd used up all his creativity helping her. So many times she had heard him say he'd put his story on the back burner and help her with one of the dime novels.

Slowly Micah stroked her dark brown hair with his free hand. "Now, don't go making a scene here in front of Mr.

Westwind and the Ranger. It ain't as if you haven't got two good men to take my place in seeing after you. I know I'm hard to replace, but the two of them should muster it."

Seth's smile widened. The old man had told the story of Seth being Westwind so many times he believed it himself.

"Thirty years ago I was in a battle near Shiloh. We thought we were all going to die before sunup. The captain placed those of us able to shoot between corpses leaned up along the line. We was hoping to fool the Yankees into not attacking. I finally got so tired I just curled down between two already cold bodies and prayed the Lord would take me fast so I wouldn't yell like I could hear others doing in the darkness."

Micah coughed, twisting his face with the pain.

His normally leathered skin was so white it looked as if it had been powdered like an old wig from a hundred years ago. "Come dawn the only thing moving on the field was the pickers snatching what they could from the bodies in both blue and gray. I figured right there and then that when my time came I'd go without swearing against God for more breath. He gave me over thirty more years, and I haven't wasted a minute of it not living."

An aging hand cupped True's face. "And he blessed me with knowing you, child. No character I could have ever written would be near the rainbow you are, darlin'. I don't mind dying knowing I've left you to remember me."

True pulled an inch away. "You're not going to die. Get some rest." Her voice was higher than usual. "You'll be better in the morning. You'll see."

"Hand me my hat." Micah sounded very weak. "Has anyone seen my cane?"

Link stepped out of the room while True went to the pile

of clothes and found Micah's hat. She brushed it smooth and shaped it as best she could.

"This was always my favorite hat of yours," she whispered. "You look mighty grand in it."

Micah's eyes were closed, but he managed a slight smile. He raised his hand from the sheet until she placed the hat beside his fingers.

The door creaked as Link entered with a cane. No one asked where he'd found it.

"Your cane, sir," the Ranger said as he lay the wood along Micah's side.

The old man gripped his hat in one hand and his cane in the other. "I won't want to meet my Maker lookin' less than proper."

True was almost blinded by tears, but she reached gently and brushed the few strands of Micah's hair into place. "As always, you look wonderful. A man who would stand out in any crowd."

"I never saw any need in being part of a crowd. So I reckon I'll go on alone now."

With one long breath, Micah relaxed. The lines in his face slowly calmed as the rise and fall of his chest stilled.

Seth, Link, and True waited. It was as though they all felt that as long as no one moved, time would stop.

True finally stood and kissed Micah's cheek. When she looked at Seth, her tears had dried. "He's gone to the next adventure," she whispered.

Pulling her to him, Seth was surprised by his need to hold her. The old man had been right. True was like a rainbow. Suddenly he didn't want to face a world of browns and grays. He wanted to know that when his time came, he could say, as Micah had, that he'd lived. In one moment Seth Atherton saw his organized life for what it was— empty and dull.

The thought of changing it made cold, hard fear climb up his spine. The two-week detour from his life was becoming reality, and Seth wasn't sure, unless he ran like hell, that he would ever be able to find the way back. Or that he even cared to return.

SEVENTEEN

Seth awoke to the smell of raw fat beneath his nose and the feel of a tiny human hand pressing into his chest. He opened one eye.

Emily was propped on his lap with a piece of uncooked bacon in her hand. She looked disappointed that he was awake.

Seth very slowly lifted her and the bacon away from him as he sat up in the chair. Without a word, he raised one eyebrow and stared at the child.

"Phillip says if I hold raw meat under a sleeping man's nose, he'll snap at it like a dog."

Seth rubbed slumber from his face and wondered if he was still asleep. It had been hours before they'd left the hospital and returned to Audrey's. Then True had lain on the couch and talked about Micah and every story he ever told her until Seth must have dozed in the chair. "Phillip's wrong," Seth mumbled, blinking at the sunshine.

"Phillip's never wrong. He told me so himself. He said it's 'cause he's ten and in double digits, whatever that means. The nuns say I'm small for my age, but I must be about eight." Emily looked disappointed, then brightened. "Want me to have Dr. Gates's housekeeper cook this for you for breakfast?" She waved the bacon. "I figure it'll be good."

"That would be nice." Seth rubbed the stubble on his chin.

The child ran toward the kitchen. "It's a good piece.

Course it was a little bigger before that cat, Wiley, got a hold on it."

Seth couldn't help but smile. He stood, wondering where everyone else had disappeared to. He was becoming accustomed to True vanishing from his arms before the sun shone, but Link and Audrey seemed also to have gone. As he stepped toward the stairs, something moved on the window seat.

Seth touched his leg for his gun before he recognized Link. The Ranger stretched and stood. "Mornin'." He ran a hand through unruly hair. His clothes were wrinkled, but he didn't sound like he'd just awakened.

Seth never wasted words before he'd had a cup of coffee. "Where's True?"

Link stretched. "She and Audrey made a great show of sneaking out of the house before dawn."

"You didn't try and stop them?"

Link looked as though he'd been called a fool. "Of course not. I knew they were going to the undertaker. Judging from the clothes they took, Micah'll be dressed in style for the funeral." Link rubbed his bandaged arm. "Besides, my job's to keep watch on you."

Seth headed up the stairs. "I think I'll clean up. I've got a piece of bacon waiting for me for breakfast."

An hour later, with Emily perched on his knee, Seth downed the best pancakes he'd ever eaten. Audrey's housekeeper might never say a word, but she could cook.

Audrey opened the back door with her arms loaded down with supplies. Link stood to assist her without a word of greeting.

Seth didn't miss the way she avoided Link's gaze even as she accepted his help. "Morning," she said, looking at Seth and the child. "My Granny Gates always said the main reason God invented laps were to hold young'uns."

Emily giggled. "The nuns sent me in with the milkman this morning to have you bandage my arm again. They said you wouldn't mind."

"Of course not. I'm glad you're here. I decided I'd better buy more food. With all the company I've been having, I might have to postpone my trip to Alaska for a few weeks." She handed two bags to Marie but never stopped smiling at Emily. "I'll just put these office supplies up and be right with you."

Audrey crossed the room, with Link following, and entered her office. "Set them down anywhere, Lincoln. I'll put them away later."

He did as asked, but made no move to leave. Folding his arms over his chest, he leaned against the table and watched her.

As before, his stillness bothered her, making her more nervous than a schoolgirl on her first outing.

She couldn't allow herself to behave so ridiculously. She was a woman past her prime, with enough sense not to make a fool of herself over any man. Why didn't he leave? Why didn't he say something?

Finally, she could endure the tension no longer. She turned and faced him. Link simply stared at her with brown eyes that promised something she had no intention of accepting.

"Thank you for your help." Audrey kept her voice formal.

"You're welcome," he said but didn't move.

Audrey pulled off her jacket and reached for the white coat she always wore. The coat made her feel professional. It was her armor against the world.

Link's hand closed over hers and the coat before she could remove it from the hook. Audrey jumped. "Could you make a little more noise when you move? You're constantly startling me."

"Sorry." Link took the coat from her hand and held it for her.

Audrey straightened. "No, *I'm* sorry. I'm just on edge this morning. I didn't get enough sleep."

"We'll all feel it this morning."

She tried not to notice that his hands rested on her shoulders a moment longer than necessary as he straightened her coat. Maybe she was only thinking they had. After all these years why should Lincoln Raine treat her any different than he always had?

"Miss Audrey," Emily's voice came from the doorway, "are you ready for me yet?"

Audrey buttoned her coat. "Yes, dear, I'm ready for you."

Seth followed the child into the office. "That was a great breakfast. You may miss fresh eggs when you get to Alaska."

Both Link and Audrey looked at him without saying a word.

Seth thought it wise to change the subject. "Is Miss McCormick still at the undertaker's?"

"No," Audrey said as she cut the bandages off the child's arm. "She wanted me to tell you to meet her at the Harvey House for lunch. She has several things to do this morning."

Seth frowned. He didn't like the idea of letting True out of his sight. There was no telling what she'd be up to. Somehow in the few days they'd known each other she'd gotten under his skin, and he couldn't remember what he'd thought about before she was in his life. Or what he'd worried about.

He could hardly wait to tell her he'd shared his breakfast with her lover, Wiley the cat. He'd almost believed that story she'd told him the first night he'd kissed her, because she'd named her lover so quickly. He'd learned from Link that Wiley had been the name of Audrey's great love, who'd come to Texas some twenty years ago and was never seen again. Audrey apparently looked for him for several years before naming a cat after him and settling in Galveston.

When Link and Seth walked out of the doctor's place an hour before noon, they were both lost in private thoughts. Neither wanted to talk and each had a woman on his mind.

They walked half a block not caring where they were going. When they passed one of the town's never closing bars, Seth shrugged. "Feel like having a drink?"

Link nodded. "I feel like having a bottle."

Without another word they walked into the dingy place and ordered two bottles. By lunchtime, Seth felt as if his head were swimming in wet cotton, and Link wasn't doing any better.

Both tried very hard to walk straight out of the bar. When they reached the sunshine, Seth found out that the wet cotton in his brain had been soaked in kerosene, and someone set it afire. He could do nothing but try to walk until the pain burned out beneath his skull.

"Did you know, Westwind, the Indians who lived on this island when the first white man stepped foot on Galveston were cannibals? They've been extinct for over two hundred years or more by now." Whiskey seemed to have loosened the Ranger's tongue. "They were a mean, lazy lot who would starve rather than farm. They'd capture the enemy and herd them naked like cattle until they'd eaten them all one by one."

"Sounds like a friendly welcoming committee to Texas," Seth mumbled.

"They were lazy, filthy, savage, and heartless. The tribe traveled in small groups and didn't even get along with other families within the Karankawa tribe. There wasn't another tribe of Indians in Texas who would have anything to do with them. They only had one rule they lived by—fidelity. A Karankawa male picked one woman and never slept with another. If he did, he was the main course for supper. Early priests wrote of seeing hands and feet slow cooking on spits when they entered the Karankawa camp-site."

"So you think the reason they died away is that they were the lowlife bottom of civilization?" Seth asked.

"No." Link laughed. "I think it was the trying to get along with one woman that did it to them."

Seth laughed. "Maybe you're right," he agreed, as they took the steps of the Harvey House none too steadily.

Both men tried to look sober as the headwaitress checked their weapons and showed them to a table close to the kitchen. Seth usually preferred to sit by windows, but today it might be wiser to have an exit handy. If trouble came calling again, he planned to be ready.

True was already waiting for them. She looked beautiful even in her black funeral dress with only a touch of white lace showing at the collar and cuffs. Her eyes were puffy from crying, but she held herself in check, the porcelain lady as always.

"I've made plans to have Micah buried in a few hours. We had to turn the town upside down, but we finally found a Confederate uniform in good condition to dress him in. I think he'd like it that way." She looked closely at the two men and tried to figure out what was wrong with them.

Both were determined to hold their liquor as they sat very still and ordered coffee. From all outward appearances, no one in the room could have guessed they'd downed two bottles of whiskey.

True folded her napkin over her lap. "It's a little warm for coffee, gentleman. The lemonade here is wonderful." She watched them both, but they remained silent. "I ordered finger sandwiches as an appetizer for us."

"Finger sandwiches," Link whispered as laughter bubbled from him like lava from a formerly plugged volcano.

Seth tried to keep himself in control. This was a sad day for True. He needed to be supportive and caring, but the image of a Karankawa meal came to mind and the whiskey blocked all reason from his brain. He joined Link in laughter. Deep, rolling laughter that only men who find little in life to laugh about can summon.

True stared at both men as though they'd lost their minds. The more they laughed, the angrier she got, until she considered pulling out her pistol and silencing them both.

A Harvey girl brought the coffee and saved both men from total self-destruction. Seth downed the coffee as fast as she refilled the cup, not caring that it was scalding his throat. When she left to refill the pot, he was sober enough to apologize.

True glared at him with no understanding in her blue eyes. "Are you telling me you two spent the morning drinking?"

Seth thought for a minute, hoping some other answer would come to him, then finally replied, "Yes."

Link helped him out. "It was our way of saying farewell to Micah. I think the old man would have approved."

Seth was the only one at the table who agreed with the Ranger.

"The two of you hardly knew the man—" She stopped as the Harvey girl returned. The young woman refilled both coffee cups, then slowly moved True's glass to the other side of her plate.

When the girl walked away, True stared at the glass. "Something's wrong," she whispered. "Very wrong."

Seth leaned forward. "Why, because we had a drink?"

"No." True looked up with alarm in her eyes. "Did you see what the girl did to my glass? A Harvey girl would never move a glass to the wrong side of the plate. It's part of the cup code they learn the first day they're hired. Each drink has an exact place. A Harvey girl never, ever forgets the code."

"Are you saying our waitress is not a Harvey girl?"

"She's either an impostor, or she's trying to warn us of something."

Seth looked around the half-empty room. "If this is another one of your cheap tricks, True, I'm not playing. Half the cavalry at Fort Davis can ride in here, but I'm not fighting."

"This is no trick!"

Link leaned low and pulled the Navy Colt he kept hidden in his boot. He didn't know anything about a cup code, but he could smell trouble in the calm air.

Seth stood. "I'll get my guns from the front." As he moved from the table, a crash sounded from the kitchen only a few feet away. The scream that followed was muffled, but they all heard it.

True pulled her pistol from the pocket of her mourning dress and rushed through the door leading to the kitchen. If one of the Harvey people was hurt, she had to help.

As the door swung closed behind her, a coarse hand gripped her mouth. A huge arm twisted around her arms and shoulders, then jerked. The violence forced the air from her lungs and caused the gun to fall from her fingers.

Her attacker pulled her away from the door with far more force than needed. Several other men stood in wait for the next victim to fall into their trap. True fought wildly, knowing that a few ounces more pressure and the stranger would crack her ribs with his grip, but she had to break free.

The door swung again and Seth rushed in. For a moment he stared at her captured in another man's grip, then he reacted with all the anger of a wild animal defending its young. He took one step toward her before another attacker stepped from behind the door and slammed an iron frying pan into the side of his head. Seth fell like a great pine brought down with one blow of an ax.

True kicked and fought the man who held her as two men pulled Seth from the doorway. She knew the door would swing again in seconds and it would be Link. Twisting to free her mouth, she tried to scream through the filthy fingers bruising her face.

Like a nightmare come to life, Link swung the door open. His gun was ready, and with lighting quickness he pulled off two rounds before several men opened fire on him. The blast knocked him back through the swinging door and splattered his blood across his clothes.

True fought now like a wild woman, thinking of all the horrible things she'd do to these men when she was free. She could hear the screams from the dining room, but no one else tried the door.

The troop of outlaws moved out the backdoor swiftly, to a waiting wagon. Two threw Seth into a box that looked to be little more than a coffin, while a third tied True's hands. Another shoved a gag into her mouth as they dropped her into the long box with Seth.

"Leave her!" the driver shouted.

"No," another said. "The boss might like to have some fun with her after he kills Westwind. You know how murder always makes him feel like he has to have a woman."

One of the men reached into the box and squeezed her breasts. "And she's a ripe one. Fiery, too, just like he used to like them in his wilder days."

"All right," the driver agreed. "We ain't got time to argue."

True watched in panic as a lid was lifted over the pine box. It was then nailed down with a few quick strokes.

EIGHTEEN

Officer Lincoln Raine came awake one pain at a time. He felt cold, really cold for one of the few times in his life. There were so many parts of his body shooting pain to his brain with every heartbeat that he couldn't tell where he'd been wounded.

"You awake?" Audrey Gates's voice drifted through the icy hell he was in. "Lincoln, can you answer a few questions?"

Link nodded and was punished with a throbbing that seemed to travel all the way to his toes and back. He closed his eyes and tried to remember the last thing he'd seen before the gunfight. The image of True being held by a man who was smiling like he'd gladly break her in two on a bet, and Granite Westwind, the man Link had been hired to protect, lying on the floor, flashed into Link's thoughts. He'd fired once, no twice, before several blasts knocked him back through the door.

Audrey's voice sounded again. "I've patched you up, Ranger, as best I can. You took a bullet in one leg, another in the shoulder just left of your heart. Looks like you also cut your forehead in the fall and sliced a piece of glass into your hand."

Link couldn't help but smile. He remembered the way his dad used to look at life when everything went wrong. "Other than that how was the lunch?" he whispered, knowing no one but his father would understand his words.

"Lincoln?" Audrey leaned close and touched his unbandaged hand. "Do you know who I am?"

He grasped her fingers tightly as he tried to focus through the torment. "They'll have to shoot me a few more times before I'll forget you, Doc." He could feel her free hand brush the hair away from his eyes.

"I think you're going to make it, Lincoln. I'd like you to rest, but first Colonel McCormick needs some information from you. You're the only one who saw the men who took True and Granite. All the kitchen help are too frightened to remember anything."

Link closed his eyes. "Colonel, it was my fault." He believed in owning blame when it was his. "It was all my fault."

Worry colored Austin's face. "We'll talk about that later, Link. Right now we need any information you have."

Mustering all the skill he'd developed since childhood, Link related a description of each man down to the type of gun in his hand. He'd only seen the kitchen for maybe three seconds, but it was tattooed onto his memory.

When he finished, he looked at Audrey. "How long till I can ride?"

"Not this time," Austin said. "I'm putting you on leave for a few weeks. Much as we need you, I'll not have you killing yourself trying to find True. You dripped enough blood from the hotel to here to paint the walk. If you don't stay here with Audrey, I'll check you into the hospital."

"He'll stay," Audrey answered, "even if I have to tie him to the bed. With Marie's help, I should be able to take better care of him than they could at the hospital. I was about to decide to wait until fall to travel anyway."

Austin smiled. "Marie's that housekeeper of yours who looks like she's a direct descendant of the pirates who landed here years ago? Most folks would be afraid to sleep in the same house with a woman who acts like a knife between her teeth might improve her looks."

"She's a good nurse." Audrey glanced at Link. "Or warden if need be."

"One other thing," Link said, as if he weren't even listening to their discussion. "The man holding True had on boots like I've seen the shrimpers wear. If that's any help."

Austin patted Link's shoulder. "Don't worry, we'll find them. The outlaws don't know what they got when they captured those two. My guess is they'll free themselves before we can catch up to them."

The coldness around Link made him too sleepy to keep his eyes open. He could hear the Colonel and Audrey talking, but he could no longer make out what they were saying.

Just before he passed over into the blackness promising a rest from his pain, he thought he felt Audrey pull a blanket over him and kiss him gently on the cheek. He thought he must already be dreaming. She'd never do such a thing.

Seth felt the sensation of a boat's gentle rocking beneath him as he opened his eyes to total blackness. His head throbbed in pain. When he raised his hand to brush away some of the ache, he touched a warm body lying next to him.

His hand slid along the linen covering a woman's form. As he touched her, True moved, causing more parts of her body to brush against his.

"True?" he whispered, trying to guess where they were. He'd know the feel of her beside him anywhere, but all else was foreign.

She only mumbled and wiggled against him.

"True, are you all right?" he whispered, needing to know that she hadn't been hurt.

She wiggled more, pushing against him with her shoulder.

"Easy, True." Seth gripped her arm. "You don't have to pick a fight, just tell me what's wrong." His finger slid along the sleeve of her dress. As she rolled against him, his hands moved around her waist and he felt the ropes.

"You're tied up." He whispered the obvious as he pulled at the ropes that tied her hands behind her. "Why didn't you say so?"

She mumbled what he guessed to be an oath and moved her face against his cheek so he could feel the gag in her mouth.

Seth swore to himself. Sight didn't seem to be the only sense he'd lost. Part of his brain must have fallen out when someone hit him from behind.

Using only touch to guide him, Seth untied her hands and pulled the gag from her mouth.

"They shot Link!" she cried as soon as she could speak. "They've killed Link, and I've been trapped in this box afraid you were dying also."

Seth felt her face in the darkness and wiped the tears away. He knew the tears were for Link, but he wished just one could fall for him. She was shaking so badly her teeth were rattling. "Shhhh, True. I'm here. I'm not as easy to kill as you may think."

The crate they were in suddenly tilted to one side, then straightened out in a rocking motion. "We've no time to cry, darling. Right now, we've got to figure out where we are."

She moved her cheek against his and held tightly to him for a long moment before she spoke. "They put us in this box hours ago, but only bothered to hammer a few nails into it. I tried to guess from the direction and sounds where we were going, but this blackness turns me around. Some light was coming in between the cracks, but by now it must be dark outside."

He felt the boundaries of the crate with his legs and hands. There was barely enough room for them both. "How many men?" Seth whispered as he pulled her against him, wishing he could protect her.

"Five," she answered. "Six, counting the man who drove the wagon. I think two of them were hurt by shots Link got off before he was killed. After leaving us in what smelled like a cotton storage warehouse, they carried us down to the dock and put us in a boat. Only two men climbed in with us. Guessing from how much we rocked when the men stepped in, I think it must be a very small boat."

Seth touched his fingers to her lips. They could hear the soft splash of oars moving in and out of water. For a long while he listened, trying to hear anything else, but the men in the boat with them only spoke in mumbles.

"They're taking you to their boss so he can kill you himself. My guess is he wants all the fame that would come with shooting the great Granite Westwind. I don't think he has a fair fight planned, because I think he's ill or wounded, by the way they were talking."

"Why are you along?" Seth's voice was angry. This one time he wished she'd stayed behind.

"I'm going to be the dessert after the killing, it seems," she answered back just as angrily. "Besides, what makes you think you've got a right to get into trouble without me along?"

"This is no game, True. We could end up dead."

"I know that. Stop acting like I have a loose grip on reality. I've had time to think of a plan, and I know just what Granite Westwind would do."

"Spare me," Seth answered. "I've told you before, I'm no hero."

"But you would be interested in saving your own neck?"

"I would."

"Well, since it seems to be attached to a body everyone thinks is Westwind's, why not try my idea?"

"What's the plan?"

"Follow me," she said as if they were off on another adventure. She suddenly rolled from one side of the box to the other. "We may not have much time. My guess is this little boat is taking us to a ship anchored several hundred yards out."

The sudden shift of their weight rocked the boat. When they rolled the second time, they could hear the men shouting and trying to stop them by pounding on the top of the box.

Seth pulled her against him and rolled again, protecting her as much as he could from his weight.

The third roll sent the box splashing into the water. The boat must have capsized, for Seth could also hear the men shouting and splashing from what sounded like several feet away.

"We're free!" True sounded triumphant.

"We're sinking," Seth answered, as water seeped through all the corners.

"Kick off the lid!" True yelled, trying to push the water back with her hands. Two inches of the gulf already filled the box and more was coming in fast.

Seth kicked at the lid and more water rushed in.

"What do we do now?" she asked as if the plan had been his from the beginning. "They'll find us at any minute."

"We sink and hope they're too busy trying to stay alive to worry about us," he answered, bracing his back against the fast dampening wood to allow himself better mobility. He doubled his legs up and braced his feet against the lid. "Once we're below the surface, I'll kick the lid off and we can swim out. Between the choppy water and the night, they just might not see us moving away from where the box sunk."

Seth shoved the lid and water rushed in faster.

Water now covered half of True's body. "Only one problem with your great plan of escape." Fear and anger made her voice high. "I can't swim."

NINETEEN

Seth kicked at the crate's lid as hard as he could in the cramped space. "Hold your breath, True, and I'll get you out!"

There was no time for her to answer. He could feel them sinking as the last bit of air bubbled out of the box. He knew any moment they'd be beneath the water.

He kicked again, forgetting all else but survival. He'd worry about the men catching them when they once more had air. He wrapped his arm around True, protecting her from his quick movements.

A third shove knocked out the few nails loosely holding the lid. Seth scrambled out, pulling True beside him. She hadn't panicked as he'd expected her to do when the air ran out. She'd simply closed her eyes and pushed her face against his chest, as if trusting him completely with the last few moments of her life.

Pulling her up, he swam at an angle from where the crate had sunk. There was little air left in his lungs, but if they were going to have a fighting chance, they had to come out above water several feet from where they'd gone under.

For a second after he surfaced, he didn't realize True's head still remained against his chest. With one sudden jerk, he pulled her face above the water. "Breathe!" he ordered.

True took a gulp of night air. The oxygen filled her with fight. She splashed and kicked, trying to climb atop him as they floated in the choppy gulf.

Seth fought to calm her, but she pulled at him in panic,

dragging them both beneath the water. This time he went down without drawing a breath while she spit and gulped beside him.

Struggling with each other, they drifted farther under. Forcing the last air from his lungs, Seth floated slowly downward.

True released his sinking body immediately.

An instant later, Seth clawed upward with powerful arms. On the surface again, fighting to save both their lives, he violently swung his fist into the bottom of her chin.

True fell backward from the force of the blow, floating in unconsciousness as she'd never been able to do while awake.

Seth gently cupped her face in his hand, careful to keep her mouth and nose above water. Slowly he swam toward the outline of a shore. The water seemed inky and bottomless in the pale moonlight. Luckily, he heard no sound of a boat coming toward them. He thought he heard men several yards away yelling at one another, but all that mattered was getting True to shore as quickly as possible.

He couldn't help but smile when he looked at her. She'd be madder than hell at him when she came to. True would probably also be disappointed that she hadn't drowned him. Trying to get him killed seemed to have developed into an occupation for her. She'd attempted every way to murder him but fire, and he had a feeling he'd fight one of those before his days with Miss McCormick were over.

But he didn't care. He felt more alive with her than he ever had. Sometimes at night back home he'd been afraid he might die before dawn and not notice it for a week. Nonfeeling had become so comfortable he hadn't noticed when he'd stagnated.

True had changed all that. He'd told her he was no hero, but maybe there'd been even less to him than he'd thought.

He hadn't even been a man. Somewhere in the years of work, the fighter in him who'd dreamed had washed out like a sandy gully after a spring storm. It had taken him ten years to look for his brother's killer, when he should have ridden out after the funeral. Hawk Sloan was probably an old man by now or turned to dust in a grave marked "Unknown." Seth realized that if he'd waited any longer, he never would have taken the train he'd ridden to Galveston a week ago.

The shoreline drew closer. Because of the low clouds, Seth had no idea what time it was. Since there were no lights on the island, he guessed he was heading toward one of the many tiny strips of land around Galveston. As he pulled True toward the beach, he wished he had a weapon, for some of the islands were inhabited by folks too mean even to live in Texas.

Seth's foot touched land, and he pulled True into his arms as he walked out of the gulf. The water pulled them back, making her heavy and his own legs seem ten times their weight. The beach was sandy at first, littered with shells, but then turned marshy. Huge clumps of plants were anchored in patches between mud.

Seth slowed his pace. He guessed there would be pockets of quicksand around large enough to swallow a horse. Snakes also liked the marshy lands of these strips. Carefully, he picked his way to a black rock that jutted out from the sand like the bow of a ship.

Groping the darkness, Seth tested the safety of the rock. The surface felt cool and smooth to his touch. Very gently he placed True down, using his arm for her pillow. Exhausted, he pulled her against him, to keep her warm, and closed his eyes to the night.

As the warmth of the sun brushed her cheek, True awoke slowly. Her wet clothes lay heavy against her skin, but she didn't feel cold. She could sense the slow rise and fall of

Seth's chest at her side. His strong arm protected her even as she slept.

Slowly, she slipped from his embrace and sat up. Ahead of her in the clear morning she saw nothing but water. Far off to her left were the tiny dots that even without her glasses she knew were the huge warehouses along Galveston's port.

A flock of pelicans flew over, screaming their song to the morning. Seth moved beside her, reaching for her naturally, as if he had every morning of his life.

"Good morning," she said as though they'd spent the night in a feather bed and not on a rock.

Seth didn't look as if he found one thing good about the morning. He frowned into the sun as he stood and stretched. Though his clothes were wrinkled, and his boots mud-covered, he'd never been more handsome to her. With his hair shining in the sun and the shadow of whiskers dusting his chin, he looked like a pirate. His blue-gray eyes turned toward her, and she saw the hint of a smile brush his lips.

"You look like a drowned rat," he said.

True opened her mouth to argue, but when she glanced down at her mud-splattered dress, she realized he was right.

He knelt and pulled one of the combs from her hair. "I'm sorry," he said, still laughing. "I guess that's not a polite thing to say to a lady I've just spent the night on a rock with. How's your chin?"

True touched the tender skin along her jaw. She could tell that it was bruised all the way to the bone. "Sore," she answered. "I must have hit it on something in the water."

"Something," he whispered without adding more. "The tide's dangerous."

"I guess I'm not the first drowned rat you've slept with, so you should know."

"Oh, you're the first." Seth smiled, thinking how much he

wanted to kiss her. Even covered in mud, with her hair half in tangles and half in her face, she looked more appealing than any woman he'd ever seen. He folded his arms over his chest to keep from reaching for her. "Have any idea where we are?"

True looked behind her at the thick growth of vines. She couldn't tell without her glasses if the bushes were almost tree high or the trees merely squatty. "Sure I know where we are," she answered without volunteering any more information. With effort she began dragging her hair combs through the tangled damp mass of her curls.

Seth sat beside her. "Want to share your knowledge, or am I just supposed to guess our whereabouts?"

"I don't care what you do as long as you stop grinning at me." True pulled the last of her curls free of pins. "We're on a place called Pelican Island. The pirate Jean Laffite used to bring men who stole from him over here and hang them. According to legend, he'd leave their bodies hanging until they were bones. Early settlers used to call this place Skull Island."

"Sounds delightful," Seth said. "Not only ghosts, but probably snakes amid the bones and buried treasure."

"No snakes. This place is covered with pelican nests. I sailed past here once, and if I remember, there's a hard-packed sandy beach on the other side. It would make a better camp."

Pointing with her comb, she added, "We'll make better time following the water line then trying to wade across the marsh. Once we're there, it should be easy to spot any boats passing by." True looked down at her dress. "But I'll never make it with the mud on this dress dragging me down."

Before Seth could think of what to say, she unbuttoned the top of her heavy black mourning dress and slipped it down over her hips. Her underclothes were still damp and clinging to her body, revealing every inch of the curves he'd touched in the night.

A fire started inside Seth as if someone were setting off fireworks along his veins. He'd always thought of himself as a rational man, but at this moment he was having trouble remembering to breathe. Her undergarments were silk and lace, molding over her like paint. He could see the outline of her breasts and the gentle curve of her hips. Just the sight made his hands bend to the shape in longing to mold against her.

True glanced up at him as she bent to roll her dress into a bundle. "Stop looking at me like I'm not still fully covered. You've seen me in my nightgown. Surely this can be no more shocking?"

She was doing it again, he thought. Leaving him speechless. How could he explain that he'd been raised by a father and brother with no women around, and that during the short time he'd been married, his wife never dressed or undressed within his sight? The few times he'd seen her underthings, they'd been durable cotton. Now a woman stood before him wearing lacy things he wasn't even sure what to call and looking at him like he was the crazy one.

She pulled off her shoes and stockings, leaving her legs bare from the knee down. "If I were you, I'd pull off those boots. It'll make walking along the shore easier."

Seth forced his gaze from her to his feet. He didn't care about walking right now. He was finding it hard to stand. The most beautiful woman he'd ever seen stood before him in her undergarments, frowning at him as though he were a stubborn child.

"When we get to the other side, I'll wash out some of the mud from this dress if my attire bothers you. It'll dry fast as soon as the sun's high. Then all we have to do is wait on the beach until a boat comes close enough for us to flag down."

Seth struggled for something to say. He wanted to tell her she could burn the dress and bother him all day, but he didn't think she'd agree. Her body might be made for touching, but her voice told him she was back to being Miss McCormick again. "Did it ever cross that organized mind of yours that I might also have a plan? You seem to think someone named you as director of my life."

"All right, cowboy, what's your plan?"

Seth sat and pulled off his boots. "We walk to the other side of the island and wait for a boat."

"Great plan," she said as she moved off the rock and walked along the sandy edge of the water without waiting for him.

They found the tiny beach just as she'd said they would, but no boats came close as the sun grew hotter. Without a word, Seth removed his shirt and placed it over her sun-burned shoulders.

As he spread the cotton over her back, he could feel the warmth of her skin through the material. Her underclothes were dry now and not as revealing as they had been, but the need to touch her hadn't cooled within him.

By mid-afternoon, the sun had driven them off the beach and into the shade of a tree. Seth pulled away vines beneath the branches, and they lay in the cool sand.

At first she seemed hesitant, but finally she rested her head against his arm.

"Don't be afraid. We'll find help," Seth whispered into her hair, which still smelled of the gulf.

"I'm not," she lied. "I've been in worse trouble. One time I—"

"Don't," he interrupted. "Don't go making up some story that sounds like Westwind wrote it."

"But one time I really was in worse shape," True

answered. "I was with Link out near a place the Indians call Enchanted Rock. It's up around New Braunfels."

He noticed her head tilting slightly as she talked.

"We were out of drinking water and had been for two days. Link went up on top of the rock to look for the men we'd been following. I went along, of course, to give him a hand."

True paused as if waiting for him to argue, but Seth was silent. "Well, about the time we started down, a whole war party of rattlers came out from hiding. We couldn't get past them, and we couldn't stay forever on the mountain. Link had plenty of bullets, but one shot would have told the entire country where we were."

"Don't tell me. You both died on Enchanted Rock that day?" Seth said, still disbelieving her story.

"No!" True poked him in the ribs. "We emptied out the powder from his bullets and set it afire. The snakes struck at the blaze, then shriveled away. We ran off the hill in the time it took the powder to burn."

Seth closed his eyes. He had no idea if the story was true or not. Part of him didn't care.

She rolled on her side and rested her chin on his chest. He could feel her breath against his skin. The softness of her breast was pressed into his chest, branding him forever with a need greater than any hunger he'd ever felt.

"The reason I'm not afraid now is that I'm with you," she whispered as her hand lightly brushed the roughness of his jawline.

"True, I'm no hero," Seth answered as he moved his hand over her hair.

"Yes, you are." Her words were light against his throat. "You're the only person who's ever made me feel safe. Somehow you saved me last night. Water is one thing I can't fight my way out of. You pulled me to shore."

She wanted to tell him she'd dreamed of lying next to him for over half of her life. He was the one man she'd longed for and wanted as a lover. Him alone. Closing her eyes, she allowed the soft sway of the branches above to fan her to sleep.

He was not so lucky. Seth should have been thinking about how they were going to get off the island, or how he was going to stay away from the men who seemed so determined to kill him. But all he could think about was True. He knew she had him mixed up with the Granite Westwind whose novels she typed. How could she think he was a hero? He'd never been anyone's hero.

He had no idea how they were going to find food or water if a boat didn't come by soon. But a part of him wanted to stay on the island just a few hours longer because here he had True all to himself. He closed his eyes and wished he could be the hero True seemed so sure he was.

The branches moved above him, but he didn't open his eyes until the warm barrel of a shotgun nudged against his ribs.

TWENTY

Seth reached for his absent Colt as he rolled an inch away from the shotgun barrel pointed toward him. He glanced up into the afternoon sun. A stout man, with a beard half down to his waist and eyes that shone black as a raven's, stood over him. The only covering the man wore other than a worn pair of sailor pants was tattoos across both arms.

"If you folks are just out for a swim, I suggest you start back to the Galveston shore and get off my island."

True raised on one elbow, far more curious than afraid. "I can't swim," she answered directly. "Our boat overturned. We didn't know there was anyone on the island." Without allowing him time to comment, she asked, "Where'd you get all those tattoos? Did it hurt? I heard someone say once that the ink poison darkens a man's blood forever."

The stranger didn't lower his weapon. His sharp eyes watched True as if he'd just met his first rabid human. He finally glanced toward Seth. "Is this your woman, son?"

Seth wasn't sure what to say. If he said no, the man might take her or shoot her on the spot. If he said yes, True would probably kill him. She looked as if she might stand any minute and try to touch the stranger's tattoos. "More accurately, I'm her man," he finally said and placed his hand on her knee to make sure she stayed put.

From the stranger's laughter, it seemed he either understood, or had decided they were both crazy.

True sat cross-legged and looked at the stout little man with interest. "You're Three Leg Sam, aren't you? I've heard the sailors talk about you. I heard you got in big trouble in Galveston and disappeared years ago before the law could knot a noose around you."

The man tapped the gun barrel against the wooden stump that decended from his knee. "That's me, and there ain't no trouble Three Leg Sam can't get out of." He seemed pleased she'd heard of him. "Took a fall from the mast when I was still in me teens. The leg healed, but wouldn't straighten out, so I just strapped this wood on and used the bent part of me leg as a rudder."

Though he was talking with True, he still kept the gun pointed at Seth. "Who might you two be, little miss?"

True explained the kidnapping and boat capsizing in far more detail than Seth thought necessary, but he couldn't find a spot to interrupt her. She added so much to the story, he found himself wishing he'd been there to see all she described. When she finished, she turned her hand palm-up toward Seth. "Thanks to Granite Westwind, I'm still alive, because something must have hit me while I was in the water and knocked me cold. He brought me to shore."

The stout man looked impressed. "Can't say as I've ever heard of you, fellow, but what you did was something. Saving the little lady and all. Especially, you already knowing what a talker she was."

Seth fought the urge to say it wasn't near as much as True boasted. He smiled up at the old sailor. "You wouldn't happen to have a boat you'd loan us? My guess is half the lawmen in this part of Texas are looking for us by now. It might be to your advantage to help us get off your island if you enjoy your peace."

Three Leg Sam finally lifted the gun over his shoulder and stroked his beard. "You have a point. I might have a boat at that. We could talk money over a meal. My woman's got some crawdad stew cooking that'll put hair on your navel, and when she's a mind to, she can make potato patties that melt in your mouth."

The old sailor marched ahead of them, and True started to follow.

Seth pulled her back. "Don't you think you'd better put on your dress?" He'd seen the greed in the crippled man's eyes and hoped it was for the money he was about to make and not for True. Seth was willing to bet the wet cash in his pocket that the only reason they'd been invited to supper was so Sam could have a little time to figure out just how much he could ask for the boat.

"Why?" True looked puzzled. "I've got more clothes on than he does."

"But most folks don't go to dinner in their underthings."

"Does it bother you?"

"Yes," Seth answered before he saw the spark of mischief in her gaze.

"Too bad, cowboy." She laughed and hurried to follow Sam.

Seth pulled her dress from the branch where they'd hung it to dry and followed, wondering how he'd signed on to play nursemaid to this crazy brat hiding inside a woman's body. Right now he'd have given the money he'd made to have the proper Miss McCormick back.

When they reached the shack Sam called home, Seth noticed that if anything, he and True were overdressed. Sam's woman only wore a long thin cotton shirt with the sleeves cut out. Her hair was matted and the dirty color of dried seaweed.

"Find something else that washed up on shore?" she grunted at Sam without even looking closely at True and Seth. "I ain't figuring on having two more for supper." She pulled a spoon from the pot she'd been stirring and tasted her cooking. After washing the hot stew around in her mouth, she spit most of it back onto the spoon before using it to stir once more.

True glanced at Seth and touched her lips, silently saying she had no intention of staying for supper. He nodded slightly in total agreement.

Sam didn't seem to notice the exchange as he put his gun against the wall of the shack and slapped his woman on the bottom. "Hush your griping. These folks be thinking of rentin' me boat."

A female, no more than fifteen, appeared in the doorway. She was willow-thin, with eyes rimmed in red from crying.

The old woman's sour anger turned toward the newcomer. "Get back in there, Allie. These folks don't want to see the likes of you."

The girl vanished into the blackness of the shack, and the mother waved her hand as if to erase her from their sight. She smoothed a dirty strand of hair back from her face and smiled a toothless grin at True. "Don't pay her no never mind. She ain't nothin' but trash. After we raised her and fed her, all she can think about is running off with some no-account who stops by here now and again. He ain't offering marriage, though, and he don't want no kids. Which she keeps havin'. This is the third birthin' I've had to clean up after." The old woman's laugh was a sharp snort. "If we weren't stuck on this island, she'd have gone to him by now. And I'd be raising that last brat she had a few weeks ago."

The girl called Allie appeared in the doorway again, watching more from the shadows now. True could hear a baby whimpering in the background, but noticed Allie paid no mind.

"About that boat!" Three Leg Sam yelled above the noise. "I might be willing to let you have it if the price's right. Or I could rent it to you, but it would cost because I'd have to go with you and bring it back."

True watched the mother and daughter carefully as the baby began to cry louder. Neither of them seemed to notice, much less care.

As Seth raised his finger to make an offer, True stepped around him, her shoulders stiff and her hands balled for a fight. "How much for the baby?"

"What!" both men said at once.

True's eyes were fixed on the young mother. "How much for the baby, Allie?"

Hope sparkled in the girl's eyes as she looked from True to her mother.

The older woman was far more practiced at bargaining. "I can't believe you'd say such a thing, miss! Offering to buy a flesh-and-blood baby. He ain't no calf, you know."

"What happened to the other two children?" True moved to the doorway and addressed only the young woman. With a closer inspection the girl looked older than True had thought at first glance, maybe even out of her teens.

"They died." Allie shrugged. "I ain't got time to mess with no cryin' babies."

Sam swore under his breath. "Yeah, but you got time to mess with ever' sailor who comes ashore. For a few dollars I'd sell ever one—"

True's voice cut him off. "How much for the baby, Allie?"

"Money won't do me no good. Pa'd just take it from me when you leave."

"What if I offered you a ride to Galveston?"

Allie shook her head. "I ain't leaving this place. Pa says there's men in Galveston far worse then him, and I reckon he's right. I might sell the baby if you had something worth trading, but I ain't going to town, where I'd have to work all day for enough food to fill me."

True glanced at Seth, who was still holding her dress. "I'll trade you the baby for my dress. That fellow of yours would probably offer marriage if he saw you in it. Then you wouldn't have to work or stay on the island."

True's elbow jabbed into Seth's ribs as he opened his mouth to object to her last statement.

Allie's eyes brightened as Seth straightened and silently handed her the garment. "Would you throw in those fancy things you're wearing to go underneath it?"

"Now wait . . . ," Seth started.

"Yes," True answered without hesitation.

An hour later True was sitting in the middle of Three Leg Sam's tiny boat. She wore only Seth's long dress shirt, which ended just below her knees. The baby lay cuddled in her arms with Seth's jacket for a blanket. Though her legs were muddy and bare, her hair wild with curls, Seth knew she'd never looked more beautiful. He realized with a sudden groan that he'd never wanted to hold a woman as much in his life as he wanted to hold her. His need for her was a weakness he wouldn't allow himself.

"It's wrong to bargain for a baby," he said as he pulled the boat into the tide. It had cost him more to buy the boat, but he couldn't stand the thought of having to put up with Sam another moment.

"Would it have been right to leave him there, where no one cared, and he'd starve to death like her other two children?"

"Yeah, but to bargain?"

"Do you think she would have given him to me if I'd told her it was for the baby's own good? No." True answered her own question. "I had to do what I could to help the child before it was too late."

"But, True," Seth said, seeing her point, but not sure they'd made the right choice, "the baby might be safer on an island than going back to Galveston with us. In case you forgot, someone's trying to kill us."

"Not us. You." True smiled. "I was brought along for dessert, remember."

Seth couldn't help but smile. "And a nice dessert you'd make wearing only my shirt."

"I'm no longer on the menu."

"Too bad," Seth whispered to himself as he slid into the boat and lifted the oars. It had been years since he'd rowed a boat, and he didn't remember having much skill then. He tried to look as if he knew what he was doing as he continued talking. "A woman who keeps saving children is hard to resist."

"You don't think I'm strange?"

"Oh, I think you're strange, all right. Everything about you is unique. You're a one-of-a-kind woman, True McCormick. Micah was right about you being a rainbow."

"Does it bother you?"

The setting sun behind her kept him from seeing her eyes, but by her tone he guessed the question was very important to her.

"No." His voice was low. "Right now nothing about you bothers me."

She didn't ask any more questions as he turned the boat toward Galveston. The air was hot with July, and not even the splash of the water cooled him. She looked so desirable against the dying day. Wonderful and magical, he thought. And as untouchable as the sunset. A woman like her would have no place for a man like him in her life. If she knew the truth about him, she'd probably make him jump ship here in the middle of the gulf. He hated the game of playing someone he wasn't, and somehow he guessed she'd hate him for it also. He was no gunfighter, no outlaw, no hero.

True kissed the baby's forehead and whispered to Seth,

"When we reach the shore, we'd best stay low until it's late, then try to move toward the orphanage."

Seth laughed. "The way you look, staying out of sight seems like the only sensible thing to do."

"What's wrong with the way I look?"

Despite the pretended anger, he could hear the laughter in her voice.

"I think the shirt looks better on me than it does on you."

Seth didn't argue. He pulled the boat through the water, hoping he remembered how to row before they drifted too far from land.

TWENTY-ONE

"Shut up and take your medicine!" Audrey Gates ordered, losing all the bedside manner she'd ever mustered. It was almost midnight. Her day and her patience were at an end.

Ranger Lincoln Raine looked up at her. His dark Indian eyes filled with fury. "Leave that bottle of whiskey Marie brought earlier and I'll handle the pain myself. I don't want any of that tar you're peddling as a cure." He closed his lips and folded his arms over his bandaged chest, leaving no doubt that stubbornness was about to collide with determination.

Audrey hesitated as if debating her ability to force the Ranger to take the medicine. She could see little of the boy who would have done anything she'd asked of him. This man before her had a mind, and a will, of his own. Finally, she lowered the spoon. "All right, Lincoln, have it your way."

"You keep saying that, Doc, like it's an option." He watched her move around to the other side of the bed she and the housekeeper had set up in the corner of her office, which was serving as his sickroom. "Every time I've needed something today, all I've seen is that housekeeper of yours, Bloody Marie, who has the bedside manner of a wide-mouthed toad." Link couldn't help but smile. "Too bad she doesn't have the looks."

Audrey didn't answer as she checked the bandage on his leg and tried to keep from laughing. The white cloth contrasted with the deep tan of his muscular thigh. No new

blood stained the wound. He'd been lucky. It had been a
clean shot through the flesh and would heal fast.

She moved to the bandage at his shoulder. He hadn't been
so lucky there. She'd dug the bullet out, and the wound was
still staining the cotton over what promised to be yet another
nasty scar.

As she worked, Link never took his gaze from her face.
She'd always been his definition of perfection, with her
thick red hair and her straightforward manner. No woman
he'd met in Texas could ever compare to his Doc. At first
he'd had a schoolboy crush on her, following her around and
usually making a fool of himself trying to talk to her. Then,
as he'd become a man, he'd loved her as a man loves a
statue, or a portrait of beauty, never hoping that he'd have
a chance with her.

"I think the wrappings should hold the shoulder still
while you get some sleep." Audrey straightened beside the
bed. "I'll check on you in the morning. If you need
anything, yell. I may not hear you, but Marie can hear dust
collect. She'll wake me if there's trouble."

"You mean if I'm trouble," he corrected. "I was such a
bother today, I have the feeling Sweet Marie plans to
smother me in my sleep tonight."

Audrey put the supplies away and turned off all but one
light in the room. "If I thought you'd be more trouble than
I could handle, I'd have you moved to the hospital. And
Marie is kinder than she looks."

"She'd have to be," Link grumbled.

"Try to get some sleep, Lincoln."

"What about my head wound?"

She leaned close. So close he could smell the fresh scent
that was hers alone. "It's little more than a bump and a
scrape along your hairline." Absently, she brushed his black

hair away from the cotton. "You were very lucky, Ranger. If the bullet in your chest had been a few inches over—"

"It would have harmed nothing," he interrupted, "for you've already shattered my heart."

"Don't be ridiculous," Audrey answered without smiling. Her voice was so hard it seemed to crack the tenseness between them. "I'm sure there's many a girl in Texas who's had the honor of trying to break your heart."

"Many," Link repeated. "So many I can't remember a one."

When she stood to leave, he didn't try to stop her. Worry over True was on both their minds. There would be time to tell Dr. Gates how he felt later. First, he must do his duty.

"You'll be stronger tomorrow," she said as she lowered the light and nodded her good night.

Link only watched her go. He wanted nothing more than to force himself from the bed and follow her upstairs. He knew he had the power within him to do just that, but he wasn't sure he'd have enough energy left for anything else when he reached the top of the stairs.

No matter how dearly he wanted to hold her, he must store his strength and sleep. Tomorrow he'd be stronger. Tomorrow he'd be gone.

TWENTY-TWO

"Where did you learn to row?" True shouted above the baby's crying.

Seth pushed the oars into the water and pulled with all his strength. He'd paddled around a lake a few times while fishing near Timber Creek, but he'd never tried to fight anything like the choppy waters of the gulf. "I'm doing the best I can," he answered between clenched teeth. The night was almost as black as the water. He was glad she couldn't see the anger and frustration in his face. Around her he wanted to do everything right, and he wasn't about to admit he knew little about boats, even if it was obvious to both of them by now.

"The best you can is going to get us killed," True yelled back. "We'll be lucky if we reach the shore before we starve at this rate."

"I don't remember rowing being named as one of the requirements for this job." Seth was more angry at himself than her, but he couldn't allow it to show. "Or having to listen to your constant complaining. If you think you can do better, you're welcome to try, Miss McCormick."

True nestled the baby between rolls of canvas low in the boat. "I haven't the strength to pull the oars against the sea, but I can guide you. If I don't, we'll be in New Orleans by the time you reach land."

Before he could protest, she crawled in front of him. To his shock, True turned her back to him and sat down on the tiny bit of bench left open between his legs. She snuggled close against him, aligning her back with the front of his body. Her arms spread out over his until her fingers gripped the oars just above his hands.

"Now follow what I do, cowboy, before we both get tossed overboard again."

With slow, even strokes she pulled the oars, gently letting up on one oar while digging the other deeper into the choppy water.

Seth followed her lead, and within a few minutes they moved like dancers in unison. She seemed to be concentrating on the line of lights along the shore, but all he could think about was her body pressing so closely against his own. He'd thought his muscles were tired from trying to row, but now he responded to her every silent command. Her fingers brushed his hands, applying the amount of pressure she wanted him to use with each stroke. Her back pressed against his bare chest as he drew the wood through the water, and he was sure she could feel his heart pounding.

Seth tried not to think about her bare hips nestled between his legs. But with each pull, their rhythmic touches drove him mad with a need to be even closer.

True's hair feathered across his face as they worked slowly cutting the distance to shore. He didn't need to fall out of the boat to drown, he felt he was going down for the third time gladly, in an ocean of desire for the woman in front of him.

She seemed to have no idea what she was doing to him every time the oars carved through the water. Her fingers moved along the muscles of his arms as if they were connected to the oars and not flesh.

They were only a few hundred yards out when she nudged his hands. "Rest a moment," True whispered. "I want to make sure there's no one on the beach when we go in. It'll be safer if we drift for a while, until it's well after midnight."

Seth racked the oars and opened his grip for the first time in over an hour. His palms felt raw and tingled with sudden blood flow. He could barely see the baby between the bundles. The little thing had finally gone to sleep. If he'd only stay that way for a few hours, True would have the infant settled in a warm bed with milk in his belly. Seth had no doubt she'd find the child a home and food, if she had to steal and lie to get them.

He brushed a kiss against her hair. "Where'd you learn to maneuver a boat like that?" he whispered.

"Would you believe I was once kidnapped and taken to sea by a band of gold-smuggling gypsies?"

"No."

True shrugged as though it were his loss. "All right. When I was little, I'd go out with a friend of my father's to check new boats coming into harbor. The sailor used to show me how it was done. I was so little I could stand in front of him and control the oars just like I did tonight."

"I like you seated in front of me better."

True leaned into his back. "It's warmer here in your arms."

Seth folded his arms around her, pulling her even closer.

"And safe," she added. "Sometimes I feel as if nothing in the world can hurt me as long as you're so near."

"I wish I could make it so," Seth answered.

He brushed the hair away from her throat and gently kissed the side of her neck.

She didn't pull away as he'd expected.

His hands rested lightly on her bare legs. Slowly, as if treasuring every inch, he moved upward along the sides of her legs to her thighs and beneath the shirt she wore. *His* shirt, he thought, as if wearing his clothes made her somehow belong to him.

As his hands spread wide over the skin at her waist, True arched backward, pressing against him with pleasure. She cried softly, lost in passion as his hands grew bolder.

Seth felt his heart shatter. How could she cry out for his touch as if it were a need she must beg for? Didn't she know the longing was far greater within him than her? Had she no idea the heaven she offered by allowing him to touch her? He was the needy one, not she, but True was asking, almost begging with her every move, for his touch. The knowledge made him long to please her.

His hands gently brushed the lower half of her breasts. With a cry of joy, she moved her head along his shoulder, exposing her throat, silently offering herself. After the brush with death they'd survived, she needed to feel alive.

In all her years of writing, thousands of words had tumbled from her mind, but she couldn't find a single word to tell him how dearly she needed his caresses. He was a fantasy come to life, all strong and tender at the same time. As they floated just yards away from shore, she needed the dream that he could care for her. She needed to feel alive.

Seth couldn't resist tasting the tender skin of her neck as his fingers teased her breasts, stroking just below the peaks. She tasted of magic and wonder and woman. She felt of passion and life and longing. His large hands moved over her body, slowly pressing into her flesh, warming, loving.

True danced beneath his touch. A timeless dance to music heard only by lovers. Her movements pressed against the core of his need for her. She swayed in passion to the gentle rocking of the boat; her back moved against his chest, her hips slid along the inside of his thighs until the pleasure drove him insane with need.

He played with the fullness of her breasts, lifting slightly, stroking, cupping as he pressed his lips against the pulse at her throat. Her flesh swelled within his grip, and the points hardened as if pleading to be tasted. His open mouth hungered at her neck. But he continued to tease with his touch, loving the way each part of her seemed to compete for his attention.

When she cried softly once more, he moved to her ear. "Tell me what you want." He wanted to give her all the passion he'd built inside, but he couldn't frighten her. If she were only playing a game of lovemaking, she might be angry if he went further.

As she had earlier with the oars, she moved her hands to his fingers hidden beneath the material of her shirt. The cloth separated their touch, but she could feel the warmth of his hands.

She hesitated, and he pressed slightly against her, pulling her full into the warmth of his arms. "Unbutton the shirt, True, and open it for me."

True did as he ordered until the shirt hung open to her waist. He could feel her tremble slightly with each button, but she didn't stop. She was offering him a gift. A gift he'd always cherish.

Her back stiffened from what he guessed was more excitement than fear. As if she were afraid of her own boldness, she cuddled closer to him for comfort. She'd silently asked for his touch, and now she lay her head against his shoulder in waiting.

"Place your hands over mine." He breathed the words into her ear. His fingers were tight bands just below her breasts, but his kisses were feather-soft along her throat.

When her small hands moved over his, she laughed with pleasure. He felt her take a deep breath. Her breasts seemed to swell slightly above his hands, and her back relaxed

against the warm wall of his chest. He loved the feel of her
hands atop his as his fingers began once more to explore.

Seth could see little in the blackness. He longed to turn
her to face him, but the pleasure her hips were bringing him
delayed his need to see her before him with the oversized
shirt she wore hanging open.

For a moment she was still and he wasn't sure she wanted
to continue. Then her hands pressed firmly over his fingers
and moved his palms upward. As his hand covered her
breasts, she cried out once more, shoving his fingers into the
softness of her flesh.

Tasting her neck, Seth smiled at the way she moved
beneath his touch. His hands circled and molded her
fullness. Her hands rode atop his own, no longer giving
direction, but now gently pressing, as if capturing his touch
and drawing it to her.

Seth had never held something so wonderful in his arms.
Sex in his marriage had been a cold politeness between little
more than strangers. And passion, passion had been nonex-
istent. Marcy had tolerated their lovemaking with the
kindness of a dutiful wife, but True was drowning him with
pleasure. The more he touched her, the more her need grew.

He pressed his palm hard against her breasts, pulling her
tightly to his chest, branding the feel of her forever in his
memory. The need to taste her overwhelmed him.

He found himself whispering the words before he even
thought about how outrageous they might sound.

Seth could feel heat rising up his throat. The cold breeze
from the water did nothing to cool his skin.

Removing her hands from his, she pulled away. True
seemed to melt into the darkness like a wish he'd been
afraid to say out loud. He wanted to capture her and pull her
back, but he knew he couldn't, any more than one could
recapture a dream.

Seth raised his head to the starless sky, knowing he'd gone too far. He couldn't believe what he'd asked her. A woman who'd told him his arms made her feel safe. How safe would she feel now, knowing his thoughts? She was a lady, and ladies are never asked such a question by gentlemen.

He was aware of her moving very carefully so as not to rock the boat. She'd have probably run from him if there had been a place to run. If she'd been able to swim, he guessed she'd have already been in the water swimming toward the shore. A man just didn't ask for such a pleasure as to taste a woman. His request belonged in a brothel, not said to True McCormick. Her father would probably kill him if the lady didn't do the job first with one of those pearl-handled Colts she was so fond of carrying.

"You'll have to sit in the bottom of the boat." True's words drew him from his thoughts.

"What?"

Laughter filled the inky space between them. "I'm afraid to stand in the boat. You'll have to sit in the bottom."

Seth crossed his legs and slid from the bench. He wished he could see her face. Her voice gave nothing away of what she was thinking. He wasn't sure if she was planning to grant his request or hit him with one of the oars.

The outline of her body moved carefully before him, a shadow of perfection. She was so close he could feel the warmth of her skin, but he didn't reach for her. She knelt in front of him, her head only slightly taller than his.

Seth lifted his hands, lightly brushing the sides of her arms. No shirt hindered his touch. He slid his fingers over her shoulders. Dear God! His mind exploded. She'd removed the shirt.

"Touch me," she whispered as she rested her arms on his shoulders. "Taste me."

He pulled her to him, loving the feel of her breasts on either side of his face. She giggled as he brushed his scratchy chin against her soft flesh. With long strokes, his fingers moved along her back, cupping her bottom and pulling her to him until her lower body pressed gently against his chest. The feel of her against him shattered all barriers in his proper, dull life. There was no world but True now. And death, death would be her absence from his arms.

He tasted her then as he'd longed to taste her. Full and completely. He held her tightly as she cried in pleasure when his mouth covered her body. His hands moved down to her legs and explored while his tongue savored her peaks.

They were running wild on the streets of passion now. Children in a game of desire despite their years.

Their bodies were so warm with need for each other they didn't notice the rain until they were soaked.

"We'd better pull to shore," True whispered as she moved from his arms.

Seth knew the shore she spoke of was more than the land before them.

TWENTY-THREE

Just after midnight a slow rain started to patter along the sand of the coastline. Seth sheltered True as best he could with his arm while they walked parallel with the shore to the orphanage. Broken shells that the tide had scattered in the sand kept making True jump in pain. The third time she hopped on one foot and fought back an oath, Seth lifted both her and the baby in his arms.

"I can walk!" she shouted above the sound of the waves and rain.

"I know," he answered, "but you'll be bloody by the time we get to the sisters."

She didn't protest further. The warmth of his arms was always a welcome to her. Pressing her cheek against his chest she listened to the pounding of his heart and tried to forget all the times she'd been alone. But even her earliest recollections were bruised.

The memory of a childhood friend came rolling across her mind. Henry had been almost her age, but he'd had a family to go to when their adventures were over each day. One night she needed to talk to him. She'd gone to his window, planning to tap lightly.

Henry was curled in his mother's arms. The woman sat on the edge of the bed and rocked him slowly back and forth. True couldn't hear what she was saying—maybe she'd been singing—but the mother tenderly stroked Henry's hair until he fell asleep. True watched Henry's mother tuck him into bed with loving hands. Long after the woman had turned down the light and left the room, True stared in the window. Henry's house was only a farmer's shack, but True felt she was staring into Heaven's home. A home she'd never find the door to.

True would have given up every adventure she'd ever had to have someone hold her at night and to know that person would be near when morning came. Reality forced its way into her thoughts. Seth would never be such a person. He was molded of shifting sand with wanderlust blood. She'd seen his kind a hundred times in the train stations across the country. Men born to leave, with nowhere as home and "on down the tracks" as their destination. Yet he was the only kind of man who would even try to understand her. Other men, stable men, would never take the time to get to know a woman like her. A woman who needed no roots and wanted no boundaries.

"Jump up," Seth whispered as he lifted her onto the orphanage's wide porch.

"Aren't you coming in?"

"I'm not too sure the nuns would like to see me without a shirt."

His modesty surprised her. "I'll toss you the jacket as soon as I get the baby inside." She winked. "Can't say I've minded you shirtless all day."

True ran toward the door before he could see her blush.

Seth's smile was slow and easy. He guessed she shocked herself with her words more than she did him. From where he stood, he had a clear view of her bare legs as she crossed the porch. The memory of them pressing against the inside of his thighs warmed him despite the rain. He couldn't even picture a woman of Timber Creek selling her clothes to save a baby's life, then walking barefoot in the rain with only a shirt to cover her. The women back home would probably organize a committee to study the problem. But not True;

she'd acted. Nothing about True McCormick shocked him anymore. Everything about her was uniquely beautiful.

Before he realized time had passed, True tossed him the jacket and ran back inside. "I've clothes in the attic!" she yelled back. "I'll be dressed and down before our stew cools."

Seth walked to the front door held open by one of the nuns. She didn't speak but simply pointed toward the kitchen. He nodded his thanks, thinking she had a soft, pretty face that already made her look more angel than woman. Her eyes were the kind of tired a week's sleep wouldn't rest.

As he walked into the huge kitchen, his gaze was caught by two bowls of stew on the table, with a half loaf of bread between them. Seth took one chair and tried to wait politely for True, but the smell finally won him over.

He'd finished his first bowl by the time she came in dressed in pants and an oversized shirt only slightly smaller than his had been on her frame. Though her feet were still bare, her hair had been combed and pulled back. She'd tossed his shirt over her shoulder.

"How's the stew?" She joined him with none of the ladylike hesitancy he'd seen her show when she was wearing a dress.

"It would be perfect if I'd found even a sliver of meat in it," Seth answered as he took the shirt from her shoulder.

"Meat's not easy to come by." True pulled a piece of bread off and dunked it in the bowl. "Maybe you'd like to have another talk with the butcher about donating some?"

Seth laughed. "I just might do that, but right now we need to think of a place to stay the night."

"We can't go back to the Harvey House. That's the first place they'll look."

Seth agreed. "And we can't stay here. It would put the children in too much danger."

"We could stay with Audrey."

After downing half a glass of milk, Seth shook his head. "No. If they've been watching us for long, they may have seen us leaving her house. It could be risky. Another hotel is out. I gave most of my money to Sam for the boat."

"We could go to my father."

"Not yet," Seth reasoned. "If they were willing to kill one Ranger, they'd be willing to kill more. I'll be safer sending a message to your father and staying away. Right now even the alleys are less of a risk than going to anyone we know."

"What about me?" True frowned.

"They don't want to kill you. They only want Granite Westwind. I see no reason why you couldn't go back."

True fought the urge to scream, I am Granite Westwind, but now was not the time to tell him. Besides he probably wouldn't believe her anyway. Neither would anyone else except her father and Audrey, and they couldn't go to either of them. "I'm staying with you," she announced.

"But—"

"I'm staying with you."

Seth wanted to argue, but in truth he wanted her with him. "All right, but we play this my way. No more crazy plans like rocking the box and capsizing the boat."

"It freed us."

"It almost got us killed."

True forgot her meal and stood. "You haven't thanked me once for saving your life."

"And you haven't thanked me for knocking you out and saving you from drowning." The words were out before he realized what he'd confessed to.

"You hit me!"

"It was either that or leave you in the middle of the Gulf."

The door opened suddenly, interrupting their argument. "True!" Emily shouted as she bolted across the room. "Mr. Westwind! You're alive."

True hugged the child, then passed her to Seth. She climbed into his lap and patted his face with both her hands as if proving to herself he was real.

"I thought you two might have been shot by the bad men like the Ranger was. I cried so hard I got the hiccups."

Seth gently pulled her hands off his face. "We were lucky. The bad men only threw us in the Gulf and took our clothes."

"Ranger Lincoln told me you'd get away, but I didn't think it would be so fast. I figured it would take days and days to fight your way out of an outlaw hideout or the cave they probably put you in. Phillip says it wouldn't take the great Granite Westwind days and days, but I figured you had True to slow you down."

Seth laughed, but when he glanced at True, her face was white. She stood by her chair with her hands in fists at her side.

"Did you say Lincoln is alive?" True's voice was only a whisper, as though she were afraid to hope.

"He was this afternoon when I went by the Doc's house. He was yelling and screaming that Doc was going to finish the job of killing him."

One huge tear bubbled over True's lashes. "He's alive," she whispered to herself.

Emily shrugged as if the thought had never occurred to her that he might really die. "Phillip says it takes more than a few bullets to kill a Ranger. I figure it might take a cannon."

Seth lifted Emily to the chair next to him. She was talking about all the excitement their kidnapping had caused and didn't seem to notice True and Seth's silence.

When Seth stood, True moved into his arms. "Link's alive," she whispered again.

Seth laughed as he hugged her. "For someone who claims to dislike the man, you sure seem happy he's not six feet under." Seth couldn't help but wonder if she'd have been half as glad if he'd been the one gunned down but alive. It would almost be worth getting shot to find out. "If I remember right, about the last thing you said to him was that you planned to kill him for drinking all morning."

True laughed. "That seems like a long time ago."

Seth kissed the top of her head. He liked the way she came into his arms so easily. A week ago he would have said he didn't care if he hugged another woman again for as long as he lived. Now just thinking about not being with True made his arms ache, and he was still holding her.

True wiped her cheek with her palm. "I know." She pulled away, looking embarrassed at her own tears. "I must need some sleep. Crying over Link being alive seems foolish."

"You can have my bed," Emily offered, "but there's three already in it. And one of the Bostock twins wets every night."

Seth's large hand slid over her curls. "Thanks, but we need a place no one will look for us for a few days."

Emily shrugged as if she'd made the best offer, and helped herself to the last of the bread on the table. "There's a hotel further down the beach. It closed a while back but's gonna be open again soon. We helped the night watchman look for his dog last night. It's got lots of rooms, and no one's there but a few people looking after the place. They live on the first floor by the kitchen. If you and True wanta go, I could show you how Phillip and me climbed in and looked around last night just for fun. No one would know you were there."

Seth glanced at True. "You think we could talk the watchman into putting us up for a night?"

Emily didn't give True time to answer. "You don't have to even ask him. I know a way in, and the watchdog licks my hand when he sees me. The night watchman won't even know you're in the hotel."

Seth winked at True and tilted his head toward Emily. "You sure this little one doesn't belong to you?"

"I only wish she did," True answered.

"I could," Emily joined in. "Phillip says if you two got married, you could adopt me. And I'd tell you Phillip was my brother so he'd get to come along, too. Ain't nobody goin' adopt us, 'cause we eat too much."

"But we're not getting married," True corrected the child before she got carried away with the fantasy.

"Are you already married to someone else?"

"No," True answered slowly. "But folks only marry when they want to spend the rest of their lives together."

"Well, at the rate you two are going, I'm not sure the rest of your life is too long a time. So you might get to thinking about it."

True looked to Seth for help, but he was silent. His blue-gray eyes seemed to be looking all the way to her soul. Even though he was tired and worn from the day, the lines in his face didn't seem as deep as they had the day she'd met him.

When he'd rolled from his bunk in the cell and stared at her, there had been a hardness in his face. She would have sworn he hadn't smiled in months, maybe years.

"As soon as I lace on my moccasins, you can show me the hotel. We'll talk about marriage later. Tonight we've got to worry about staying alive."

An hour later they were climbing up the wet porch lattice work to the second floor of the Beach Front Hotel, with the

watchman's dog wagging his tail below them. The roof to
the hotel slanted steeply, and water ran in a steady stream at
one corner of the balcony, splashing enough to muffle any
sound they made.

Emily showed True to one of the rooms that was all ready
for the grand reopening. Long French doors opened out onto
a balcony, allowing the watery moonlight to shadow the
room in shades of gray on gray. The interior smelled clean,
and a quilt covered the bed. There was even water in the
pitcher on the washstand. A balcony connected another
room, which Emily assigned Seth.

"When I get my hands on any money, I'll pay for this
room," True whispered as she kissed Emily good night.

"Just remember," Emily warned. "Don't light a fire or a
lamp. Even if no one saw it, this place already had one fire
scare a few weeks ago."

"Good night, Mother Emily," Seth said as he lowered her
over the balcony as far as he could reach. She dropped softly
to the sand and disappeared.

"That child's growing on you, isn't she?" True whispered
from behind Seth.

"That she is," he answered. "Do all girls talk as much as
that one?"

True laughed. "I guess so."

Neither of them seemed in a hurry to go inside. The soft
rain thinly veiled them from the rest of the world, but they
could still hear the sound of the waves.

"The rain's not showing much sign of letting up." True
walked to the edge of the balcony. "This seems a lonely
place to spend a holiday. The water almost reaches the
porch in the back when the tide's high. I wouldn't think
there would be much to do."

"It'll be different when the sun is shining and every room
is filled." Seth tried to lighten the mood. "Folks will come

from Houston to enjoy the cool breeze. There will be dancing in some room downstairs and laughing in the dining rooms."

"I guess." True leaned against a pole and closed her eyes listening to the waves.

Seth tugged up on his shirttail. "If it wouldn't embarrass you, I think I'll wash up in this stream of rainwater."

He'd expected her to excuse herself and go inside, but she stood as if planted on the balcony. "It won't embarrass me." Her voice cracked slightly, giving her lie away.

He looked at her a long moment. "Do you plan on watching, Miss McCormick?"

"Would you mind?"

Seth didn't know what to say. After all they'd been through, after the way he'd touched her on the boat, after sleeping wrapped in each other's arms, it seemed foolish to answer yes. But he'd never stood totally nude in front of a woman. His father had told him years ago that the gentlemanly thing to do when your wife even passed the door while you were bathing was to cover yourself as much as possible. Seth even remembered his father saying that his grandfather had parented eight children and boasted that his wife had never seen him without his trousers. Now this woman he'd known less than a week was planning to stand a few feet away and watch him undress.

Seth smiled. Let her! He wasn't going to be the one to turn away like some old maid. If she wanted to watch, he might as well give her something to see.

Slowly, he pulled his shirt over his head and faced the water. "Mind handing me the soap? My guess is it'll be by the pitcher on the washstand."

"Not at all," True answered.

He could hear her moving and would have bet his ranch she was fighting to keep from running.

While she was gone, he pulled off his boots and socks.

"Here you go," True extended her arm full length. "The soap."

"Thanks," Seth answered and met her gaze. He saw it then, that sparkle of adventure in her eyes. Watching him bathe rated up there with walking the streets at night or shaking hands with a dead man.

Seth unbuckled his belt. He didn't pull it from the trousers, but let each end hang open as he unbuttoned the two waist buttons.

True took a step backward, but didn't turn around. He could no longer see her face, but the outline of her body stood very still. He couldn't help but smile. If the night was silhouetting her, it had to be doing the same for him.

He turned his back and stripped off his pants. Head first he stepped into the stream of water, allowing the cold rain to cool his blood. Leaning his head back, he let the water splash his shoulders and chest.

True stood in silence, watching. All the air left her lungs, and she couldn't seem to loosen her chest enough to take in a deep breath. Seth stood before her, a pale shadow in the moonlight. Water shot like tiny stars off his black hair and bounced over the hard muscles of his shoulders. His feet were wide apart, making the view of his bare hips and waist seem more angular. His movements were slow as he rubbed the soap onto his chest and arms. She could almost feel her hands sliding behind the bar of soap, feeling the hardness of the muscles and the tickle of damp chest hair.

The smell of soap blended with the rain as she watched him wash. His hands seemed large and dark as they moved over the untanned parts of his frame. When one hand crossed his chest, she remembered the feel of his fingers sliding over her body.

He moved slightly so that the water washed across his

back. Liquid silver flowed over the muscles. As he leaned his head back and shoved his fingers into his dark hair, she saw him fully. Every inch of him was beautiful.

Seth shook the water from his hair and dared to glance in True's direction. He'd been bolder than he'd thought he'd ever be in front of a woman, and he hadn't heard her say a word. He was sure he found the knowledge that she was watching him far more exciting than she found the view.

He stepped from the stream of water and listened. He'd expected True to say something, even yell at him for being so immodest. Silence.

A fan of dark and light shadows crossed both corners of the balcony as he looked around him for True. Only the sound of the dripping rain from the roof threatened the silence.

The cool air blew in from off the water, chilling his skin. One thing was clear even in the darkness of night. True had vanished.

TWENTY-FOUR

Seth moved his head back into the stream of water. He couldn't believe how bold he'd been. She'd dared him to strip before her, and he'd been just fool enough and tired enough to do it.

That was it in one sentence. He couldn't seem to go an hour, much less a day, without making a total fool of himself. If he told her he owned one of the most prosperous businesses in Texas, she'd never believe him. She'd probably offer to buy his son away from him if she knew about Johnny, thinking no such idiot should raise a child.

The stream of water decreased to a drizzle. Seth turned slowly, wishing he'd thought of asking her to bring a towel along with the soap. She'd never want to face him again. A fine hero he'd turned out to be. He'd never saved her when they were being shot, he hadn't fought hard enough when they'd been kidnapped, and now he'd stood in front of her naked and wet as a newborn calf without the sense God gave groundhogs.

Raking his fingers through his wet hair, he moved to his room. The wide French doors stood open, but no one welcomed him. His quarters, unlike True's, looked small, with heavy furniture that seemed to crowd the space. The shadows of the bed and wardrobe cut into any extra area.

Seth walked to the washstand in the corner. Everything was laid out as though the room were ready to be occupied. The reopening of the hotel couldn't be more than a few days away.

Everything was there except a towel. Both racks were empty.

Seth glanced toward the bed, then at the hooks lining one wall. All empty. He had no intention of looking for a towel in True's room. That left only one choice. He'd have to find his clothes on the balcony and put them on while he was still wet.

As he turned back toward the French windows, something moved on silent feet from the shadows. Lifting the towels, she moved toward him.

Seth took one and wrapped it tightly around his waist without taking the time to dry himself. He was glad the room was so dark. He wasn't sure he could have faced her otherwise. "Thank you," he managed to say as she took another step toward him.

"Sit down on the corner of the bed, and I'll dry your hair."

He knew what she was doing. She was playing with fire. Pushing danger as far as she dared.

He followed her orders. The mattress sank with his weight. A heartbeat later he felt her knee press against his leg as the towel she carried covered his head.

She rubbed the water from his hair. Her movements were brisk one moment and caressing the next.

He could feel her leg move along his side, and her breasts brushed lightly against his shoulder.

Feelings were exploding inside him. He loved the way she touched him, with the care of a lover long comfortable with his nearness.

She pushed the towel to his shoulders. Her hand combed his damp hair back. With each stroke she seemed unaware that her body brushed lightly against him.

The memory of their touching on the boat returned to him as his fingers lightly brushed her shoulders. Slowly, hesitantly, he turned toward her. His hand moved into the softness of her hair and pulled her lips to meet his mouth. At first their kiss was feather light, an introduction. Tenderly, they explored. Her mouth parted in welcome as his lips pressed harder with desire.

Tenderness turned to passion. Seth felt all control burned away by desire. One hand spread wide across her back while the other cupped her bottom. He wanted her breasts crushed against the wall of his chest, flattened so he could feel her peaks harden with the rise and fall of each breath he took. He longed for her to be even nearer, so close there was no beginning of one or ending of the other.

She cried softly with pleasure, and his hold tightened. Her fingers dug into his hair as he tasted the softness of her neck.

"Stay with me tonight," he whispered, his words tickling her throat. "Stay in my bed as a lover as well as a friend."

Knowing she was caught up in the wild adventure of feelings, he communicated his longing with his hand. No one would ever dare touch the proper Miss McCormick, but he would set the untamed True afire with her own passion. Making her long for his touch as dearly as he longed for hers was his one goal. He wanted to love her so completely that she'd cry his name even in her sleep, while dreaming for more.

Before she could answer, he guided her backward atop the covers and spread his body over her. His lips found hers, and he kissed her deep and hard.

When he pulled away, both were out of breath. "Touch me," he whispered, wanting to feel her hands move over him.

Lightly, her fingers rested on his back. He whispered his need for her as her hands explored from his waist to his shoulders.

His body felt as wonderful as she'd imagined. The skin was warm, and she could feel the strength beneath her touch. His frame was hard, and the fresh smell of rain lingered on him. As her touch grew bolder, he rewarded her with long, warm kisses. Deep, forever-lasting kisses that made her want to melt against him.

For the first time in her life she wasn't just imagining adventure, she was touching it. There was no need to run through the night looking for a thrill that made her blood rush and her heart pound. Seth lived a day-by-day life of danger. He walked on the edge of violence that she'd only been able to write about. And somehow she'd captured that danger, that adventure in her arms.

True pulled him closer. She'd not let him go. Not tonight. Tonight she'd believe she was a part of the excitement. A small fraction of the adventure.

She knew he'd been right about her only playing a game. Holding Seth was no different from holding Granite Westwind in her mind. Neither relationship would go anywhere. Both were built on smoky dreams. Except, Seth felt solid in her arms. She could almost believe he'd be there in the morning, and every morning for the rest of her life. Almost believe.

Suddenly she wanted to live the dream for a night. She wanted to believe forever was an option for her. True longed to feel him beside her without barriers. He might disappear, but she'd always have the one wild night of loving to remember.

"Love me," she whispered.

Every muscle in his body seemed to tighten at once.

Digging her fingers into his back as if she could mold him to her, True pleaded, "Love me tonight."

He pulled away, not seeming to notice how she clawed into his back. For a long moment he held himself above her. She could still feel the warmth of his flesh and the softness of his breathing against her face, but he was no longer touching her.

"I can't see your eyes," he answered, his voice low with desire. "God, True, I need to see your eyes."

"Why?" She dared to move her hands over his chest, loving the way he lost his breath as she touched him.

He shoved the hair away from her face. "I have to know that you want this between us as much as I do."

"How much do you want me?" Her hands tugged at the towel around his waist. "Enough to play the game if a game is all I offer."

"I want you more than I've ever wanted anything, and longer than any game rules allow play." He lightly brushed the side of her face with his knuckles.

"I think about touching you with every heartbeat. So much I sometimes believe I must be mad. Maybe I already am crazy. Somehow you've shattered all reason in my life and made my longing for you so deep, I'd sacrifice air or water before giving up being with you." He plowed his long fingers into her thick hair. "But I'll not start it and have you stop halfway through to tell me you were only dancing near the fire."

His hand twisted into a fist, tying her curls inside his grip. "I have to know you're seeing *me,* loving *me,* not some fictional character. Not Granite Westwind."

"Come closer," she ordered.

Her fingernails raked across his chest, making him forget how to speak. With a low groan, he did as she'd requested.

Her mouth opened slightly as his lips claimed her and he captured her sigh of pleasure.

She shoved the towel free and ran her fingers over the warm flesh that blanketed her.

Suddenly Seth didn't care if she were making love to Granite Westwind or him. He was making love to True.

With one mighty jerk he ripped open the shirt she wore. Her breasts were full with need for him. He shifted to her side without breaking the kiss, yet allowing him to touch heaven. With a cry of pleasure she arched her back slightly and dropped her arms to her sides.

When his mouth moved to taste, his fingers also gripped lower and removed her pants.

She laughed when the moccasins she wore hampered his progress. Without a word she shoved him away and slid to the edge of the bed.

As she unlaced her leather shoes, he studied her in the moonlight. She was perfection.

When True stood to allow the pants to drop to the floor, she turned to face him. As she raised a knee to climb back into bed, he lifted his hand and stopped her.

"No," he whispered, feeling very much as if he might die any moment of the fever running through his blood. "Let me look at you."

True laughed. "You can't see. It's dark."

"I can see your outline in the moonlight and you're wonderful. You're the most beautiful woman in the world."

True laughed again. "Of course," she teased. "I've noticed the way men keep dropping at my feet on the street. I'm attacked by passionate lovers all the time. It's getting to be quite a bother being the most beautiful."

It surprised Seth she didn't believe him. How could she not see her own beauty?

"Well." He sat up and caught her hand. "You're about to be attacked by a passionate lover tonight, and you won't see it as a bother."

He pulled her to him, capturing her in his arms and turning her so that her back was against his chest. "I enjoyed this in the boat," he whispered, "but I think I like it much better now."

Seth moved his hands over her body, loving the way his touch made her sigh. He rolled away only long enough for her to stretch onto her back, then he lowered himself over her.

There could be no more words between them. Passion was a mindless fever that captured them both.

He'd meant to go slow, but they were running at full speed, hearts pounding, a hunger devouring all sense of time.

His hands were caring and gentle as he lead her into passion. When she hesitated, he placed his warm fingers over her hands and showed her how to touch him. She was a fast study and wanted more of each pleasure. Her body grew warm and welcoming beneath him.

When he shoved into her, he felt her jerk in pain, but it was too late to stop. His body and mind seemed to explode. The last ounce of reason told him he'd been the first to love her, and she'd be the only woman he'd ever love, if he lived to be a thousand.

TWENTY-FIVE

Seth rolled away from her slowly. The cool breeze brushed over his sweaty body, but he hardly noticed. His heart was still pounding against the inside of his rib cage, and all his muscles felt as if he'd been swimming for hours without resting.

True lay still, her eyes closed, her pale limbs twisted on the dark covers. Just as words had failed him when they'd made love, they failed him now. How could he ever tell her that she'd been the first for him also? He'd been married for two years, but he'd never tasted passion. The act of lovemaking was an easy pleasure to be indulged in if time permitted. Most of the months he and Marcy had been married she'd either been pregnant or in poor health. A polite kiss each morning had been the only intimacy they'd shared. But after one hour with True, Seth knew his arms would ache to hold her every night for the rest of his life.

As quietly as he could, Seth rolled off the bed and lifted the comforter that had fallen to the floor. He placed it tenderly over her body then lay atop it next to her.

Seth's hand shook slightly as he pushed soft hair from her face. Moisture dampened his fingers. Salty, silent tears.

"True," he whispered, longing to pull her closer but suddenly finding himself shy. "True, I'm sorry. Did I hurt you?"

"No." Her voice was so soft it sounded more than a few inches away. "Will you hold me the rest of the night . . . promise."

He pulled her against him, wrapping the covers around her. "I'll hold you for as long as you like," he answered. He wanted to scream, "Don't leave me, True. Believe in more than just one night." How could their loving have made her cry when it had been his first touch of paradise? What lay hidden in her past that kept her from believing in the future? She was a complex woman, and somehow when he was near her Seth felt there was more to him also.

She rested her head on his shoulder. "I know there is no forever between us, but I need there to be tonight."

Seth blinked hard. This woman was ripping apart every wall he'd built around his heart. She was saying the very thing he didn't want to hear. There would be no forever, maybe not even a tomorrow. Everything in his life seemed to go on endlessly. Everything except True.

"True." He kissed her forehead. "You have to believe me. I've never made love like we did just now."

"Are you saying we didn't do it right?"

Seth couldn't stop the smile. "If we didn't, I don't know what else there could be. For me it was wonderful, but I know I caused you pain. I don't think there will be any discomfort next time."

Next time. He let the words rattle around in his thoughts. If there were a next time.

"I know," True answered as her cheek rocked against his arm. "You forget, I have three mothers. Over the years since my eighteenth birthday, they've all felt the need to fill me in on the facts of being a woman. Audrey even provided a chart she found in a medical book."

"But you never explored until now?"

"I thought of it a few times, but it never felt right. I knew from the way you held me that first night on the docks, when we slept among the cotton bales, it would be right with you."

She lay very still, as if waiting for him to say something, but Seth couldn't think of anything. There was so much in his heart, but he'd never been good at putting feelings into words.

She lifted her head. "Don't go getting nervous and thinking I'll try to tie you down. I know men like you can't stay in one place too long."

"I—"

"Don't make any promises you can't keep," True interrupted. "All I ask for is tonight."

"And tomorrow?"

"Tomorrow we step back into our regular life."

Seth wanted to tell her he was the kind of man who would settle down and stay in one place. But settling down with True in a town like Timber Creek would be like putting her in a cage. She was where she belonged, roaming around the West with the real Granite Westwind. Typing his stories while her imagination made up a life she lived only in her dreams.

After tonight, Seth knew he would be part of that dream life. A memory molded into fantasy for proper Miss McCormick to keep hidden away from the real world.

"Our regular life?" Seth stared at the ceiling. "Let me see. That would be the dull ordinary one where we're being chased by a group of men with an unknown leader who wants to kill me. The one where we have no money, few clothes, and not a friend we can turn to."

True laughed. "I didn't say this job would be easy."

"Sometimes I think it would be easier to die a hero than to try and stay alive as just a man."

True fought down the giggles. "Someone sure is trying to make it easy for you."

"Go to sleep, True." He kissed her forehead. "I'll hold you till dawn."

He felt her relax in his arms. She cuddled close to him. As the night aged, she molded against him as if she belonged at his side.

Seth never bothered to close his eyes. Sleeping would have been impossible. The realization that this might be the last night he held her in his arms made him treasure every minute. He tried to remember if he'd been happy before he'd left home and boarded the train to Galveston. He couldn't recall now if he'd even thought of being alive much less of being happy.

Now in a few days Seth would go back to the life he'd built so carefully for himself. He'd work at his store, read to Johnny by the fire every night after supper, sleep alone in the house where he'd been born. But life wouldn't be the same. Something would be missing . . . True.

An hour passed, and Seth realized what he had to do. First, he had to get her to safety, and the only safety was away from him. Second, he had to find the real Granite Westwind and get him to come forward. If he were some old man who'd spent his life dreaming, the outlaws who wanted to kill him would realize what fools they'd been. If Granite Westwind turned out to be the man the legend had been molded from, a few men hunting for him shouldn't prove such a threat. Either way Seth would be free to go back and resume his life. And more importantly, True would be *safe*.

When he was sure she was asleep, Seth moved away. He shoved his pillow close against her so she'd think he was still beside her. His clothes lay wrinkled and damp on the balcony, but he put them on as if they were his Sunday best. It didn't matter anymore how he looked.

He moved through the sleeping town toward Audrey's place. If Officer Raine was still there, he might be a great help in locating Granite Westwind. Link was also the only man he trusted with True's whereabouts.

As he neared Audrey's house, Seth noticed only one light burning in her windows. A low lamp had been set in the office window, as though a mother waited for her child to come home.

Moving toward the brightness, Seth felt as though it had been a year since he'd seen Link and a lifetime since he'd been home.

He found the door to the office unlocked and slipped inside without making a sound. The window light did little to brighten the interior.

Three steps into the room Link's cold voice shattered the silence. "Come another foot closer, mister, and you'll be walking with the angels."

"Link?"

"Westwind?"

Neither man spoke for a moment, then Link turned up the lamp. "I can't believe it's you. I thought you were a dead man for sure."

Seth laughed. "Me! The last time I saw you you were flying out of the kitchen, decorated in bullet holes."

Link lowered himself to the bed. The action of standing had cost him greatly. "Doc fixed me up. I'll be good as new in a few days."

"Or weeks." Seth didn't miss the gray lines around the Ranger's face.

"It's nothing." Link tried to wave away Seth's concern. "What's important is that you and True are alive."

"As you can see, I'm fine, and so is True. She's somewhere safe, resting. I came because I need your help. You're the only one I can trust."

"You have it, Mr. Westwind. What can I do?"

Seth was bothered that Link called him Mr. Westwind. He might as well face the problem. "First stop calling me Mr. Westwind."

"All right, Granite."

"No." Seth moved closer. "Not Granite either. My name's Seth Atherton, and the closest I ever got to a Westwind novel was forging his name on the front page of his book."

For one of the few times in his life Link looked shocked. "Does True know this?"

"She's the one who put me up to it." Seth knew the Ranger wouldn't be satisfied until he was filled in on all the details.

Link showed no emotion as Seth talked.

When Seth stopped, Link rubbed his bandaged shoulder. "This tops anything True has ever done. Did she and Westwind really think they could get away with passing off a counterfeit? It wasn't fair to throw you in the line of fire like that."

"I don't think they knew anything about the trouble coming. It's too late to matter," Seth answered. "Right now I only have two things to worry about—keeping True safe and talking the real Westwind into stepping forward. If he can make a public statement, I'll stop being hunted."

"The real Granite Westwind!"

Audrey's voice startled them from the doorway. "Are you both sure you want to meet the *real* Granite Westwind?"

"How bad can he be?" Seth stood and nodded his greeting to the doctor. "He must have lived quite a life to write all those adventures. He'd probably make short order of this gang who wants to shoot him."

Link watched Audrey closely. "Do you know the real Granite Westwind?"

"Can you get word to him?" Seth added.

Audrey moved to Link's side and seemed to ignore Seth's question. "I've known Granite Westwind for some time. But before I introduce you to him, I have one question. Where's True?"

"She's safe."

"Can you take me to her?"

Seth nodded.

"Then I'll get my jacket."

Link pushed himself from the bed. "I'm going, too."

Both Seth and Audrey said, "No," at once.

Link pulled his trousers over his bandaged leg. "I'm going if I have to crawl behind the two of you. I may not be much good at walking, but I can still shoot if there's trouble."

Audrey pressed her lips together, readying for a fight. "You are about the most hardheaded man I've ever met. I'd argue, but in the end I figure you'd just follow us anyway, leaving blood all over the street." She glanced at Seth. "Help him get dressed while I grab my coat and wake Marie. We can hitch up the buggy by the time you can get his boots on. If nothing else, the Ranger can sit in the buggy outside and warn us if there's trouble coming."

She was at the door when she turned around to add the final words, "But if you die on me, I swear I'll kill you, Lincoln Raine."

Both men laughed as she disappeared.

"I think I love that woman." Link winked at Seth.

Seth shook his head. "I can see why. So sweet talking and endearing."

"Couldn't you hear it in her voice? She's crazy about me."

Seth didn't argue but decided the Ranger must have lost too much blood to his brain. The doctor treated him with about as much kindness as a rattler treats a rabbit. But one thing would ease his mind—if Link was with True, he could help protect her while Seth looked for Westwind. And right now Audrey seemed to be willing to make the introductions.

TWENTY-SIX

True stretched in her sleep and reached for Seth. Only his cold pillow filled her fingers. He'd vanished from her side as though he'd been a dream and nothing more. Curling into a ball, True tried to force the disappointment from her heart. She'd thought she'd have at least one last night before he left her.

A shout came from somewhere deep in the hotel, pulling her full awake. True shoved the hair from her eyes and sat up in bed. Seth was gone; moping wouldn't change the fact. He'd left her when he'd promised before she fell asleep that he'd stay. Seth had abandoned her sleeping and unprotected in this shadowy place.

True angrily shoved the tears off her cheek. She hadn't cried when her mother left all those years ago. She'd promised she'd never cry because she was alone. "I can take care of myself," she whispered.

A noise sounded again from below. Someone was running through the hotel, shouting. The waves beneath the balcony of her room drowned out the sense of their words, but she could hear the voices. Footsteps pounded on the stairs, and a door slammed from the floor below.

Self-preservation sprang True into action. She climbed from the bed and darted toward the door. Having made sure it was locked, she ran and latched the windows. "Safe," she whispered as she grabbed the shirt Seth had ripped from her earlier, then wrapped it around her. Pulling a blanket and one pillow from the bed, she hurried to the wardrobe. "Even if someone breaks into this room, they wouldn't find me." She knew where to hide.

As she closed the door to the wardrobe, more voices shouted and she thought she saw a bright light reflect on the water outside her window.

"I'll be safe," she whispered, remembering all the times she'd hidden in a wardrobe when she was so small she could stretch out in the bottom and sleep until morning. Three young Harvey girls had taken her in. They'd hidden True in the storage space in one of the rooms where Harvey employees stayed. At the time True thought the roomy chest delightful. It was warm, safe, and best of all private. No one could get close enough to hurt her. There was only enough space for one, and as long as she was alone no one could hurt her, as Seth had tonight.

True pushed all thought of Seth's leaving aside. She didn't want to think that she was wrong about him. Finally she'd dared to put her belief in someone and he'd abandoned her the moment she'd fallen asleep. True shoved the blanket into the cracks of the wardrobe so that not even sound could intrude. "I should have been smarter than to allow a gunfighter who can't even row a boat to touch me."

Curling on the floor of the wardrobe, True pulled the pillow over her head. "Go away, world!" she shouted. "Go away!"

Audrey's buggy moved almost silently through the sleeping streets of Galveston. Though all looked quiet, Seth kept checking behind him. He couldn't see anything, but he could feel someone following them. He'd felt it from the time they'd loaded Link into the wagon. A barn door had creaked somewhere in the blackness. It could have been the wind, or a cat rubbing against a door someone had left unlatched. But there was a possibility someone waited in the darkness to follow them, hoping to catch Westwind alone and unarmed.

Seth looked forward just as Audrey turned toward the beach. He saw flames rising from the Beach Front Hotel even before he heard people shouting. The huge wooden structure lit the sky bright as dawn, but only parts of it were fully burning.

"Fire!" A man yelled the obvious as he ran past the buggy.

"True!" Seth shouted as he jumped at full run from his seat. "True's in the hotel!"

Audrey threw Link the reins and followed Seth. "Wait! Westwind, wait!"

"I know True's still in there!" Seth shouted as he passed several men trying to organize to fight the fire. "I'll get her out and send word when we're safe."

The fire looked as though it had started on the far side of the hotel from where they'd taken a room. If True were sleeping soundly, the room might fill with smoke before she realized it.

"I'm going in!" Seth announced as he pushed past two men with badges on their vests. "Let me pass."

The two huge deputies grabbed Seth as he tried to shove them aside. "Hold on there!" one yelled. "This is close enough. You're not going any closer."

"But someone's still in there!" Seth could feel the heat from the flames.

"No, mister," the deputy shouted. "Everyone's out. There weren't but a few kitchen helpers and a night watchman." Though they were trying to pull Seth backward, his heels plowed deep into the sand, stopping their efforts.

"There was a woman!" Seth jerked wildly, trying to pull his arms free of both men.

"If anyone else is in there, she's dead by now. Ain't no way someone could stand that smoke and heat."

Seth fought to pull away, but both men were accustomed to handling madmen and drunks.

He glanced at Audrey. "Give me a hand, Doc!" he yelled.

If Audrey hesitated, it was for too short a time to notice. With one quick swing, she slugged the deputy nearest her with a punch that would have put most men out.

The huge deputy turned loose of Seth's arm and grabbed for the doc. That was all the aid Seth needed. He plowed his free fist into the face of the man holding him, then broke free. Out of the corner of one eye, Seth noticed that Audrey was putting up a gallant fight and maybe even winning against the deputy who tried to restrain her.

"I'll get word," he repeated his promise to Audrey, knowing they would be separated in the crowd.

"I'll probably be waiting in jail." Audrey shouted as she slugged the deputy again with a right hook that almost knocked the man to his knees.

Seth didn't pay any attention to the shouting as he ran toward the fire. The air was hot enough to sunburn his face as he moved through the wet sand to the back of the hotel. The fire seemed to be passing from balcony to balcony, crawling across the wood with an endless hunger.

"True!" he shouted, feeling each breath burn his lungs. "True!"

No answer came from the shadows along the beach.

When he reached the back of the hotel, the tide was so high it almost came to the back steps. Seth fell into the water, crawling his way around burning pieces of wood that seemed to fly off the fire only to drown in the sea.

The spot where he'd climbed down an hour before was still intact, but flames were already licking their way from another balcony to where he'd stood and showered.

Seth climbed the wood. In only a few minutes the whole structure would be aflame. Somehow he knew True was still in the room. When he'd left, he'd thought she'd be safe. If he didn't get to her fast, she'd be dead. Anger and fear blanketed his senses from the heat as he kicked the French doors open and stormed inside.

The room was a dark, smoky hole surrounded by the light from the fire outside. Seth buried his nose into the bend of his elbow and pushed into the heat.

"True!" he shouted, feeling his throat raw from the boiling air.

Running to the bed, he dragged his hands across the covers. Nothing! Seth pulled again madly, ripping the blankets apart.

"True!" he shouted, knowing she had to be somewhere in the room.

He ran around the bed and knocked over the dressing stand as he felt the wall for the door. Finally, he touched the brass knob already hot from the flames in the hallway. The door was still locked from the inside. She hadn't gone that way. If she'd jumped from the balcony, he would have passed her, and she wouldn't have taken the time to close and lock the French doors. She must be here!

"True," he whispered as his hands moved aimlessly in the blackness. He could see the flames from the balcony now and knew if he didn't leave, he'd die in the inferno. But he couldn't force himself to run for freedom. Not without her.

His fingers brushed the wardrobe. "True," he whispered as an ounce of hope flooded his despair.

Seth jerked the door to the wardrobe open. Something tumbled out at his feet. The air was too black with smoke even to see her, but he heard her cry in fear.

Lifting her, he ran toward the balcony. There was no time to question. A moment's hesitation might be his last. When

Seth reached the French doors, he was running at full speed with True in his arms.

The floor of the balcony crumbled as he shattered the railing and jumped. He wasn't sure he could jump far enough to reach the water, but he'd rather die in a fall than a fire. As they sailed through the smoky air, Seth twisted so that his body would hit the ground first. It seemed they drifted an eternity in a hot, black void. He could feel True wriggling, trying to get away, and he heard a scream that seemed to last the entire jump.

Suddenly he hit the water with a mighty splash. A second later the world went black, blacker than even the smoke that surrounded them. The smoke no longer hurt his lungs. The fire didn't sting against his face. He couldn't even feel True in his arms.

True held her breath as water covered her face. She wanted to scream again as the salty water stung her eyes and filled her mouth. Kicking free of Seth, she stood in the shallow tide and slung her hair out of her face. Anger replaced fear as she turned to Seth.

He floated on his stomach with the waves toward shore. His lean body was lifeless as the water pulled him first one direction then another.

"Seth!" True screamed, forgetting her anger. She waded to him and pulled his head from the water. His eyes were closed. Warm blood dripped onto her fingers from the back of his head.

Frantically she pulled him through the water toward shore. The incoming wave made her job easy, but when the water receded, it tried to claim his body once more.

When she finally reached the rocky sand, True rolled Seth onto his back and tried to push water from his lungs. She wasn't sure what to do.

"Wake up!" she cried as she hit him hard in the chest. "Or

I swear I'll throw you back in the gulf." She doubled both hands and hit him again.

Seth coughed and shoved her away. He spit water and took a deep breath. When True moved closer, he held up his palm to her. "Stay away or I may die from the rescue."

"Are you going to be all right?"

"Yes." Seth touched the back of his head. He felt like a train must have tunneled through behind his ears, and his eyes had trouble focusing on anything. "I must have hit a rock in the fall."

"That was no fall," True corrected. "As I remember it, you jumped."

"I didn't hear you objecting," Seth protested.

"I was too busy screaming."

"It was the only way I could think of saving us."

"You almost got me killed!"

"I saved your life," he answered, thinking he must not be the only one with a head injury.

"You almost got me burned alive in that fire." True kicked at the water with her bare legs.

"Now, hold on." Seth held the side of his head, wondering if her yelling were some kind of slow death he'd been assigned for trying to be a hero he wasn't. "I'm the one who climbed a burning building and carried you out."

"You're the one who left me there in the first place."

"I had to talk to Link," Seth's reason didn't sound as solid as it had when he'd left her sleeping.

"You promised not to leave me."

"Darling, don't you see? We have to do something. I can't go the rest of my life looking over my shoulder. I don't even know who wants to kill Westwind, but I'm not willing to wait around to give him another chance."

True twisted her hair trying to drain the water from it as

they walked onto dry sand. "Waiting around doesn't seem to me your strong suit."

"Granite Westwind may die, but not while this tour is going on." He lowered his voice as he noticed several folks moving around the burning building.

"Mr. Westwind," someone whispered in awe. "You're the great Granite Westwind!"

Seth took True's hand and moved away from the light. The last thing he wanted to see was a fan or a reporter asking questions.

"Mr. Westwind?" A man carrying a box camera over his shoulder and a tripod in one hand hurried toward Seth. "It is you, isn't it, sir?"

Seth looked at the sky and fought to keep from swearing. It was his own fault for mentioning Westwind's name. Now he had to get True away before they were swamped with reporters.

Seth turned to face the young man. He was shorter than most men but appeared to be trying to make up for it by walking on his tiptoes. "Yes." Seth stepped in front of True. "I'm Granite Westwind, but I'm asking you to keep it quiet. I'd just as soon no one knew."

"Everyone in town knows about your kidnapping." The cameraman tried to keep down the excitement in his voice. "They'll be real happy to know your alive. I know I am. I'm one of your greatest fans."

"Thank you," Seth said as he moved more into the shadows. "My secretary and I've escaped from the kidnappers, but we still need to get to safety." He debated slugging the little man as hard as he could and running. Surely if he'd got away from the deputy, he could fight off a reporter.

"How can I help, Mr. Westwind?" The man was almost dancing with excitement. "I've read everything you've ever written, and I'd be honored to help you out of this scrap.

Name's Dan Miller. It'll be easy to spell if you put me in the book." He let out a hoot. "Wouldn't that be something, to be in the next Westwind adventure."

True moved around Seth. "Would you loan me your coat, Mr. Miller? I was asleep when Mr. Westwind saved me, and I'm afraid I'm not properly dressed for a stroll."

"Yes, miss." Dan sat his camera down and stripped off his long duster. "I'd be mighty pleased if you'd wear it. I saw him run off the porch with you in his arms. I guess you must be Miss McCormick, Mr. Westwind's secretary. I read of you in the report about the kidnapping. You're just about as brave as your boss."

"Thanks," True said without any sincerity in her voice. But her smile was genuine as she pulled on the coat. "Do you remember the Westwind story called *Danger's Shelter*?"

"Oh, yes, miss." Dan walked with them away from the fire. "Westwind was hunted by a gang of eight brothers who blamed him for their pa dying years back. I'll never forget that last scene when Granite filled his gun and shoved two extra bullets into his pocket as he went out to face all eight brothers in a shoot-out."

Seth wanted to ask how the hero could possibly get out of such a mess. Even if he killed the first six brothers, surely the other two could get him while he reloaded. But Seth couldn't ask. After all, he was the one who was supposed to have written the book.

True leaned closer to Dan. "Well, we need a hideout like Granite found in that book."

"You mean the fake wall in the old Civil War widow's house where they used to hide runaway slaves, or the box canyon where you could only enter by rolling a rock away from a tiny tunnel?"

Seth shook his head. He had a feeling they were going to be one widow and one box canyon short tonight.

True's voice suddenly filled with hope. "Yes, that's just what we need. Somewhere safe to stay out of harm's way. And no one but you, Mr. Miller, is to know where we are."

"You trust me?" The little man seemed to grow an inch before their eyes.

"Of course," True answered. "You've got blue eyes and blue-eyed people can never lie without looking away."

Seth glanced at True as if she'd just said the dumbest thing he'd ever heard. Dan Miller looked at her as if she was spouting some old sage saying he hadn't heard until this very moment.

"Is that so?" Dan whispered, amazed.

"It's true." Seth tried to sound as if he believed such a ridiculous statement. "You're the only one we trust to help us find a hideout."

"So where can we hide?" True asked.

Dan sighed. "I don't know of anywhere like the canyon or the widow's place around here. About the best I could do is offer you the basement of the newspaper office for the rest of the night."

He smiled at his own idea. "Then I could put you on the first train out of here in the morning. I'll be working all night. No one can get to the basement without passing my desk. I might not be able to stop them, but I'd make enough racket so's they didn't catch you by surprise."

"That sounds grand." Seth didn't like the idea of staying anywhere near Galveston, but they couldn't very well leave with True dressed as she was. "I'll give you a note for a Dr. Audrey Gates. She'll get Miss McCormick a change of clothes—but she's not to know where we are. The less people who know the better." He could just see Audrey and Link showing up tonight.

Seth couldn't shake the feeling they'd been followed

from Audrey's house earlier tonight. Audrey might lead someone to them if she knew where they were.

With a backward glance, he checked to make sure they were alone on the beach.

For a moment he thought he saw a man melt into the darkness between two rocks. But nothing moved near them. Everyone awake at this hour was still running around the fire.

"We'll be safe till dawn," Seth whispered to True. "Then, if we can make it to the train, I know a place where no one will find us."

TWENTY-SEVEN

Folks call the basement of most newspaper offices "the morgue," a place where old news goes to die. True could smell years of rotting paper and see shadowy piles stacked higher than her head. Wooden file cabinets lined one wall where someone had made an effort years ago to organize the place.

"It's not as bad as it looks." Dan smiled as he handed True a medicine kit. "People do get lost down here, but they usually find their way out in a few days."

Seth glanced at the young reporter just to make sure he was kidding. "This will be fine." Any place that was dry and away from the fire would do.

"There's a few blankets in the back, but I wouldn't swear how clean they are." Dan picked up his camera and suddenly seemed in a hurry to be gone. He'd pumped them with questions all the way from the beach, and now he had nothing more to say. "Remember if anyone walks in while I'm working, I'll stomp twice on the floor. That way you'll know to keep hidden and blow out the light."

"We got it." Seth took the candle from Dan. "Don't worry about us. Just make sure you send a message to Dr. Gates to have a bag for True at the train station in the morning."

"Yes, sir." Dan looked as if he wanted to salute but wasn't sure he should. "I'll see you in a few hours." He disappeared up the stairs.

Seth glanced at True, who stood a few steps higher up than him. "Do you think we can trust him?"

"As much as we can trust anyone." True looked lovely in the light of a single candle, but her voice was sharp. "Probably more than I can trust you."

Her words stung. Seth could not remember a time when anyone he knew wouldn't trust him. He'd gone out of his way in the years he'd managed the store always to be fair.

"I tried to explain to you on the beach. I thought I'd go over and talk with Link while it was still dark. If it hadn't been for the fire, I'd have been back before you woke up."

"I only asked for you to hold me till dawn." True raised her chin slightly. "You needn't worry, I'll never ask something as impossible of you again."

Seth had never wanted to hold anyone as dearly as he ached to hold her now. She was standing two steps away from him, but she might as well have been a mile. All he'd wanted to do was love her and he'd let her down.

"I didn't intend to hurt you," he finally said. "The time we were together tonight was—"

"There was no time between us," True interrupted. "It never happened." She sat the medicine kit down and began looking for supplies to clean the small cut on the back of Seth's head.

He moved a step closer. "You can't do that with life, True. You can't just rip the page out like you can in a book. What happens, happens. It's real even if you call it a game and never talk of it."

"It never happened if I say it never did." Guiding his shoulder, True turned him around so she could look at his cut. "Life's just a story we tell ourselves each day. Do you really think all the stories and memories folks talk about are true? No. They're just versions of what people wish happened or what they'd like to believe."

"But not us." Seth fought the urge to shake her and make her see just how real he was.

True dabbed at the cut with alcohol. "Oh, of course not us. You're everything you appear to be, Mr. Westwind. And me, I'm exactly what you see."

"Don't call me Westwind," Seth demanded.

"Don't try and make me believe anything between us could be real." She gave up her effort at doctoring. The wound was obviously of little worry to him. "We've both only been caught up in a story, an adventure, nothing more."

He wanted to scream that everything between them was real. That she was the only real thing in his life and all the rest was a walking dream. He wanted to tell her that the time they'd spent in the hotel was the most alive he'd ever been or would ever be if he lived a hundred years.

"This is real," he whispered as he leaned and kissed her cheek.

He'd thought she'd pull away and yell at him for kissing her again without asking, but she remained like stone.

"And this is real," he added as his lips moved lightly against hers. The knowledge that she could pull away at any moment was intoxicating.

She stared at him as if determined to ignore his actions and prove to him that the kiss was not part of her world.

Seth leaned and placed the candle on a higher step behind her. Now her face was in shadows, but he could still see her mouth pouting like a stubborn child's.

His finger slid along the front of the unbuttoned duster she wore and shoved the coat open. Her town shirt was little armor against the warmth of his caress. With a feather-light touch he moved his hands to the sides of her body then from hip to shoulder.

"So you're not real, True McCormick. You're only a story I tell myself."

Her body trembled slightly as he brushed the tips of her breasts.

"I'm having the most wonderful adventure in my mind." His fingers grew bolder, warming her skin through the shirt she wore. "I'm imagining the most beautiful woman in the world is standing before me." He kissed her mouth, lightly pulling at her bottom lip. "She's silently begging for my touch. A touch that she'll never forget, no matter how much she says it never happened. And the reason she'll never forget is I'll always hold the memory of her in my heart and soul until the day I die."

He brushed her hair away from her ear and kissed her neck. "Stop me, True, if you don't want this to be real."

She moved closer with a tiny cry of need. As he pressed his mouth against hers, her lips opened in welcome.

He tasted her deep and full, as if she were the only meal of passion he'd ever have. His fingers slid down her chest and cupped a full breast in his grip. As his hand tightened, she cried softly with pleasure against his mouth.

Suddenly he couldn't stand the material of the shirt between them. He shoved the cotton aside and felt the perfection of her flesh. She was alive and real in his hands. A woman of fire and passion. A real woman. She could play all the make-believe she liked, he needed only the reality of her so near.

He'd never thought about couples making love anywhere except their beds, but he wanted to love her here and now on the steps. If they went any lower into the room, they'd be in the filth of the basement. If they climbed any higher, they'd be in danger. This was the nowhere land where they'd have to make heaven.

"Sit back," he whispered as his hand spread across her abdomen. He loved the feel of her. He would have never believed that just the slightest touch of a woman could make him forget how to breathe.

When she opened her mouth to question, he kissed her

and gently lowered her to the steps. The long duster buffered the wood against her back. He was careful not to rest his weight on her. He knelt between her legs and gently kissed her breasts.

When she arched her back in response, he pulled a peak into his mouth. One hand spread across the inside of her thigh while he braced her back with his other arm.

As she cried softly in pleasure, he returned to her mouth for a long kiss. He could feel her body growing warm in his hands. Her breasts strained for his touch, and her legs circled around his waist. He wanted the kiss to satisfy her, and though he wanted more, he could wait as long as his fingers could explore every inch of her body. Her arms wrapped around his neck and pulled him closer as if she had to have one more taste, one more embrace before life pulled them forever apart.

Her fingers plowed into his hair. When he flinched as her nails touched his wound, her caress turned loving and her lips softened to velvet.

Finally, he broke the kiss and pulled her up off the stairs. Sitting down on the step, he drew her into his arms. As perfect as a dream, she came to him, soft and loving and warm.

He liked the freedom she had now to show him of her pleasure. When he kissed her deeply, she pressed her breasts against him. When he stroked her gently, she moved her bottom back and forth in his lap.

"True," he whispered. "You're driving me insane."

She laughed as she unbuttoned his shirt. "Maybe it's my way of making you pay for leaving me tonight."

"Then pull away now if it's only revenge because I plan on making love to you."

"I'm too interested to see how."

Seth pulled her mouth back to his as her fingers moved

against the wall of his chest. Her hands were small and warm, with nails just long enough to tickle as they raked across his chest.

"I can't get enough of the feel of you," he whispered as his hands moved over her.

Laughing, she agreed. "I know what you mean." She lightly brushed her hands over the hair across his chest. "I . . ."

A pounding silenced True. Someone upstairs was stomping around deliberately trying to make noise.

"That's Dan's warning," Seth whispered as he leaned above them and pinched out the candle.

As silently as they could, they stood. True tied her shirt closed and pulled on the duster.

"Do we go up and see who it is, or down and hide?"

He could hear the excitement in her voice.

"We can't stay here," he answered, not sure which way to turn. If they went up, they could be walking into a fight. If they went down, he wasn't sure how True would react to one of the many rats he'd caught glimpses of in the basement.

"I hate rats." True read his mind. "I'll bet the basement is full of them."

"Then we fight," Seth answered.

He took two steps toward the door before she stopped him. "Wait. If we were followed here, they'll be armed. We wouldn't have a chance. My guns are at Audrey's place, and you checked yours at the Harvey House before we were kidnapped."

Seth had a sick feeling in the pit of his stomach that he'd regret asking, but he whispered, "What's your plan?" He couldn't see her face in the darkness, but he'd have bet her eyes were dancing.

"Micah told me once that some of these old newspaper

shops have a secret way out in case an angry citizen comes running in demanding to see a reporter."

"Great!" Seth sighed as he followed her down the steps.

"A secret way out would naturally be in the basement," she reasoned aloud.

"Or up the chimney, or out the back door." Seth tried to keep from laughing. "Or maybe there's a secret panel where we could hide. Who knows, maybe the Civil War widow built it the last time she passed through Galveston. Or better yet, the basement covers a box canyon entrance."

"Don't you dare laugh at those stories," True pulled him between the stacks of newspapers. "That was a great plot twist. The readers loved it."

Seth followed, trying to sound serious. "Answer me one question. If there is a secret way out of this place, why didn't Dan tell us about it?"

"Maybe he's too young to know. They don't just tell everyone who works on the paper, or it wouldn't be secret."

Seth tried to see the logic, but in the dark, dodging stacks of dusty paper and listening for rats, it wasn't easy.

"If I were putting in a secret exit," True continued, "I'd put it by that old wood-burning heater."

Seth had noticed an old Sunshine stove in one corner when they entered. It looked as if no one had burned anything in it for years. True pulled him in the direction of the stove.

Another loud pounding came from above, as though something the weight of a body had hit the floor. They heard someone running.

"No." Seth pulled at her arm. "If I were building a way out, it would open into the alley."

"If you were building," True repeated. "How many offices have you put up in your lifetime?"

Seth wanted to answer. "More than I can count," but he doubted she'd believe him.

"If I remember from glancing around when we came down, the walls are rock everywhere we could see. That leaves only one place for a wood wall and an escape door. Behind the steps."

True hesitated.

"That's also the only place they could come and go from this room without being seen from the door on the ground floor," Seth added. "The only safe exit."

She moved with him behind the stairs. Staying as close as she could to him, she still couldn't block out the sound of small rodents rushing past her bare toes.

Seth raised his hands and began to pound lightly on the wall.

"They'll hear you," True whispered.

"If they're here for us, they'll be down in a few minutes anyway. If they're not, they'll think we're only noisy rats."

True pressed against his back. "I wish you wouldn't use that word."

"What word?"

"Rats."

The third time Seth tapped he heard the hollow sound of a passageway behind the board. "You were right," he said, genuinely surprised. "There may be a secret passage."

"Would I lie?" True asked, as if offended that he ever questioned her word.

Seth didn't answer; he was too occupied with feeling along the wall for a way to open the door. To his amazement the wall slid open as smoothly and silently as a drawing room door. "Nice work," he whispered, admiring whoever had built the exit.

"Shall we go?" True was suddenly impatient.

They stepped through the porthole a moment before the

basement door opened from above. As Seth slid the panel back into place, he heard four men thundering down the stairs. Light flooded the basement, but the intruders would have to reach the bottom of the stairs to see the passageway. Seth closed the door.

He waited for a moment in total darkness, listening to the shouts of men just beyond the wood.

True moved behind him, feeling her way. "It looks like whoever built the escape spent most of his time on the door and left the passageway mud." She could feel cool, wet dirt pushing up between her toes.

Bending forward, Seth moved up the sharp incline toward the outside world. "If this gets any smaller, I'll be on my knees."

True moved on, hating the way the mud weighted her feet and legs as she packed layer after layer on with every step. "I hope Dan's all right."

"We'll find out later," Seth answered as he felt ahead of True for the end of the tunnel. "If he's unharmed, my guess is he'll meet us at the train station. He said he had to work all night and couldn't leave until the morning edition went out."

"Morning," she whispered, knowing that by then they'd either be safe, or dead.

TWENTY-EIGHT

Seth pressed his shoulder against the door to the outside entrance of the passage and shoved as hard as he could. The door gave only a few inches, but cool night air drifted into the tunnel.

"Something's blocking the exit," he whispered as he shoved again and gained only an inch.

True reached her hand through the opening and pulled back a broken bottle. "There's trash piled up outside. I guess it's been a few years since anyone used this way out."

Seth shoved again, but with each try the door moved only slightly. He pushed his arm through the opening and tried once more, but little movement happened. He was not only trying to open a door that had been weather-beaten for years, but trying to move the trash in front of it as well. With each inch he gained, the trash's weight seemed to double.

"Let me help." True dug her toes into the mud and pushed with all her might. Only the movement of her feet sliding deeper into the mud changed with her effort.

Seth let out a long breath. "It's no use. We'll have to stay here until the men in the basement leave, then go back the way we came."

As he finished, the hollow sound of someone pounding on the basement walls echoed in the tunnel.

"They're looking for the passageway!" True whispered in panic.

"Well, if we found it, they'll find it," Seth answered as he tried once more to open the jammed door.

"Move out of the way." True stripped off the duster she wore and pressed past Seth. "I think I can make it through the opening."

"No," Seth said, but he moved aside. "It's impossible."

True threaded her body through the space an inch at a time.

"Watch out for broken glass," Seth whispered when he realized she might have a chance of squeezing through.

"Don't worry." True laughed. "With the amount of mud I've got on my legs, I might as well be wearing moccasins."

Seth watched her melt away. She'd made it! True was safe. "Run," he whispered to the open space where she'd stood only a moment before. "Run, my darling."

The pounding below grew louder. It would only be a few heartbeats before the men found the sliding door. Seth would be an easy target when they threw light into the tunnel.

He turned slowly to face his destiny. He wasn't a hero, but he wouldn't die begging for his life. Even if this were the end for him, he didn't regret coming to Galveston. If he hadn't taken the train, he'd never have met True. He'd been looking for his brother's killer, but he'd found his own life. Seth had lived more in these few days with True than he could have lived if he'd stayed in Timber Creek into his old age.

A rush of air brushed past him, telling Seth that they'd opened the silent sliding door at the bottom of the tunnel. Any moment light would fill the space and he'd hear gunfire.

Seth closed his eyes and took his last deep breath. He could hear voices from below. Men were coming in. He held True's face in his mind, wanting his last thoughts to be of her.

Something touched his sleeve. "Seth," True whispered. "Try again."

Guided only by the sound of her voice, Seth shoved once more at the door. It gave slightly. He could hear True on the other side frantically throwing trash out of the way.

"Again!" she insisted.

The door gave another few inches, then another.

Seth shoved his shoulder through the opening, then his leg. He tried to move carefully past the rough door, but True pulled him to her.

As his head cleared the opening, he saw light flood the tunnel.

True grabbed his hand. "Run!" she ordered.

Seth followed her. They ran again, madly, wildly, through the streets of Galveston. He had no idea where they were going. He realized it didn't matter. He was alive and with True.

They ran for what seemed hours, resting in dark corners, moving like shadows through the town. When they felt safe enough, they would talk and try to reason out a safe place to hide. Most of the time they walked silently, giving no one a reason to notice their passing.

"If we can get out of Galveston," Seth finally said, "I know a place were we can hole up a few days." He knew taking her back to Timber Creek would make a lie of what she believed him to be, but it was the only safe place he could think of. What difference did a lie make if she were killed?

True smiled. "If we're going to get out, we have to reach the train yard before dawn. I'll never get past folks unnoticed once it's daylight."

Seth agreed. Between the ripped shirt and the mud, she was a sight. Nothing remained of the proper Miss McCormick he'd met. The creature before him was as wild and free as the night wind, and more beautiful than midnight lightning.

They moved around the corner of the Harvey House. Seth could already hear the early crew in the kitchen preparing breakfast. The smell of baked bread and ham frying blended with the oil and smoke of the train yard.

True darted across the open yard and into her private car. The railroad men had pushed the car to a side track waiting for her orders.

Seth looked around before he followed. Nothing was out of order. A few railroad employees stood several yards away, near the engine, and a porter slept on an empty baggage cart, but none of the passengers had arrived.

As Seth took the first step up to the car, True leaned out the window. She'd taken the cover off one of the pullman sleepers and was using it as a shawl. "Tell someone I need to talk to Smokey Shelburn."

Seth looked around. "Tell who?" He didn't want to go anywhere but inside. It had been so long since he'd slept, the world was starting to look fuzzy all around him.

"There're men already eating in the Harvey House kitchen. One of them will know who Smokey is. He's got to make arrangements to hitch this car up if we plan to leave this morning."

Seth backed off the train. "Anything else?"

"Yes. Ask Smoky if he can have one of the boys at the Harvey House deliver me some hot water. I have to have a bath." True giggled. "That's something I never thought I'd say. There was a time during my childhood when I avoided bathing."

Seth was too tired to see any humor. "Anything else?"

"Breakfast," True added. "Ask the house to make us breakfast and put it on my bill."

Seth started walking off before she came up with any more orders.

"Wait!" True shouted.

Seth turned around. "What else?"

"Nothing," she said hesitantly making it obvious that there had been something else, but that she had wisely decided not to ask. "We'll have to work on your problem with taking orders later."

"Maybe we'll work on your not giving so many," Seth mumbled as he walked off trying to remember everything she'd told him.

By the time he'd found Smokey, ordered breakfast, and talked someone into delivering water, the horizon had turned a light purple color. People were arriving for the first train out. A few early salesmen who probably hadn't slept well in the hotel milled about, along with several college boys dressed in A&M uniforms, who looked as if they hadn't gone to bed at all.

Seth watched for trouble without taking his attention off True's car. He guessed she needed a little privacy, but he didn't feel comfortable without her in his sight. He bought a paper and leaned against the corner of the building.

"Psst," someone whispered from behind him. "Psst, Mr. Westwind."

Seth looked around but saw no one. He rubbed his whiskery face hard. He'd been so long without sleep, he was starting to hear things. No wonder. In the last two days he'd been in a gunfight, kidnapped, almost drowned, and survived a fire. If voices were all that bothered him, Seth figured he was well ahead of the game.

"Psst," the voice came again. "Mr. Westwind."

Again Seth looked around him. Nothing.

"Look down," the voice ordered.

Seth looked at the platform on which he stood. Between the cracks he could barely make out a tiny face. "Emily?"

"Hello, Mr. Westwind."

"What are you doing there?"

"Audrey had Marie bring True's stuff over as soon as she got the note from the newspaperman. Marie told me to stay here sitting on it until you or True came along. I fell asleep once and was afraid I missed you."

Seth laughed aloud and watched a few salesman fold up their papers and move farther from him. For a moment he stared at them, then he realized what a picture he must be. A muddy man in wrinkled, smoke-stained clothes standing on an empty platform talking to himself. No wonder they moved away.

"Meet me at the steps," he whispered to Emily.

He walked slowly to the end of the platform and glanced around until he was sure no one was looking. Then quickly he stepped off the wooden walkway and crawled into the dark space below.

Emily jumped into his arms. "Mr. Westwind. I was so worried about you and True when I saw the fire. I figured you were both dead for sure this time."

She rubbed her hand along his chin. "Mr. Westwind, you look terrible. Did you have to sleep in the alley last night?"

Seth lifted her hand off his face. "I wish I'd had the chance."

Emily's eyes widened with sadness for a moment before she brightened. "The doc packed you and True all kinds of things in this bag."

Seth lifted the bag. "Feels like a cannon in here. How come you ended up over at Doc's house?"

Emily took his free hand as they walked toward the train. "'Cause somebody was up using the chamber pot." She paused and wrinkled her nose. "Someone's always up using the chamber pot at night. So I figure they must have seen the fire and screamed, 'cause before I knew what was going on, everyone was yelling and screaming.

"Anyway, I started running on account of you being there. But by the time I got to the hotel, no one would let me near the place. The doc passed by me while I was sitting in the sand crying. Two men looked like they were arresting her. I didn't know what to do so I grabbed onto her leg and cried louder."

Seth looked down at the child. He could almost see the sight. "So what happened?"

"The men felt sorry for the doc on account of her having such a screamin' kid, I figure. They talked to her real mean then let her go."

Seth laughed. The deputies were willing to fight with one angry doctor, but the cries of a child were too much for them. He lifted the little girl onto the steps of True's car.

"Doc said if I waited until you got here, I could stay for breakfast."

"Then you must join us." He wondered if even now at the orphanage Emily had enough to eat. He'd seen the children sit down in shifts at the table, and their plates never looked full.

When they walked into the car, Seth could hear True in the back splashing. A Harvey girl had just finished spreading on the table a breakfast that looked like enough for ten people. She turned and faced Seth. "Will that be all, sir?"

She'd been well trained, he thought. She treated him with the same respect she would have shown if he'd been dressed in his best.

"Yes," he said and held the door for her, "and thank you."

"Oh, you're welcome, Mr. Westwind," the waitress answered. "And may I say we're very glad you and True are back and safe. I placed the guns you left with us yesterday on the back of your chair."

Seth looked puzzled as she left. "Gossip must travel fast around here," he whispered to Emily. "She didn't even look surprised to see me alive."

"Why should she?" Emily asked as she stole a roll from the table. "Everyone's been talking about you since the paper hit the corners about five this morning."

"What paper?"

"The one you got under your arm." Emily eyed the fruit basket. "I can't read, but the picture tells it all."

Seth dropped the suitcase and opened the morning newspaper he'd forgotten he carried. There on the front page was a photo of the Beach Front Hotel fire. The headline suggested that the fire might have been set, and Dan Miller had the byline. But what stopped Seth's heart was the picture.

The camera must have been flashed as he broke the balcony railing. Fire was all around him and smoke bellowed from both sides of the French doors, but anyone could see him clearly as he held True in his arms and jumped.

Below the picture the caption read, "Westwind saves woman from certain death."

"You saved her, didn't you, Mr. Westwind? Just like you do in your books, you saved her."

Seth's eyes blurred as he tried to read Dan Miller's account of the fire and the rescue. The reporter even told about how they'd managed to escape from the kidnappers. The only thing he'd left out was that they were leaving by train this morning.

The noise that had panicked them in the basement probably hadn't been the kidnappers at all. It had probably only been the early shift coming to work so they could get the paper out by morning.

Emily broke into Seth's thoughts. "I heard one of the salesman say that he figured that photo will be delivered to every whistle-stop along the rails in twenty-four hours."

"That's it!" Seth slapped the newspaper against his leg. "This charade has got to end today."

He stormed off toward the back of the car.

Emily only smiled down when she heard True's angry scream. The child figured Mr. Westwind and True had some fighting to do and she might as well start breakfast before it got cold.

TWENTY-NINE

"Get out of here!" A bar of soap missed Seth's head by an inch.

"Not until we've talked." Seth slammed the tin door closed and planted his feet wide apart in the tiny space referred to only as the necessary room. He tried to force himself to look anywhere except at the hip tub True was sitting in. Unfortunately his eyes didn't seem to want to cooperate. "We have to get this mess about Westwind straightened out now," he said, forcing his voice to sound calmer than he felt.

True smiled, loving the sight of him turning red. He might be trying to look calm, but she could see the muscle along his jaw twitching. "Can't it wait until I've finished my bath?" She had several towels within reach, but she didn't cover herself. It didn't seem any great crime to allow him to see what he'd already touched in the shadows of night.

"It's waited for too long now." Seth forced himself to stand his ground, but the sight of her was intoxicating. He felt as if his brain had dried to jerky from the heat generated by just looking at her. Her hair was wet and pulled up off her shoulders by a wide blue ribbon. Her skin was creamy and covered in patches with soap bubbles. When the bubbles popped, she seemed to sparkle for a moment. Her breasts floated just above the water. They were shiny with moisture and peaked to perfection. The gentleman in him wanted to ask her to cover herself; the man in him would never make such a foolish suggestion.

"So you're just going to stand there and watch me bathe?" She leaned back in the tub, revealing even more of the body he loved so dearly to touch.

He didn't answer. He wasn't sure he could force any words past the lump in his throat. All he could do was watch the water lap gently against her flesh, caressing her with tender strokes. The room was warm with moisture, but he felt as if he were standing in an oven.

True smiled and lifted her leg out of the water. With long movements she soaped her limb. "Well, what is it that's so important you have to invade my privacy to discuss it?"

"I . . ." Seth couldn't continue. He'd lost the ability to form words. She was the most beautiful thing he'd ever seen, and the knowledge that she didn't seem the least embarrassed to have him watch her was more than he could comprehend. True should be yelling at him. He should be leaving. But no. She was enjoying his shock, and he was loving her performance.

True rinsed her leg and started washing the other one as though he were nothing more than a paper man standing before her. "So," she whispered almost casually, "you want to get this Westwind thing straightened out?"

"Yes." Seth attempted to pull himself together. He was no pup at his first saloon show. He'd seen postcards of women who didn't have much more on than True did now. And he'd been to the stockyard saloons in Forth Worth where they had a picture of a completely nude woman hanging right over the bar. He could handle this discussion if she could. "Westwind has got to come forward right away."

True washed the soap off her leg and watched him closely. "Is that the only way?"

"Yes." Seth wet his lips as he watched drops of water slowly trickle down her calf and plop into the tub. He wanted to kiss her so badly. Not on the cheek or mouth, where everyone else kisses, but all over. He wanted to taste the skin she'd just washed and run his tongue along the inside of her thigh, where the smell of her soap must linger.

"All right. What's your plan?" True stood slowly, letting the bubbly water slide down her body. As she reached for a towel, she turned her backside to him.

Seth had to order every muscle to freeze. His hands knotted into fists from the need to touch her. This discussion had to happen if they were both going to stay alive, but right now he'd have rather died in her arms. No postcard or nude painting had had the effect on him that watching True did.

Pulling the towel around her, True pushed her breasts closer together. She twisted a knot just high enough over her cleavage to hold up the towel. Tugging the ribbon from her hair, she shook out the clean, damp curls.

"True." Seth held himself in check but felt his very nerves mutinying from his body as they strained toward her. "Tell me where Westwind is and I'll talk to him. Whatever it takes, I'll make him understand that he can't risk our lives any longer. He's got to come forward and tell the press who he really is."

True looked at him closely. For the first time since he'd entered the room, the laughter left her expression. "I can't," she said simply, as if that were the end of the discussion.

Seth saw something he thought he'd never see in True McCormick's eyes. Fear.

"Tell me where he is," Seth said more gently. "You've no need to be afraid of him." Seth couldn't believe Westwind was the kind of man to instill such fear in True. "I'll see that he doesn't hurt you." What had Westwind threatened to do if she told his whereabouts? Whatever it was, Seth would find a way to protect her.

"I'm not afraid *of* Westwind." True raised her chin. "I'm afraid *for* him."

Seth couldn't believe she was willing to face all the danger for her boss. Wasn't he a man? Couldn't he take care of himself? "Westwind will be all right. The law can take care of him just like they try to do us." Seth suddenly realized that the law wasn't doing to good a job of watching after them. Maybe True had a right to be worried about Westwind. Maybe he was old and alone. Maybe he couldn't take care of himself.

Seth couldn't stand the pain in her blue eyes any longer. He moved slowly toward her, knowing that he was still covered in dirt, but he had to hold her. "Don't worry, darling. I'll stay with Westwind awhile if need be. I'll make sure he comes to no harm. He just has to step forward with the truth. Then this will all blow over and folks will forget all about who is the real Westwind."

She swallowed hard and moved into his arms. "I can't," she whispered. "My career will be over."

Seth pulled her tight. "Don't worry about that. You'll find a secretarial job somewhere else if that's what you want." She felt so good in his arms. She smelled of honey and roses. He wished he could find the words to tell her that she didn't have to worry about working at all. He wanted to take care of her. But now wasn't the time to think of forever, and she'd already told him what she thought of marriage.

"There will never be another Westwind book." True pushed away and turned toward the windows. "You don't understand; there are people depending on the money from the next Westwind book and the one after that and the one after that."

"That's not your problem." Seth wanted to pull her back in his arms, but she was pacing now. The word "marriage" kept rolling around in his thoughts, as if it had always been there but never found a place to come out. He had to fight not to say it.

"Yes, it is my problem," she shouted. "You can't just come in and tell Westwind to step forward. It may seem simple to you, but it's not. Westwind had kept his identity a secret for too many years to have the truth explode now."

Seth could see there was no use talking with her. Her loyalty to Westwind was too great. She was willing to risk her life and his to protect the man. He admired her loyalty and was jealous of whoever this writer was that he could hold such control over her. "All right." Seth finally held up his palms in surrender. "Don't tell me. I can find out for myself. Audrey told me she'd make the introduction to Westwind if I needed one. I don't need your help."

"Audrey promised not to tell anyone!" True's voice held an ounce of panic.

"She'll tell me when she realizes she may be saving your life."

True hesitated. She knew he was right; he could see it in the way she bit back her bottom lip. "If she tells you, I'll never speak to her again."

"If you're dead, you'll never talk to her either. I think Audrey would rather face you angry than dead silent." He reached for the door lever.

"You can't go now. The train will be leaving in a few minutes."

"I've got time to get to Audrey's and back." Seth knew he was bluffing. He would be lucky to get to the street and back before the train pulled out.

"They'll be looking for you. They'll shoot you down in the streets." Worry made True's voice a bit higher.

Seth took a step toward her, as if he'd finally made her see what had to be done. He gripped her shoulder and made her face him directly. "Then you tell me who he is. I've got to see him before we're both dead."

True moved away from his touch, but the red imprint of

his fingers remained on her skin. "All right!" she shouted. "I'll tell you."

She took a step away and touched the knot holding her towel together. "How would you like to see all of Granite Westwind?"

Seth had no idea what she was doing. He watched as she untied the towel and let it drop to the floor. She stood before him proud and angry.

"Don't play games with me. Where is he, True?" Seth had to see them safe before he touched her, no matter how she tortured him.

"He's right before you," she answered. "I'm Granite Westwind."

"What!" An invisible railroad tie must have slapped silently against his forehead, for he felt the blow though he didn't see or hear it.

"I wrote all those books." She moved closer. "So tell me what you need to. I'm Granite Westwind."

"You can't . . . ," Seth started and regretted the words as soon as they passed his lips.

Fire warmed her cheeks. "Why? Because I'm a woman. Because I'm helpless? Why couldn't I have written those books?"

He felt as if he were standing on the only inch of solid ground in miles. He wasn't about to say a word and step off into the quicksand.

"I've listened to lawmen and railroaders tell stories all my life. But I knew that, like you, New York would never believe a woman could write a novel about the West. So I made up Westwind. I made him up so real that I almost believed he lived."

True lifted her towel, but didn't cover herself as she took a step closer. "Then I walked into the jail a few days ago and Westwind did come to life. You're him. You're everything

I've always thought he'd be. Right down to his faults. You're overprotective, stubborn, and a no-account drifter who would never allow anyone to mean anything to you. You're a fighter who'll never be tied down. How dare you come in here telling me you have a right to ruin my life?"

She grabbed the end of the towel and hit him hard across the face with it. "Get out!"

The railroad car jerked as it hooked onto the rest of the train. Seth shifted to steady himself. He pulled the towel from his eyes and turned.

"Get out!" she screamed.

He didn't know what to say. He felt as if all hope had been shot from him. He'd hesitated to dream that True might be happy with him when he thought she was a secretary, but now that he knew she was one of the hottest dime novelists in the country, there was no hope. He was tired and hungry and dirty. He didn't want to think. For the first time, he was afraid to think.

Seth walked out of the room without a word.

True pulled her clothes from the suitcase he'd brought while she muttered every swear word in every language she'd ever heard. She had known this would happen if she told him what her pen name was. No man was able to accept the fact that the small woman before him could tell tall tales that would interest every adventurous soul in the country. He thought her a freak. She might as well have shown him another head growing out of her back.

Without giving much thought to what her hands did, True assembled the Winchester "take down" rifle Audrey had packed in the suitcase.

She couldn't get the look on his face out of her mind. That "Oh, my God!" Look that told her she was no longer a woman he wanted to hold, but a curiosity folks were charged to see at the fair.

Once the rifle was loaded, True set it aside and pulled on her clothes. She took great care in putting up her hair. Micah was right. He'd told her over and over to tell no one. No man will ever look at you the same after he knows, Micah used to say. And no matter how good the stories are, men won't read them if they think a woman wrote them.

She stood staring out the window. Seth didn't seem to want to look at her at all once he knew. The sight of her body had driven him mad before, but once he knew she was Westwind, he couldn't get out of the room fast enough.

"It doesn't matter," True lied to herself. "I have to do what I have to do."

Someone tapped on the door, and True felt hope dance across her nerves. Maybe he'd understand if she explained where all her money from the Westwind novels went.

But Emily was the only guest waiting when True opened the door.

"Hello." Emily smiled as if she'd just dropped by for a visit and they weren't on a train leaving town. "Mr. Westwind told me to come in here and tell you I forgot to get off before the train started."

True smiled remembering how she'd used that lie a few times herself when she was Emily's age. "And what else did he say?"

"Nothing." Emily walked around the room looking at everything. "I think he had something else on his mind, but he didn't say anything. I figured he must be mad at the chair, though, 'cause he kicked it several times before he sat down."

Emily handed True a biscuit. "I brought you a biscuit with some bacon in it."

"Thanks." True took the offering. "That was kind."

"Just repaying an old debt." Emily winked. "Besides, maybe I'm your guardian angel this time. Looks like you and Mr. Westwind could use one. I figure I'd best tag along and try to keep the two of you out of trouble."

True looked out of the window at the passing countryside. "It doesn't look like we have much of a choice. I'll ask the porter to wire the doc that you're with us."

"Great." Emily relaxed. "What could happen to the two of you with me along to keep an eye out?"

True was afraid even to think about the answer.

THIRTY

Seth stepped off the train before it came to a full stop. He had to get away. He wasn't sure if he wanted to run from True McCormick, or from the truth. His plan to keep her safe by having the real Granite Westwind come forward had been a joke. If she told who she was, she might live but her career would die, and for some reason she wasn't about to let that happen.

"The train's only stoppin' for twenty minutes!" the conductor yelled. "Make sure you're back."

Seth didn't know if he was coming back. Maybe he should just walk out of her life now and save all the trouble. She could tell everyone Westwind had been kidnapped again, and he could go back to Timber Creek. In a few months the law would stop looking for Westwind and True could start writing more books. Everything would be back to normal for her.

But nothing would ever be back to normal for Seth. She'd turned his life upside down and made him love more deeply than he'd thought possible. Then she'd stomped on his heart. He'd fallen in love with a wild young girl who was beautiful and bright and full of a dizzy kind of madness that made him laugh. Now he knew she was also famous and, no doubt, richer than he'd ever be. He couldn't ask the country's most well-known writer to settle down in a little town where the biggest excitement was a Saturday night barn dance.

He paused a moment when he reached the street in this

town too small to bother putting a name on the water storage beside the station. A cafe was on the right, a saloon on the left. Most of the passengers were lining up outside the cafe to take anything offered called lunch. Seth turned left.

Maybe if he had a few drinks he could get back on the train long enough to reach Timber Creek. He'd told the conductor that was as far as he and True were going, but now he'd be the only one getting off. She could go on as far as she wanted.

Seth downed a drink in one long swallow and ordered another. He'd been crazy to think she needed him. She didn't need anyone. About all he could do to help her was tell no one the real identity of Granite Westwind. Once Seth was away from her side, she'd be safe enough by herself. After all, no one wanted Miss McCormick dead.

Motioning for his third drink, it dawned on Seth that he had no money. This was it, he thought, the bottom. He might as well go into Timber Creek drunk and ruin what little of his life was left. He kept the bottle when the bartender passed. With no food or sleep for two days, the liquid had its desired effect on his mind within minutes.

At least he didn't have to worry about them throwing him in jail for not paying. This town was too small to have a jail.

True waited until the whistle blew a second time before she decided to look for Seth. She knew the conductor would hold the train as long as he could. How far could Seth have wandered in a town so small? Lifting the Winchester, she left the private car.

"I saw him go in that saloon when he walked away from the train." Emily danced at her side as True marched down the street. "Something's wrong with Mr. Westwind. I figure he's real bad sick, maybe even dying. He hasn't said a word all morning and he told me I could eat his breakfast."

True opened the saloon door in time to see the bartender plow his fist into Seth's face.

"I'll teach you to try and cheat me!" the bartender yelled as he hit Seth again.

"Stop!" True shouted and raised the rifle to shoulder level.

The bartender held Seth's limp body up with one beefy hand. His eyes traveled the length of the weapon's barrel before he decided to follow her order. "He's trying to leave without paying."

True pulled from her pocket money Audrey had included with her clothes. "I'll pay you what he owes if you'll help me get him to the train."

"I'll be glad to, miss. We don't want the likes of him around here."

Emily let out a scream when she saw her hero's face. She kicked at the bartender as he lifted Seth over his shoulder. "You bully," she cried. "You shouldn't hurt Granite Westwind. If he weren't sick, he'd kill you twice right now."

The bartender brushed her aside as if she were a gnat, but several men in the saloon whispered the name of Westwind.

True, the bartender, and Emily marched back across the street. The train was just starting to move as the bartender tossed Seth onto the platform and walked away counting his money.

True and Emily pulled him into the sitting room while the train took on speed.

"Get some water from the other room," True ordered. "Maybe we can clean up his face some."

"Should we wake him up?"

"No," True answered. She needed time to think of what she planned to do. It was obvious that Seth didn't plan to help her any longer. Even though he knew who she was, the men who kidnapped her didn't, and if they found Seth, they'd kill him before he had time to explain. Somehow she had to keep her secret and protect him as well. She must find a safe place for them both.

True brushed the side of his face gently with her fingers. He was like a Christmas present a child sees in a window, but knows he'll never own. He was a gunfighter, the last of a free type of men who were quickly dying in the West. She would destroy him if she asked too much of him, and if she held him again she wasn't sure she could ever let go.

Seth slept as hours passed and the train made another stop. When they pulled into a little town by the name of Timber Creek, the conductor stopped by to ask if True still planned to get off.

"Yes," True answered. "If you can get someone to help me with Mr. Westwind." She wasn't sure why Seth had wanted to stop in this little town, but he must have had his reasons. It was as good as any place to hole up for a few hours.

True packed her bag and waited only minutes before a young man appeared at the door and tipped a hat that looked older than him. "Welcome to Timber Creek, folks. May I be of some assistance? I got a wagon for hire waiting outside."

True stood to give the man orders. But he was already kneeling over Seth. When she turned to hand him her bag, he wasn't even looking at her.

"Lord, Lord, Mr. Atherton, what happened to you?" The young man tried to wake Seth up. "You look like something the cat drug in and Momma threw out again."

True moved closer. "You know him?"

"Of course, Miss. I reckon everyone in this town knows Mr. Seth Atherton."

"Then we must be at the right place." She wasn't sure what to say. The local man seemed to treat Seth with no small degree of respect. He also didn't appear overly afraid of Seth, which might mean the respect had been earned rather than bought with a gun. True decided to play along. "Mr. Atherton's been real ill. He took a bad fall in the last town." She thought of adding "in the mud," but that might have made her lie overwritten. "I'm his cousin from Galveston, and I decided to accompany him just to make sure he made it." She glanced at Emily. "And this is my daughter. Could you take us to the hotel?"

The young man laughed. "I don't see no use in that when you could go to Mr. Atherton's house here in town or out to the farm. It ain't but a mile to the north. He'd never allow one of his kin to spend the night in what passes as a hotel in these parts. I'm Floyd Wilkins, Luke's oldest boy. You can trust me, miss, to get you wherever you want to go safely."

"The farm," Emily chimed in. "Please, the farm, Mama."

True looked at the child. She had picked up the game quickly. "All right. The country air would probably be best for Cousin Seth."

The young man named Floyd loaded Seth onto his shoulders and staggered as he walked down the steps. "He must be real bad. The medicine he's taking smells worse than my granddad's moonshine. If I didn't know better, I'd think Mr. Atherton has taken to drinking after a lifetime of being sober."

True didn't dare say a word. She prayed Seth would stay passed out until they could get to the farm. A million questions drifted through her mind, and she planned to ask them as soon as she got Seth alone. Like how on earth did a whole town know this gunfighter's drinking habits?

When they reached Seth's land, the sun was spreading across rolling hills made for farming. The huge house looked as if it belonged in a picture and couldn't be real. A wide porch ran the length of the front, as if it had been built for a large family to congregate on and watch the sun die each day. Fruit trees and a garden large enough to feed several families stretched out behind the house.

"I'll help you get Mr. Atherton inside." Floyd jumped from the wagon. "I don't reckon there's much in the way of supplies in the house. I'll probably be able to find Hollis at the store and get him to pack you in a few things. He'll bring them by and leave them on the back porch on his way home."

"Thank you, Floyd." True climbed down from the wagon and helped Emily. "How much do I owe you?"

Floyd looked puzzled. "Why, nothing, miss. I'm glad to do it. I'll put the groceries on the Atherton bill. I might take money from strangers passing through, but I'd never dream of taking something from Mr. Atherton."

"How long have you known Mr. Atherton?" True held the door as Floyd carried him in.

"Why, all my life, miss. Or all of it so far." Floyd smiled and stepped through the door. "There ain't much in the way of furniture in this place. I ain't never been inside, but I heard folks talk about how Mr. Atherton lost all interest in doin' up the place after his wife died. He built a house big enough for more than a dozen children and doesn't even furnish most of it. He comes out here and stays sometimes, though. I've seen his father working in the garden when I pass by in the summers. The old man's funny. He likes to keep to himself. I reckon all the Athertons are that way."

"Seth must have fallen apart when his wife died." True pointed Floyd toward a long couch.

Floyd dropped his load on the one piece of furniture in the room. "I don't know about that, miss. I was only a kid, but from what I hear he more likely tried to work himself to death. Folks said he was up at his hardware store from dawn till midnight with never a day's rest except the Lord's day, of course. Then he'd go to church and spend the rest of the day out here alone, with Johnny and the old man Atherton. I don't remember him ever taking a day off work except a few short business trips until he boarded that train more'n a week ago."

True tried to hide her shock. "How is Johnny?" She wanted to scream "Who is Johnny?" but she didn't dare.

Floyd smiled. "He's fine, growing like a weed in spring. Folks was talking a few days ago about how the boy should be back in a little over a week. I bet he missed his dad something bad, being only six and all. Mr. Atherton pays a lady to keep him, but the boy is up at the store pestering his dad half the day. I think he's just lonely being an only child and all."

"I can't wait to see him," True whispered. "Does he still look just like Seth?"

"That he does," Floyd nodded. "Some of the womenfolks didn't think much of Mr. Atherton raising the boy all alone with just the old man to help, but he's done a fine job. There ain't been a morning that the boy didn't look clean and well fed, much to the old maids around here's disappointment."

True looked down at Seth. "Despite the way he looks now, he's quite a man."

"Yes, miss." Floyd added. "I reckon he's about as fine as they come. He's helped a lot of folks out, loaning them the supplies to start homesteading. Even coming out with his men and working all day to put up the frames for their homes. He takes care of a father who only wants to plant things, and raises a son, too, and I ain't never heard him complain once. I reckon he's about as near to a real hero as we'll ever have in this town."

"I'd think so," True agreed. She thought back over all the small towns she'd passed through and tried to remember what to say next. "Thank you for bringing us home. You'll be sure to stop by soon for some pie."

"I'll do that." Floyd grinned, telling True she'd said the right thing. Now if she only had an idea how to make pie.

"You want me to send out the doc to take a look at Mr. Atherton?"

"No." True walked him to the porch. "I can manage."

Floyd waved as he pulled away. "I'll drop by early and see if you need anything."

True waved until Floyd was out of sight, then headed back into the house. How dare Seth get so upset because she wasn't what she pretended to be! "Emily!" she yelled. "Can you bring some water?"

"Yes," Emily answered from somewhere upstairs where she'd been exploring. "You gonna wash Mr. Westwind?"

"No," True whispered. "I'm gonna wake him up and kill him."

THIRTY-ONE

Cold water hit Seth full force in the face, shattering him awake in one painful, icy moment. He rolled to avoid the downpour and fell two feet onto a hardwood floor.

"You lying, dirty swine!" True yelled at him loud enough to make his ears ring. "You're no more a gunfighter than I am! To think all this time I felt safe with you."

Seth wiped the water from his face and slowly opened his eyes. There she stood in all her prim and proper glory, looking very much as if she planned to have him shot at sunrise.

"What seems to be the problem, darling?" Seth's voice dripped with sarcasm. "Have a bad day killing off a few hundred outlaws with only one six-shooter? Or did the plot try to get in the way of the nonstop violence?"

If True could have killed him with her bare hands, she would have. No one had ever talked to her in such a voice. "You fake! You imposter! I'll bet you've never even killed one man in your life. You're not even a good drunk. I trusted my safety to a hardware store owner!"

Seth ran his fingers through his damp hair as he fought to control his anger. Somehow he'd gotten her home safely, but he should have known better by now than to expect a thank you. "How many men have you scalped and burned at the stake, Miss McCormick? You're far too practiced at this for me to be your first victim."

"Don't you even dare speak to me again, you low-down, small town *clerk*." She threw the pail at him, only missing by inches. "You took my money knowing I believed you to be a gunfighter. How could I have ever thought you'd be able to fill Westwind's boots?"

"What money? All I remember getting paid was a small advance, and I assure you, darling, it wasn't worth the trouble I've been through."

"Well, you don't have to worry about some crazy outlaw killing you now, because I plan on doing it myself." She came at him, but Seth had sense enough to move away.

She looked for something else to throw at him as she moved around the room. "How is it going to look if it gets out that the man playing the great Granite Westwind is a hardware store owner?"

Seth couldn't follow her logic. "The only way I'll be proved a fraud is if the public knows who the real Westwind is. How is it going to look when they find out Westwind wears a dress?"

"You won't be alive to tell anyone!"

"What have I done to make you so angry? You knew I wasn't Westwind. I told you from the first I was no hero. What difference does it make that I'm not a gunfighter? You're not a secretary."

True sat down on the couch and crossed her arms. She didn't know the answers to any of his questions, but she knew she was mad, so she said the only thing she could think to say, "I hate you, Seth Atherton."

"Oh, no." Seth's voice was mocking now. "And just when I was starting to think I was in love with you, Granite Westwind."

"Stop calling me that!"

"Why not? It's your name, isn't it? Probably just as real as True McCormick." He leaned against the back of the couch and took a long breath. He couldn't remember ever yelling so many angry words at one person in his life. They were sounding like two cross children.

"Could we stop arguing?" he said suddenly, no longer wanting to fight with her. What point would it serve? They were both not what they seemed, and all the yelling in the world wouldn't change the fact. "We've got enough problems to solve without hating each other."

True remained silent. Seth listened to her breathing as it slowed to normal. Finally, she said in a voice void of all emotion, "Don't fall in love with me, Mr. Atherton. And never call me darling again. I hate that pet name."

Seth remembered what Micah had told him just before he died. "I promise I won't fall in love with you, Miss McCormick. Any man who did would just be looking for a broken heart. As for calling you darling, I can think of a few other names if you like."

"Never mind." True stood and walked across the room as if she couldn't stand being close to him. She tried to force her voice to normal. "You have a nice farm, Mr. Atherton. It'll be a safe place to stay until morning."

Seth watched her closely. She was pulling away not just physically, but emotionally. She wanted no ties with him to remain. In her mind she was ripping up the pages they'd lived together in her life. Seth had to talk about something, anything, before he exploded at her again. "I think I can guess how we got out here. Floyd brought us. He's always near the station. Around town we have a saying, 'We don't really need telephones or telegraphs. We've got tell-Floyd.' He probably told you my entire life story on the drive out."

"Just about," True agreed. "I can't believe I was so dumb to believe that you could be a gunfighter."

Seth smiled, a slow, almost sad smile. "And I can't believe I didn't figure out that you were Westwind from the first. Micah knew, of course, and Audrey. Who else?"

"No one," True replied. "Not even my father. Micah was with me when I cooked up the idea, and he always warned me that the fewer people who knew, the better. Audrey guessed, and I couldn't hide the truth from her. She could always see me lying, even when I was a child and had already convinced everyone else."

"Can't you give up Westwind?"

"No," True answered, thinking of all the people who were depending on the money she managed to send them every year. "Writers don't make much money, but what I make, I already have spent."

Seth realized he'd lost any hope of ever having her near. He'd lost her to another man. A fictional hero he couldn't fight. A man who could never hold her as she longed to be held each night. But she was tied to him in a way Seth didn't understand. The only thing left to do was to step back like a gentleman. "I'll keep your secret, True, if that's what you want. Here in Timber Creek I'm just Seth Atherton. No one will bother me. You can make up any story you like about Westwind disappearing. You're welcome to rest for as long as you like before you move on."

True straightened into the porcelain woman she'd once been. "Thank you, but we'll be gone by morning," she whispered. There was no softness in her words or her stance. There was nothing else to say. Seth could feel his heart screaming as he stood silently watching her. He could almost see the little girl who'd run wild in the streets, always on guard for fear someone might hurt her, until finally she'd built a wall between her and the rest of the world. A wall so high she could only scale it in the late hours of the night when the need for someone to hold her was too great to be ignored.

"I told Emily she could explore the barn while I woke you up," True said as calmly as if she were in the habit of waking men with buckets of water. "I thought then we might find something for supper."

Seth looked down at his wrinkled, wet clothes. "I think I'll clean up a bit first. Go ahead and start without me. You'll find everything you need in the kitchen, and if I know Floyd, he's already had Hollis send out a box of supplies."

Seth left before he said anything else. If she wanted to be polite strangers, he could act the part. He was a gentleman, and it was about time he started behaving like one. The lady was setting the rules, and he had no choice but to follow them.

He took his time bathing and shaving. It felt good to use his own things. His razor, his soap cup, his brush. Even his clothes were a homecoming. Only the absence of a gun on his hip seemed strange. He'd gotten used to the weight of a Colt at his side. When he looked at himself in the mirror, he couldn't help but grimace. He looked as if he'd been through one of them new Western Star washers folks could order out of the Sears, Roebuck & Company catalog. No one in Timber Creek had ordered one yet, but Seth was sure they could do little more damage to his face than the past few days had done.

He pulled on his suspenders, then his four-pocket gray corduroy vest that was only a shade lighter than his trousers. Thinking it best to leave the coat off, Seth tried to part his hair. It was hopeless. The rest of him might look like a respectable businessman, but his hair seemed determined to be wild.

"I'm back to my life," he whispered, thinking of how the past week seemed like a year. He felt so much older and wiser now. He'd been thrown out of bars and into jail cells and tossed off boats and balconies. He'd fought beside a Texas Ranger and slept in the streets.

"And I've loved," he said to his reflection. "For the first

time in my life I've loved a woman so much, I'd give up the rest of my life if I could spend one more night with her in my arms."

He swallowed hard and glared into the mirror. "But you can't." He forced himself to accept each word as though his heart wouldn't hear it unless it said it aloud. "She doesn't want you to die for her. She loves another more than she could ever love you. Probably the only reason she was attracted to you was that you reminded her of him. But no longer. No one will see past the clothes now. No one will look and think they see the great Granite Westwind come to life. All anyone, including True, will see is Seth Atherton. No gunfighter. No romantic hero of the West. Just a man. A man so full of loneliness he's more afraid of living without her than he was of dying with her."

He took his pocket watch from the dresser drawer and began winding it. The photograph of Marcy looked back at him from inside the watch as it had since the day they'd married and she'd given him the timepiece.

"I don't even have a picture of True," he said to his reflection as he put the watch back in the drawer, knowing he'd never wind it again. When Johnny was old enough, Seth would give him the watch. He didn't want to look at Marcy and think of True. It wouldn't be fair to either of them.

Seth walked to the window and watched Emily playing on the swing below. The moonlight made her hair look gold. She seemed so happy, as if she belonged here. How would she react if she learned her hero did nothing more dangerous each day than balance books?

Seth forced his mind to stop torturing himself. He could get through this. True would only be here a few hours. He was an expert at hiding his feelings. Now it was time to put

himself to the test. He'd play the gentleman and host, then
see them safely on their way.

He walked down the back stairs to the kitchen, determined to remain calm.

The sight that greeted him shattered all such resolve.
Standing in the middle of the kitchen was True elbow deep
in flour. The room looked as if a longhorn had plowed
through it destroying everything in sight.

"What are you doing?" he yelled before he thought to rein
his temper.

True looked up at him with fiery eyes and answered,
"Making biscuits for supper." Everything from her stance to
her tone was a challenge to his question. "Haven't you ever
seen someone make bread?"

Seth couldn't stop himself. He laughed, harder than he'd
ever laughed in his life. And the harder he laughed the
madder she got.

"Have you ever cooked biscuits?"

"No." True jabbed at the dough as she'd seen cooks do in
the kitchens of Harvey Houses all over the West. Only her
dough fought back, with a dusting of flour flying in her
direction. "But it didn't look all that difficult. All you do is
put a little soda and salt in flour."

Seth ventured closer. "Have you ever cooked anything?"

"Tea." True held her head proudly. "I can make tea."

Seth lifted one of the aprons off a nail by the door.
"Maybe I'd better help with supper. I may not have killed
hundreds of men in gunfights, but I've managed to keep
myself from starving."

She stepped aside and watched him work. At first she
thought it strange to see a man in the kitchen. Oh, she'd seen
chefs, but that was different from watching a single man
prepare food. His strong hands cut potatoes with sure pulls
of a knife. Then he placed the whole potato in his palm and

chopped it without cutting himself. Somehow the small act seemed as amazing as a fast draw.

True watched silently. It was a little thing, cooking. Something she'd never pictured Westwind doing except in front of an open fire while out on the range. Yet she found herself enjoying watching Seth.

"How'd you learn to cook?" she asked, wishing she could think of something to do besides watch.

"My mother taught my brother and me. I don't do it much anymore. I have a lady who comes in to help with Johnny every day but Sunday. My father helps out, too. He not only grows most of our food, he trades off with the neighbors, raw vegetables and fruits for a share of their canning each fall. He was never meant to work in town, but the old guy did manage to keep the store running until I could take over."

"You have a brother?"

"Had," Seth corrected. "He was killed ten years ago while he was with the Texas Rangers. Funny thing was when we were kids, he was the better cook and I was the better shot."

As potato soup boiled and biscuits baked, they talked of little things. Of nothing. Of everyday life. Of themselves for the first time since they'd met.

True found it good to be able to share with him her life as a writer. She'd learned years ago not to hang around the "normal folks" too long. It was more than that they didn't understand creative minds; nonwriters started noticing eventually just how strange writers were. She kept waiting for that look in Seth's eyes, but it didn't come.

Finally, he pulled off the apron and tossed it aside. "You'd best call Emily in while I spoon up the soup."

True nodded and moved to the door. The night had grown cool, and the country was so quiet she found it almost frightening. "I'll never be able to sleep without the sound of a train."

Seth watched her, but he didn't speak. He didn't dare. They'd somehow been able to forge a fragile truce, and he didn't want to destroy it.

Emily hurried in, and suddenly the kitchen was filled with sound. They talked and laughed and ate until all three couldn't down another bite. Emily put her head on her arm and tried to use the corner of the table as a pillow.

Seth lifted the child in his arms. She was asleep before he reached the foot of the stairs. "I'll put her in one of the beds in Johnny's room."

When he returned, True had made an effort to clean the kitchen, but she didn't appear to be much better at it than she was at cooking.

"I think I'll say good night also, I'll sleep on the extra bed in Emily's room." She avoided his gaze as she moved to the stairs. "Good night, Mr. Atherton."

"Good night, Miss McCormick," he answered as he watched her go. When she'd disappeared, he added, "Good night, darling."

Seth worked in the kitchen for a few minutes. He didn't want to go upstairs until he was sure she'd gone to bed. He wasn't sure he could be a wall away from her and listen to the sounds of her getting ready for bed and know that she wouldn't be sleeping beside him.

He walked onto the back porch thinking of the nights they'd been together and how quickly she'd become a habit. If she came to him tonight as she had other nights, would he be able to let her go come morning? Would he be able to turn her away and save himself more heartache?

Walking toward the barn, Seth thought of all the years he'd been coming out to the farm. He'd never moved here from town. He wasn't even sure why. Maybe it was because this was the place he came to get away from everything else. Here he always found peace.

Only there was no peace tonight. He knew he wouldn't sleep soundly tonight.

He walked past the empty stalls. Seth had moved all his stock over to the Millers' place before he left so that they'd be cared for. Johnny's pony would be half wild if he didn't get her back soon. She was little, but she always thought she could run with the horses.

Smiling, Seth climbed the loft ladder. He'd always liked the barn. He liked the smell of fresh hay and the sounds the animals always made in greeting.

He liked walking around in the loft, where a collection of old, unneeded memories were stored. A saddle he'd bought as a kid with his own money and now saved for Johnny. A baby carriage Marcy had ordered all the way from St. Louis. A sewing machine his mother used to say she'd pass down to a granddaughter someday. A hundred other things that tied him to family.

Seth relaxed as he leaned against the loft door. He could see most of his land from this point, and on a clear night the lights from town twinkled in the distance. Standing very still, he let the night relax him and bring him home.

Something moved from behind Seth. A slight shifting of wood that told Seth he was no longer alone.

"Who's there?" he turned slowly, wishing he'd thought to strap on his gun. It was possible they'd been followed here.

No answer.

"Emily, is that you?" Seth looked around for something to use as a weapon. A few days ago he would never have thought about a visitor being hostile. But a few days ago he hadn't been shot at and kidnapped.

Nothing moved, but he knew he was no longer alone in

the barn. Whoever was near didn't make a sound, but he could sense someone.

Seth stepped out of the light of the loft door and into the shadows. His foot struck the handle of a pitchfork. Silently he lifted the only weapon he could find and waited.

THIRTY-TWO

True watched Seth cross the yard to the barn. He looked starched and solid in his own clothes, a businessman who'd never understand someone like her. But he hadn't judged her tonight. He hadn't even really made fun of her not knowing how to cook.

There was no reason she followed him. She only knew that she had to be close to him tonight. She'd been a few steps behind him when he'd climbed the ladder to the loft. True watched him run his hand over the furniture stored there. Then he turned and stared out the loft door as if he were looking at the great treasure called his land.

She found the knowledge that he was settled far more frightening than she'd found the belief that he was a drifter. This man had roots, deep roots.

True moved unexpectedly, making a sound she hadn't intended.

"Who's there?" Seth's voice rang cold in the darkness of the loft.

"Emily, is that you?"

True didn't answer. Maybe if she remained very still, he would think he'd only been hearing things. She wanted to watch him more. She wanted to try and understand this man and his roots. True needed to say good-bye silently to the only man who'd ever made her feel like a woman.

Seth had stepped into the shadows by the door. His location melted into the blackness around her, but he was playing in her playground now. She had spent years moving in the night.

True lifted her skirts and slowly felt for an opening between the stacks of furniture. He'd never find her in the darkness. Except for her typewriter, her pearl-handled Colts, and a few bags of clothes she enjoyed wearing, True had accumulated nothing in her life. This man had so much. He had two houses and a loft full.

She wondered why none of these treasures were in the main house. As she looked from piece to piece, she figured it out. There were all the furnishings babies and women needed. In Seth's life there were no women and therefore no babies. But he must still have hope or he would have discarded all this long ago.

Seth finally moved from the shadows. His muscles seemed tight now, as if he were no longer relaxed. He turned his back to her and leaned against the open door. "How long have you been watching me, Miss McCormick?"

His question was so direct it shocked her. She thought of not answering. Maybe he was only bluffing. But she wanted to talk to him. She wanted to part with no anger between them. "I followed you from the house."

"Why?" He didn't turn around.

"I guess I wanted to look at you once more. A writer doesn't have her main character come to life very often. Even without the guns or the clothes, you still look every inch Granite Westwind."

"But I'm not," Seth answered coldly. "No part of his life and mine cross."

He turned around to face her, guided only by her voice. "Tell me something before you go. When you look at me do you see me, Seth Atherton, or Westwind?"

True thought of lying, just to make it easier on Seth. She

knew he wanted her to see him, but fiction and reality had always mingled in her world. "I'm not sure," she answered.

Seth took a step closer. "And when I touched you, was it me making love to you, or Westwind?"

True couldn't look at him and hurt him. How could she explain that she'd loved Westwind for years? She'd lost count of the times she'd wished that he were beside her. Sometimes late at night when she was so alone, she'd almost think she could feel him near. But she could never tell Seth such a thing.

Hurrying to the ladder, True glanced back at the lean outline of a man who looked every inch a hero. "I've known him for so long," she said, trying to make Seth understand. "I've only known you a few days."

Suddenly the foolishness of her own words registered. All the other reasons she'd given everyone for never falling in love or marrying weren't true. She wasn't afraid of being some man's slave or looking for a husband strong as her adoptive father. In truth, she'd closed her heart to a real love because she was already in love with a man. A hero no flesh-and-blood man could ever compete with.

She'd molded him herself, and everything about Westwind was to her liking. He was always strong, always right, always the fighter.

Only Seth had put a crack in her vision. He'd made her see Westwind was only paper-thin. Seth had thoughts and feelings deeper than Westwind's. Even the tiny lines around Seth's eyes were proof that Westwind was only a clay mold of a man and could never be as complicated as the real thing.

She'd seen Seth strong and good like Westwind, but he'd also been frustrated and angry and sarcastic. True felt like a woman who'd always loved playing with a doll until one day someone let her hold a real baby. The doll would never be the same.

Suddenly she had to get away from Seth. He'd destroyed something she'd never be able to get back, and he didn't even know it. Nothing in her life would ever be the same. Finally someone had bested Westwind, not in a gunfight, but with reality.

She hurried down the ladder and ran through the barn, paying no heed to Seth's call. Wildly she ran across the farmyard and behind the garden, where huge trees waited to shelter her. The air was ripe with late summer and cool in darkness. True wished they were in town. She needed the sounds of nightlife on the back streets to calm her. Something about always having to be on her guard made her problems seem smaller. But there was no nightlife, no town.

She walked among the trees, listening to insects and frogs. The rush of a creek drew her deeper into the woods. When she reached the bank, True relaxed against a tree and tried to imagine that the water was the far-off swish of a train just before the engineer blows the whistle announcing his arrival.

The streets never frightened her as much as the country. Here a scream would go unheard and even a gun might not protect her from the shadowy forms that swayed with the wind.

True pressed harder against the tree and tried to make herself believe the country was the same beautiful, peaceful place at night that it was in the daytime. But to her it was so much more lonely than all the other places she'd known.

Something moved among the branches. A twig snapped, then another.

"What's there?" True whispered, not realizing she'd said her thoughts aloud.

"It's me," Seth's low voice answered. "I didn't mean to

frighten you. I was worried about you. These woods can be a little tricky in the dark if you're not familiar with them."

He moved up to the clearing where she could see his outline. "It's beautiful here with the moonlight reflecting off the water. This is one of my favorite places to come."

True wanted to argue the point, but what did it matter? Be it his heaven or her hell, this was the place she'd bury Granite Westwind tonight.

Seth walked to the edge of the water. "I wish you weren't leaving in the morning." He hesitated as if choosing his words carefully. "I promise you one thing. I'll keep your secret. No one will ever know you write those novels."

"It doesn't matter." True sounded defeated. "There'll be no more Westwind novels. I'll even go to the press if you like. Westwind is dead."

Seth leaned against a rock beside the water. He doubled one long leg up and rested his chin on his knee. "That's not what I wanted."

"The secret of Westwind doesn't matter anymore." True didn't want to think about why. "Maybe it's just time for the books to end. Westwind couldn't go on forever."

"I'm sorry."

"But it wasn't your fault. I thought up this plan of getting you to play him all by myself." She held her chin up high. "Now I'd like to bury him alone, if you don't mind leaving."

"But I do mind. I want to know why you ran out of the barn a few minutes ago."

"I didn't want to hurt you." She couldn't look at him as she spoke.

"Because I know that when you look at me you still see Westwind?"

"Yes." True wanted to add that she saw far more than Westwind.

Seth shoved his hands deep into his pockets and looked at

the stars. "What if I told you it doesn't matter to me anymore? I don't care who you see when I hold you as long as it's me holding you."

"But you do care. You've wanted me to see you from the first. How many times have you told me you're no hero?"

Seth was silent. He couldn't swallow his pride and lie, even though he knew that in a few hours he'd never hold her again. His voice sounded tired when he finally answered. "All right, I care. It hurts to think that you're dreaming of another man. A man who only lives on paper. How can I fight a man who lives only in your head? Sometimes I think he's become so real to me, I even hate him."

"I understand. I'd like to hold you once more and say good-bye to Granite Westwind. But it would be too selfish of me."

"I agree." Seth shocked her with his answer. "You're very selfish to even ask such a thing. If you and Westwind want to say a final farewell, leave me out of it." He stood to leave.

True pushed away from the tree and grabbed his arm. "Selfish is something I've never been called in my life, Mr. Atherton."

"How about spoiled or pampered?" Seth knew he was blowing on a low fire, but he'd rather go away yelling mad at her than in the melancholy manner in which she'd been speaking. It made him mad to think that even now when there were no more secrets between them, she was still thinking of Westwind when she looked at him.

"How dare you talk to me like this!"

"Tell me, Miss McCormick, have you ever thought of anyone in your entire life but yourself? Don't you realize that every time you run away from life there are people worrying about you?"

"You sound like an old man." True thought of listing all the good she did, but he'd never hear her. He was convinced that she just ran around the country doing whatever she desired.

"And you sound like a spoiled child inviting only imaginary friends to your parties and leaving out all the real people."

True leaned closer, wishing she were taller and could yell at him nose to nose. "I'll bet you never did anything spontaneous or fun in your entire life before you met me, did you, Mr. Atherton?"

Seth didn't answer.

"Well," True demanded. "Name one outrageous, wild thing you did. I can just see you going to work every day and back home again."

Seth held himself in check.

"Tell me, Mr. Atherton, what do you talk about on an average day? Oh, I know." She made her voice low. "Should I plant one or two rows of corn this spring in the garden? Or maybe, Do you think it will rain this week?"

"I have an interesting life here," he whispered in a tone so low it should have warned True of danger.

"You have a life, but you don't live. I'll leave tomorrow and you'll spend the rest of your days reliving the few hours we had together."

She was right, but he wouldn't admit it.

"You'll go back to counting nails or boards or whatever you do in that store of yours. And me, I'll be out having other adventures. In a few months I won't even remember your name."

"Then maybe you'll remember this." He lifted her so quickly, she didn't even have time to fight. In one swift swing, he tossed her into the stream. "Maybe you'll remember your first swimming lesson."

Cold water filled her mouth as she tried to scream. She splashed, trying to keep her head above water. "Seth!" she yelled as the stream pulled her along. "Seth!" The water pulled her down, depriving her of air.

A strong hand grabbed her arm and pulled her up. "You finally called the right name, darling."

For a moment True couldn't understand how he could be so still when all the water was rushing around him.

"Stand up!" he yelled as his arms steadied her.

True felt her feet touch rock and she stood. The stream was only waist-deep. He'd frightened her near to death in three feet of water. With all her strength she swung at him.

"I could have drowned!" she screamed. "I hate you, Seth Atherton. I hate you."

Seth pulled her against the warmth of his chest. "Well, that's a start. At least it's me you hate."

She pounded his chest again and again. All the tension of the day exploded inside her. He held her waist so that she didn't fall in the water, but he made no attempt to block the blows.

Finally she stopped, exhausted. She made no protest when he lifted her in his arms and waded out of the water. He carried her back to the house without a word. His arms were iron bands around her as though he never planned to let her go.

When he reached an upstairs room that could only have been his, Seth sat her on her feet. "Take off those wet clothes."

For a moment he stood still as though he planned to watch. When she didn't move, his voice softened. "You'll find a dry shirt in the top drawer. I'll go get a few towels for your hair."

True watched him leave, then looked around his room. It reminded her of most of the hotel rooms she'd stayed in over the years—everything was in order, with nothing extra to make the room belong to someone. The only exception was a bookcase filled with books.

As she unbuttoned her shirt, True moved to the case. There were all kinds of books—classics, children's books, even a cookbook.

Seth noisily stepped back into the room. He carried a towel under each arm and a lantern in each hand.

"There's enough light in this room," True said nervously as if he'd caught her looking at something private.

"It'll be brighter when I'm finished," Seth said and vanished again.

True removed her jacket and blouse. Her skirt had just hit the floor when he returned with two more lamps.

"Are you cold?" he asked as he placed the lamps on the dresser and bookcase.

"No," True answered. "And I can see quite well also, thank you. I've seen stages that weren't this well lit."

"Good," Seth said as he moved toward her. "I didn't want there to be any shadows in this room. No ghosts. No make-believe."

"You're starting to make me nervous." True wondered if he'd thought of some way to get back at her for hitting him while they stood in the stream. "There are enough lamps in this room to drive a moth crazy."

He didn't answer. She could see every tiny line in his face, the small scar over his left eye, the few whiskers he'd missed along his jawline when he'd shaved, a tiny chicken pox mark on his forehead, and another on his hand.

Very slowly Seth unbuttoned his vest. The damp cotton shirt clung to his chest as he pulled off the conservative corduroy garment. Next came the suspenders.

When he started unbuttoning his trousers, True's panic turned real. "What on earth do you think you're doing?"

"I thought you'd like to play one last game, True. It's called 'If only for tonight.'"

"I don't want to play any games."

"If only for tonight, you're going to see me, Seth Atherton, and no one else."

"I'm not playing!" True moved toward the door.

"Because you're a coward." Seth whispered the words, but they still slapped her full force. "I played the game with you that first night even before I knew the rules. Too bad you're too afraid to play it with me now."

She whirled at him. "No one has ever called me a coward. I don't mind so much the other names you called me back at the stream, but I'll not stand to be called a coward."

"Then kiss me," Seth answered without moving toward her. "Kiss me, not a character from a book. Kiss me with your eyes open in the light."

"And you think I'm afraid?" True marched toward him. "I'll show you how afraid I am."

She put her hands on his shoulders and stood on her toes. Her lips touched his hard and fast, proving her point. "There," she said.

Seth didn't lean over to meet her halfway. "I thought you'd learned more about kissing than that."

True stretched on her toes and kissed him again. "I kiss just fine, Mr. Atherton. Good-bye."

"Good-bye," he answered as he leaned forward. His lips met hers soft and full. He teased her bottom lip with his tongue. "Kiss me back, True. If only for tonight."

His fingers slid along her bare shoulders and caressed with a slight touch. When she leaned into him, his hands circled her waist and pulled her tightly against him. As her breasts pressed into his chest, she cried softly with pure pleasure. Her open mouth was his for the loving.

She felt a heat build inside of her and spread like a warm

prairie fire deep through her. Seth's hands shoved the straps from her camisole and pushed the material to her waist.

"Say my name," he whispered as his hands roamed her flesh. "Say my name!" he demanded as his fingers cupped her breasts.

"Seth," she whispered. "Love me."

He didn't love her wild and hurried as he had in the hotel in Galveston. Now he was on his land, in his house. He would love her his way, slow and passionately, watching her reactions to his touch in the light of half a dozen lamps.

He allowed her to remove his clothes slowly, exposing his body one inch at a time. There was no embarrassment in her eyes as she studied him, only a sparkle of wild adventure.

He took his time undressing her, memorizing each inch of her. When he lifted the sheet to his bed, he ordered softly, "Lay on your back with your hands above your head."

She stared up at him with eyes wide in excitement as he spread the sheet over her. Slowly, as though molding a statue, he pressed the sheet around her from her shoulders down so that the outline of her body was revealed. He knelt beside the bed and lightly moved his hand over the sheet until the warmth of her body heated the cotton and it clung to her form.

"Be perfectly still," he whispered before he kissed her long and completely.

When her breath was coming fast and hot from the kiss, he pulled away and watched the sheet rise and fall above her body.

"You can watch, but don't move," he said as his hands pressed her arms against the pillows above her head. "And don't try to touch me until I've finished." His mouth started at her cheek and moved slowly down, tasting as he explored.

She cried softly with joy as his tongue moved down her throat. His fingers spread over the sheet above her breasts. He molded her flesh as he kissed her shoulders. When his mouth moved lower, his hands pulled the sheet down, slowing revealing her to his caresses.

True was lost in pleasure. Each inch of her that was uncovered brought a new level of warmth inside her. Part of her didn't want him to move lower, for she was loving what he was doing, but another part of her was wild with anticipation of what she knew was to come.

Slowly, inch by inch, he loved her. When the sheet was completely gone, he blanketed her body with his own. "Look at me, True," he whispered against her ear as his lean form pressed above her.

She smiled into his blue-gray eyes and wrapped her arms around him. His hair was a mess and she could see tiny beads of perspiration along his forehead. His mouth opened with pleasure as she moved beneath him. She slid her fingers along his back and dug her nails into his flesh as she pulled him closer.

"Love me, Seth," she whispered as she kissed his ear. "Love me tonight."

Her words shattered all restraint. He loved her so completely the lamplight exploded into lightning. She closed her eyes and cried with pleasure. It was Seth's face she saw before her.

THIRTY-THREE

Seth awoke to a cloudy morning. The exhaustion of the past few days was gone. He'd slept soundly in his own bed. Rolling to his side, he looked around the room. Sometime during the night he'd turned out all but one of the lamps, but the memory of True was still thick in his mind. He smiled, wondering if he'd ever love her more than he did right now.

He wasn't surprised she was absent from his arms. That seemed to be her habit, but he climbed from the bed and dressed, suddenly in a hurry to see her.

"True!" he yelled as he ran down the back stairs to the kitchen, trying to guess what mess she'd made for breakfast.

The house was quiet, too quiet.

Seth felt panic plow a double row up his spine.

He stormed out to the barn and back up to the bedroom where Emily had slept. Nothing. All sign of them had vanished as if they'd never been real.

A noise came from the front, and Seth almost tore the door off its hinges in his hurry to get outside.

But only Floyd greeted him. "Mornin', Mr. Atherton. I thought I'd drop by and see how you were feeling before I headed back to town." When Seth didn't respond, Floyd added, "I took your cousin and her daughter to the train station this morning. They should be on their way by now. She asked me to deliver a suitcase to your office, said she didn't want me to wake you by dropping it off here. I told her you'd be up, but I left it on the walk in front of your store just like she told me. The store's due to open in an hour, and I've never known you to be late."

"Thanks, Floyd." Seth couldn't tell the man how he felt. His world was crumbling.

"I moved your horses over about dawn. You want me to hitch up a wagon for you?"

Seth wanted to scream that he didn't care. How could he go to the store and start his life today as if nothing had happened in the past two weeks? How could he live without True? All color was gone from his world.

"No, thanks." Seth managed to get the words out. He wanted to be alone. "I'll saddle a mount up later." He was afraid he'd fall apart in front of a man who'd always seen him as strong.

Floyd waved and continued on down the road, seeming to see nothing of Seth's pain.

Going through the motions of life for Seth was like treading water in the middle of the ocean. He saw nothing around him; he just kept moving. He walked into his office as he had every day for over ten years and looked through his mail as though he could see something before him besides True's face. He thought of going after her, but he wasn't sure how to find her. Maybe ride the rails and stop at every Harvey House along the tracks. In their days together he'd never even asked her where she lived.

"Morning, Mr. Atherton." Nell's voice greeted him with the same warmth as always. "Did you have a nice holiday?"

Seth looked up at a woman he'd spent ten hours a day with for years, and for a moment he couldn't even remember her name. He had to say something. He couldn't just stare at her. "Yes," he lied. "And you?"

Nell's smile was brilliant. "It was grand. I met the most wonderful gentleman, a friend of my aunt's family. We had the grandest time. You wouldn't believe all the things we did in only one week."

Seth hardly listened. He couldn't begin to tell Nell about what had happened to him last week.

A sudden knock at the door interrupted Nell's account of picnics and country rides. She rushed to unlock the business. "My, my, someone's in a hurry this morning."

Before Nell could stop her, a child darted through the door and ran right into Seth's arms. "Mr. Westwind, Mr. Westwind. True's in trouble!"

Seth hugged Emily tightly. "Slow down, child, and tell me what's the problem." He couldn't hide the smile or the relief he felt. They hadn't left; they were still near.

"We got to the train station a while ago. True said she had some things that needed taking care of in Galveston." Emily was talking so fast her words ran together. "She gave that man Floyd a suitcase to deliver to you. He hadn't more than stepped off the train when a big man came out from the back of the car, his gun pointed right at True and me."

"What man?" Seth paid little attention to Nell, who still held the door, her mouth wide open.

"A big guy. Old, too; older than you. He made us wait awhile, then he sent me to find you. He said to tell you he was gonna kill your woman if you didn't hurry."

Nell found her voice. "Mr. Atherton, the child is mad."

Seth kissed Emily on her tearstained cheek. "Then so am I, because I believe every word." He reached for the suitcase, hoping True had packed his gun.

"But you can't." Nell shook her head.

Seth opened the case. Both of Westwind's double-holstered guns and his brother's old Colt lay on top of a few clothes. Seth lifted his brother's worn leather gun belt and strapped it on.

"Mr. Atherton, you're not going over there!" All color drained from Nell's face. "This is a matter for the sheriff."

Seth checked the bullets in the chamber. "No, Nell, like the child said, he's got my woman."

Nell looked at her boss as if he'd gone completely mad. Never had she seen him with a gun, and he wasn't the kind of man to go looking for trouble because of a child's tale. She watched, speechless, as he marched into the street.

By the time Seth walked the short distance to the train station, half the town seemed to be following him. They were all whispering behind him, but Seth didn't care. He had to save True.

When he reached the station platform, the sheriff hurried up beside him. Sheriff Hall was an older man who'd chosen this town to retire in. "What seems to be the problem, Mr. Atherton?" He tried to maintain a degree of authority in his voice, but he wasn't going to bother one of the town's leading citizens without reason.

"Nothing I can't handle, Sheriff." Seth didn't slow his pace.

Sheriff Hall pulled a letter from his pocket as he ran to keep up. "I got the strangest letter from the Texas Rangers this morning. It's addressed to me, but it says, 'Tell Atherton if you see him, the letters to Westwind were only pranks and not to worry about them.'"

Seth had no idea what Hall was talking about, but Ranger Raine and Colonel McCormick must have figured out between the two of them that he'd brought True back to Timber Creek. He only hoped she was still alive when they got here, for he had no doubt they were on their way.

"I need your help." Seth stopped so suddenly the sheriff almost stumbled. "Keep everyone away from the private car." He glanced over his shoulder. "Including this child."

Emily opened her mouth to object.

Seth pointed one finger at her and frowned. "Don't argue, young lady. I'll not have my daughter killed in gunfire."

"Daughter!" Emily yelled.

"Gunfire," the sheriff whispered.

Seth didn't have time to explain. He jumped off the end of the platform and raced toward the private car anchored at the end of a short run of tracks.

A single shot stopped his progress and silenced the growing crowd behind him.

"That's far enough!" a man's voice hollered from inside the car.

"Let the woman go!" Seth yelled back. "She has nothing to do with this. I'm the one you want to kill."

A large man stepped onto the platform. His hair was salted with gray, and evil shone in every line of his scarred face. He was using True as a shield as he moved down the steps. Her hands were tied and her mouth gagged, but she was still fighting by kicking and wiggling. Seth moved closer.

"Stay back, Atherton, or I'll kill her. She's already been more trouble than a dozen men would have been."

"You harm her, you're a dead man." Seth's voice left no doubt that he meant every word. "Come out here alone and I'll let you draw first."

"I don't need any advantage." The man grew angry and his face twisted in hate. "I'm not so old that I can't still outdraw any man alive." He stepped down from the train, dragging True with him. "I killed one Atherton; I guess I can kill another."

The crowd behind Seth all seemed to draw in air at one time.

"Hawk Sloan," Seth almost whispered the name. He'd finally come face-to-face with his brother's murderer. "You're the one who's been trying to kill me all week."

"You should have died in that bar fight I arranged. I couldn't believe after all these years someone was still looking for me for that murder. First the Texas Rangers never seemed to quit and now you. I've had enough. I'm tired of waiting for you to come looking for me."

"You followed me?"

Hawk laughed. "Sure. I thought I could hire someone to shoot you even if you did change your name. But after he shot the wrong man, I realized I'd have to do the job myself."

A train pulled into the station a hundred yards away, but no one seemed to notice it.

"Let the woman go!" Seth shouted over the noise. "The fight's between us."

Hawk tossed True aside. "All right, Atherton. Let her watch you die. She'll see the bullet hit your heart, and the next one I'll aim for her head."

In the silence between heartbeats Hawk pulled his gun. Seth reacted. Both weapons fired at the same time, exploding the air with thunder.

Seth twisted, grabbing his arm as several women screamed from the safety of the station. He fell to one knee and switched the gun to his other hand, ready to fire again.

Hawk Sloan stared at Seth in shock. As if in slow motion, he dropped his gun and grabbed his middle. He crumbled to the ground with blood trickling through his fingers. Hawk Sloan's eyes never closed, but only death looked up at Seth from the ground. The outlaw was gone.

Seth didn't lower his gun from Hawk as he stood and moved toward True. He freed her hands and jerked the gag from her mouth.

She was in his arms before he could holster his Colt. He wanted to yell at her for leaving without telling him. He longed to tell her she could never leave again, because he loved her so much, but all he could do was hold her. He'd blamed her and Westwind for all the trouble this week, and it had been he, Seth Atherton, who was the target.

"It's all over, darling," he whispered before he kissed her full on the mouth with all the town watching.

Suddenly people were everywhere, talking all at once. The sheriff was trying to ask a few official questions, but he couldn't make himself heard over the crowd.

A sudden gunshot from the back of the near riot silenced everyone. One lone Ranger leaned heavily on his cane as he stepped forward.

"If you good people will let Mr. Atherton and his lady out of this mess, we need to get his wound seen about." Officer Raine nodded toward Sheriff Hall as though asking for the older man's assistance.

With Hall's encouragement, everyone moved aside. Seth held True's hand tightly and led her through the mob to Link. "Thanks," he whispered to the Ranger as he passed. "This is just your line, one riot—one Ranger."

"You guessed it." Link pointed with his cane toward the street. "Doc's waiting at the wagon. I'll take care of Sloan's body and meet you later."

"Audrey's here!" True broke into a run toward Floyd's wagon waiting by the platform.

Link winked at Seth. "She wouldn't hear of me coming alone. Wants to be with me, you know."

Seth raised a doubtful eyebrow. The doc and the Ranger were an unlikely match, but so were he and True.

Two hours later the sheriff had finished all his questions. Audrey had removed the bullet from Seth's arm and wrapped the wound.

When the sheriff left, the doc leaned close. "Only one other thing I got to say to you." She looked at Seth with a stern expression. "You'd better take good care of True or this won't be the only bullet hole in you."

Seth laughed. "I guess you're trying to tell me there's a few people who'll shoot me if I'm not good to her."

"No," Audrey answered without smiling. "I'm trying to tell you she'll shoot you herself. She doesn't just have those little Colts in her pockets to keep her from flying away on a windy day. She's a fine shot."

Seth raised his hand to swear. "I'll be careful."

While Audrey cleaned her tools, Seth went down the back stairs to the kitchen. He had to see True. The hours apart seemed like days.

The room was filled with food. Pies, pot roasts, fried chicken. Emily sat in the middle of it all staring at the table.

"What's this?" Seth asked.

"It just appeared," Emily answered. "About half an hour ago folks started dropping by to ask about you, and they all left something to eat. I've never seen so much food."

"Where's True?"

Emily pointed to the trees. "She could only stand about the first twenty people hugging her and welcoming her to town, then she ran out that-a-way."

Seth walked slowly through the trees. He knew True would be by the creek. He saw her before she heard him coming. For a long moment he just stood and watched her. She was so beautiful, so alive. He'd gladly die to save her, but could he live and make her happy?

"True," he whispered.

She turned and stared at him. He'd pulled a clean white shirt over his bandaged arm, but she could still see the outline of the wrappings. His dress was plain, almost formal, nothing like a hero would wear. But he'd saved her life this morning and loved her last night.

He moved toward her until he was only a foot away. He

wanted to yell at her for leaving him, but he remembered something Micah had said, "If you want to hold True, you have to do it with an open hand."

"I'd like Emily to stay with me." Seth knew it wasn't the right place to start the conversation, but he had to say something. "I'll take good care of her. We've got several empty bedrooms, and I'll see she has her own horse to ride to school."

"Will you love her?"

"I already do," Seth answered. "I'd like to adopt her and the boy, Phillip, she's friends with."

"What about the baby I bought?"

"Him, too," Seth answered. "I have a lady who looks after my son. She can take on a few more. If I need more help, I've the money to hire others. Dad grows enough food for half the town, and I could run a few cattle on the land. They'll never be hungry again."

He reached toward her pocket.

True grabbed his arm and tried to stop him, but he pulled a biscuit from the folds of her dress before she could move away. He didn't say the words; he couldn't. How could he promise her she'd never be hungry when he wanted to offer her so much more?

She stared at his hand holding the biscuit. "I have to go. I have to leave today."

"Where," he whispered, "to another town, another adventure, or just away from me?" Before he could stop himself he said the words he'd promised Micah he wouldn't say. "True, I love you. Stay with me. Marry me tonight. I love you too much to say good-bye."

"I know." She held her head high, blinking away her tears. "But don't you see I don't belong here?"

"You belong with me, not just for a night, but for a lifetime." He tossed the biscuit in the water, hating the thought that she'd ever had to worry about where her next meal was coming from. "Marry me, True, or live with me and write all the stories you want. Don't you see you belong in my arms at night and by my side all day?"

"This town would never approve of me if I lived with you."

"I don't care if people approve."

"I do for your sake. If I stayed, it would have to be as your wife." She looked at the water. "I'll go to Galveston and bring back Phillip and the baby."

"I'll go with you."

"No. I need time to decide. I'll give you my answer when I get back."

Open your hand, Seth thought to himself. If you want to hold True, open your hand.

He held his arms open to her and she moved into his embrace willingly. His kiss was warm and bittersweet. "I love you, darling . . . forever. Come back to me."

A week later Seth closed the hardware store in the middle of the afternoon and went to meet the train. At first he thought something big must be happening, like an election, because everyone in town was in their Sunday best and at the station.

"What's everyone waiting on?" Seth asked the sheriff. "The governor paying a visit?" Seth hadn't bothered to read a paper all week.

The sheriff slapped Seth on the back as if he had made a joke. "We're all waiting on our True to come home," he answered. "You didn't think you'd be the only one to welcome her, did you? Her story's been in the Galveston paper every day. Most folks in town are collecting her Westwind books."

Seth looked around. "But how did they know she's coming today?"

"Pete over in the office took your telegram message and told Floyd." The sheriff shrugged as if that were enough to end the story.

Seth didn't have time to say anything else. The train pulled into the station. He hurried out, looking for True in every window.

Emily jumped off the last car and came running into his arms. "I'm back!" she yelled. "Is my new brother Johnny here yet?"

"He'll be back tomorrow," Seth answered as he watched the crowd for True. "I can't wait till he meets you. He's always wanted a sister."

A boy walked up and stood just behind Emily. He was older than her by a few years and so thin he was almost a skeleton. Seth could see in his eyes he was fighting down fear.

"I'm Phillip," the boy whispered.

Seth extended his hand. "Hello, Phillip. I'm glad to finally meet you. Welcome."

Another boy moved beside Phillip. "Hello, sir." The boy was so frightened, his voice shook. "I'm Phillip's brother, and I wondered if there's room for me at that farm of yours."

Seth's heart crumbled. "Of course," he whispered as he knelt on one knee and pulled all three children into his arms.

"Hello, sir, I'm Amy," a voice came from behind Seth. "I'm small and I don't eat much."

"Hello, sir, I'm Andy and this is my little brother, Sam. We was hoping . . ."

Seth was surrounded by children. He tried to give each one a hug and remember their names.

He looked over their heads and saw True holding the baby they'd saved. She handed the infant to Emily and moved into Seth's arms.

"Hello, sir," she whispered. "I'm True and I'm back."

He crushed her against him. "Welcome home, darling."

"I love you, Seth Atherton. Only you."

"I know," he whispered. "I knew it the night by the stream when you called to me for help, and later when you whispered my name as we made love. I stared into your eyes and knew you saw me, because blue-eyed people can never lie without looking away."

True laughed. "We'd best get the children home."

"I'm going to need more than one buggy."

True glanced at all the folks standing around the station smiling. "I don't think that will be too much of a problem."

When Seth finally got all the children settled in the wagons, he climbed in beside True. "Let's go home," he said and kissed her cheek.

"Home," True whispered, and her words were echoed by little voices filled with hope.

Later, long after sunset, Seth welcomed his bride back. "I thought all the neighbors would never leave."

"And all the children would never go to sleep," True added as she cuddled into his arms. "But don't worry, I have a feeling we're going to have more children."

Seth laughed. "One way or the other, so do I."

Readers interested in a list of other Jodi Thomas books please send S.A.S.E. to:

Jodi Thomas
℅ The Berkley Publishing Group
200 Madison Ave.
New York, New York 10016

Jodi Thomas enjoys hearing from readers.